Praise for Vicki D

"Charming, entertaining, and smart."
—*Library Journal* (starred review)

"Delany's down-to-earth heroine wraps up this investigation with even more than her customary panache."
—*Kirkus Reviews*

"[A] well-crafted series launch from Delany. . . . Fans of culinary cozies will be sure to come back for more."
—*Publishers Weekly*

"Details about tea, baking, and running a tea shop and bed-and-breakfast are woven throughout a satisfying cozy with a beautifully described setting and a cast of charming, small-town characters. Share this new series with fans of Laura Childs' Tea Shop mysteries."
—*Booklist*

"Holmes, himself, would be quite proud!"
—*Suspense* magazine

"Delany's latest work can hold its own against anything in the genre being published today."
—*Deadly Diversions*

"It's a crime not to read Delany."
—*London Free Press*

Kensington Books by Vicki Delany

The Tea by the Sea mystery series

Tea & Treachery

Murder in a Teacup

Murder Spills the Tea

Murder in a Teacup

Vicki Delany

Kensington Publishing Corp.
www.kensingtonbooks.com

KENSINGTON BOOKS are published by
Kensington Publishing Corp.
119 West 40th Street
New York, NY 10018

All Kensington titles, imprints, and distributed lines are available at special quantity discounts for bulk purchases for sales promotion, premiums, fund-raising, educational, or institutional use.

This book is a work of fiction. Names, characters, businesses, organizations, places, events, and incidents either are the product of the author's imagination or are used fictitiously. Any resemblance to actual persons, living or dead, events, or locales is entirely coincidental.

To the extent that the image or images on the cover of this book depict a person or persons, such person or persons are merely models, and are not intended to portray any character or characters featured in the book.

Special book excerpts or customized printings can also be created to fit specific needs. For details, write or phone the office of the Kensington Sales Manager: Kensington Publishing Corp., 119 West 40th Street, New York, NY 10018. Attn. Sales Department. Phone: 1-800-221-2647.

The K and Teapot logo is a trademark of Kensington Publishing Corp.

ISBN: 978-1-4967-2511-0 (ebook)

ISBN: 978-1-4967-2510-3

First Kensington Hardcover Edition: August 2021

First Kensington Trade Paperback Printing: July 2022

10 9 8 7 6 5 4 3 2 1

Printed in the United States of America

To Barbara Fradkin, Robin Harlick, Mary Jane
Maffini, and Linda Wiken, good writers and great
friends, who've helped to keep me sane
(somewhat sane?) in these crazy times.

Acknowledgments

Like Lily Roberts, I believe afternoon tea is a treat, an indulgence, and I encourage everyone to try it at least once in their lives. Over the past year, for obvious reasons, my traveling to exotic locations to enjoy afternoon tea has been curtailed, but instead I spent my time testing out recipes in my own private bake-off, which made my family and friends very happy indeed. Some of my favorite recipes are included at the end of this book, and others can be found at Mystery Lovers Kitchen, where I post every second Friday. The chocolate chip cookie recipe is courtesy of Donna Gliona.

I'd particularly like to thank my good friend Cheryl Freedman for reading the manuscript with her keen editor's eye and her love of mysteries. Thanks to my agent extraordinaire, Kim Lionetti, for her help, encouragement, and enthusiasm for this project, and to Karen Olsen, enthusiastic lover and promoter of all things teatime who introduced me to many new blends

And Alex Delany, for her love of afternoon tea.

Chapter 1

"Do you suppose this is what heaven smells like?"

"I wouldn't be at all surprised, but I hope once I get there, I don't have to do all the work. I love baking, but I wouldn't want to think it's all I'll do throughout eternity."

Simon McCracken sipped his tea. "Maybe you'll have an enormous staff of assistant bakers and kitchen helpers. I wouldn't mind being heaven's chief gardener."

I smiled at him as I patted a ball of dough with sticky, floury hands. As I did several times a day, I was making currant scones for afternoon tea. "If we can't be in heaven, then North Augusta, Massachusetts, in late June is a pretty close second."

Simon drained his cup and put it in the dishwasher. "I'll second that. Time to get back at it. Thanks for the tea." I looked up at the hesitation in his voice, then followed the direction of his eyes.

"Yes," I said, "you may have a strawberry tart."

"You're a mind reader, Lily Roberts." He grabbed one of the delicate pastries and made his escape before I could change my mind. I bake all day, every day, for a living, and

I'm not often inclined to offer freebies to all and sundry who wander through my kitchen.

I formed the dough into a thick rectangle, reached for my cutter, and began cutting small circles. "How's it looking out there?" I asked Cheryl, one of my assistants, when she came in with a load of dirty dishes. Every morsel, I was pleased to see, had been consumed.

"Busy, but under control. Need you ask?"

"Probably not. Open that oven door for me, will you, please." Cheryl did so, and I placed the laden baking sheet inside and set the rooster timer that I use exclusively for timing scones.

"Rose made a reservation for three people for three forty-five, did you know that?" Cheryl asked.

"Yes, I did. The granddaughter of one of her friends got in late last night. The rest of her family's arriving today for a family vacation. They're from Grand Lake, Iowa, where Rose used to live, so I don't know them."

Rose Campbell is my maternal grandmother and the owner of Victoria-on-Sea, the big B & B perched at the edge of the bluffs overlooking Cape Cod Bay. My tearoom, Tea by the Sea, is on the B & B property.

"Can't think of anything I'd rather not do," Cheryl said as she loaded the dishwasher, "than spend my valuable vacation days with my family."

"Present company excepted, I hope." My other assistant, Marybeth, came into the kitchen. "One order of traditional afternoon tea for four, and a children's tea for two.

"Mom," she asked Cheryl, "can you check the air pots are full and get down a tin of Darjeeling and one of English breakfast? The children will have iced tea." She opened the fridge door. My kitchen's so small, the three of us have developed a fine-tuned dance routine when we're all in it.

Cheryl prepared the tea balls to receive the tea leaves and laid out two of our beautiful flower-patterned pink-and-green china teapots. "Present company most definitely included. I love you to bits, Marybeth, and you know that, but I spend all day with you."

Marybeth winked at me. "How about the kids?" she asked her mother.

"They can come with me. Not that summer vacation's anything but a dream for anyone who works in the Cape Cod tourist business."

"Tell me about it." Scones in the oven, I started on a batch of green-tea cupcakes. Cheryl poured boiling water from the air pots over the tea balls and set the timer to ensure they steeped properly, while Marybeth prepared glasses of iced tea. When the drinks were ready, she carried a tray out to the dining room as Cheryl began assembling the stands of food. For the adults: freshly baked scones in the center, tea sandwiches on the bottom, pastries on the top. The children's tray was smaller and the food simpler, but no less elegant or carefully prepared. I believe afternoon tea is an indulgence and it should be treated as such. Fine china, stiffly ironed white tablecloths and napkins, fresh flowers, silver cutlery, perfectly prepared food. And, most important of all, the best possible selection of teas.

A knock sounded on the back door and it swung open. Large, bright green eyes in a pale face dotted with freckles beneath a mass of curly red hair peeked in. "Hey, what's up?"

"What you see is what you get," I said. "I'm making green-tea cupcakes."

"Yum. My favorite."

"They're all your favorite, and, no, you can't have one."

"Don't need one." Bernadette Murphy, known to everyone as Bernie, came into the kitchen. She wore an above-the-knee, close-fitting, sleeveless blush-pink dress with a thin black belt that showed her long legs and well-toned arms to perfection.

"You look nice," I said. "What's up?"

"I'm glad you think so. I dressed for the occasion. I'm having tea."

"Tea? Here?"

"Where else would I go for tea? I'm joining Rose at quarter to four. The granddaughter of some friends of hers is visiting, and she invited me to join them."

I glanced at the clock on the wall. "You're early."

"So I am." Bernie leaned against the butcher block in the center of the room, where I roll out cookies and pastry and cut scones. "I hope we're having the Darjeeling-poached-chicken tea sandwiches. They're my favorite."

"You're in luck then," I said.

"I've come early because I'm stuck on my book and I need to talk it over with you."

Fortunately, I was facing away from Bernie at that moment, so she didn't see me rolling my eyes. Bernie is always stuck on her book. She's an extremely talented writer with great promise, and after publishing three short stories in literary magazines to rave reviews and high acclaim, she began work on a novel. That was two years ago, but the book didn't seem to be going anywhere. So a few weeks ago, she quit her job as a forensic accountant at a Manhattan law firm and rented a cottage on Cape Cod for the peace and quiet and the time she claimed she needed to write.

Peace and quiet she had in abundance, but Bernie is anything but an introvert and she was having trouble settling. We've been best friends since we were growing up together in Manhattan, and I'd been thrilled when she announced her plans to spend the summer in North Augusta.

I wasn't so thrilled when she kept popping into the B & B or the tearoom, while I was working, to discuss the ever-changing direction of her book but I loved her to bits and I understood that she needed to talk to someone about her ideas and problems. She'd recently given up on two years' worth of her multigenerational, New York City–set, historical saga and turned two of her characters—one a privileged daughter of a wealthy and influential family, the other a former kitchen maid from Ireland—into a female detective agency on Cape Cod in the nineteenth century.

"I'm wondering if it would ruin the dynamics if Tessa gets married," she said. Tessa was the Irishwoman.

"Yes, it would."

"You seem very sure."

"I am sure. Haven't Tessa and Rose just met? They need to establish themselves as friends and partners first." Bernie had named her aristocratic character after my grandmother.

"I'm thinking long term."

"Stop thinking *long term* and get the *short term* written, Bernie."

"And in the very short term, like right now, please get away from the fridge," Marybeth said.

"Sorry." Bernie took a step to her left the moment Cheryl came through the swinging doors.

"Whoops. Close one," Cheryl said as she swung her tray out of my friend's way.

"We're kinda busy here, Bernie," I said.

"Not a problem. I can talk while you work. What do you know about forensics in the nineteenth century?"

I poured batter into cupcake liners, slid the tray into the second oven, and set the timer. Next up: shortbread. "Hopefully, I know a heck of a lot less than you do, seeing as you're the one writing the book."

"No such thing," Cheryl said. "They didn't know about fingerprints and blood spatter and DNA back then."

"I'm wanting Tessa and Rose to be cutting edge," Bernie said.

The rooster crowed, and I checked the scones, decided they were perfect, took them out of the oven, and placed them on the cooling rack.

All the while Bernie and I were talking, I continued measuring and adding ingredients, stirring batter, and forming dough, while Marybeth and Cheryl came in and out of the kitchen, placing orders, bringing in dirty dishes, washing dirty dishes, taking out clean table settings, fresh pots of tea, and trays of food.

"Rose is here," Marybeth announced. "She and her guest have taken a table in the garden."

"Use my personal dishes for them, please." For my sixteenth birthday, my grandparents had given me a set of Royal Doulton Winthrop china. For her sixteenth birthday, two days before mine, Bernie's grandmother had given her a gold-and-diamond necklace. I liked my gift better. The dishes are stunningly beautiful—white, with a deep red border with delicate gold leaves running through it, and gold trim on the base of the cup and decorating the handle.

I kept the china in the tearoom, but only brought it out for special occasions and special guests.

Cheryl went into the pantry to get the teapot and three place settings.

"If you want to have a successful tea with Rose," I said to Bernie, "try not to ask if she has personal knowledge of forensic methods, or anything else, from the nineteenth century."

Bernie sucked in a breath. Her eyes grew wide.

I recognized that expression and it always gave me a sinking feeling in the pit of my stomach. "What?"

"England during the war. The Blitz, bomb shelters,

hearty Londoners, overly stewed pots of tea. I'm thinking the book—"

"No," I said firmly. "You are not, once again, changing the entire focus of your novel. Do you want to get the thing finished or not?"

"Yes, but—"

"No *buts*. Go and have tea. As you're a paying customer, or at least the guest of one, I won't even ask you to take the dishes of jam, butter, and clotted cream out with you."

Chapter 2

About forty-five minutes later, things were beginning to slow down in the kitchen as the end of the day approached. I continued baking, glad of the chance to get some additional things made and into the fridge for tomorrow. Tea by the Sea had opened in the spring, and so far, we'd been successful beyond my cautious dreams.

Marybeth carried another load of dirty dishes into the kitchen. "Rose is asking if you have a chance for a break. She'd like you to join them and meet her guest."

I pressed my knuckles into the small of my back and leaned against them. I groaned with pleasure. "Sounds like a good idea. Did they eat everything they were served?"

"Not a crumb left for the resident mice."

"Of which we have none, so please don't repeat that. Nothing left is always good to hear, but not in this case, as I'm starving and would like to grab the leftovers. Can you bring me a cup of Creamy Earl Grey and a couple of sandwiches, please. Whatever we can spare."

I washed my hands at the sink and then went into the pantry. I took off my apron and my hairnet and peered at myself in the tiny mirror. With my fingers, I did the best I could to comb out my straight blond hair and retied it in a high ponytail. Rose's guests this week were longtime family friends of hers, but I didn't know them. My grandmother had lived in Iowa her entire married life, and that was where my mother, Tina, had been born and raised. Mom moved to New York City before the ink on her high school diploma was dry. She'd had a moderately successful Broadway career as a singer and actor. She'd also had a short marriage to a rock drummer named Jeff Roberts, and they produced me. I'd lived in Manhattan my entire life, close to both of my parents, until I came to Cape Cod over the past winter to help Rose run her B & B and open my tearoom. Mom never took me back home to Iowa, but my grandparents visited us regularly, and we often vacationed with them on Cape Cod. Rose, English to her fingertips, missed the sea.

I walked out of the kitchen and through the main dining room. China and cutlery clinked and people laughed and chatted in low voices. "This has been absolutely perfect," a woman said to her companion as I passed, and I hoped she was talking about her tea.

I need, I thought, to get out of the kitchen more. I work so hard baking pastries and scones and preparing sandwiches, I sometimes forget that the end product isn't just food but happy customers. I walked through the small vestibule, where customers check in as they arrive, and went outside to the tearoom's garden.

Six months ago, the building that's now Tea by the Sea was nothing but an old stone cottage collapsing into the sandy soil, and what vegetation surrounded it had been a handful of tough, hardy plants struggling to survive. We'd smoothed the ground and laid flagstone blocks to create the patio and dug most of the weeds out of the cracks in the low stone wall. We scattered terra-cotta pots and iron urns overflowing with red and white geraniums, purple lobelia, white bacopa, and trailing sweet potato vines around the space, and placed smaller pots on the half-height stone wall enclosing the garden. The flagstone floor was now dotted with tables and chairs, some of them under pink and blue umbrellas. As a finishing touch, I'd hung a multitude of cracked and mismatched teacups from the branches of the old oak that occupied pride of place in the center of the garden. The wind was light today, but when it blows off the bay, the cups make a delightful tinkling sound.

My grandmother and her two guests were seated at a table for four tucked into the far corner next to the wall. Bernie saw me approaching and gave me a wave. Before taking my seat, I gave my grandmother a kiss on her papery cheek.

"Good afternoon, love," she said. "I'm chuffed you could find the time to join us." Rose has lived in America for fifty years, but memories of Yorkshire are still strong in her voice.

"It's my pleasure." I turned to the woman seated across from Rose. "Hi. I'm Lily."

She got to her feet. "Heather French. Pleased to meet you at last. Rose can't stop talking about you." She stretched out her hand, and I leaned across the table to shake it. Heather was about Bernie's and my age, early thirties, but unlike us, the word that instantly came to mind was *money*. Her blond hair was slightly darker than mine and expertly streaked and highlighted; her nails were long and red, her hands sleek, her makeup subdued but perfect. She wore a white silk top cropped a couple of inches above a taut belly button pierced by a single jewel, a gold lamé jacket in a vaguely military style, and short (very short) white shorts. Her bare tanned legs ended in high-heeled gold sandals.

"Please have a seat," she said, as though she were the hostess and this wasn't my place.

I sat.

I glanced across the table at Bernie. She avoided my eyes.

Cheryl placed a cup of tea, already prepared the way I like it with a splash of milk and a few grains of sugar, and a plate of sandwiches in front of me. "Can I get you anything else, Rose?"

"More tea, Heather? Bernadette?"

They both said, "No, thank you."

Heather lifted her arms and held them out to her sides. "You own this marvelous place, Lily. Aren't you the lucky one? It's absolutely adorable. Almost as adorable as Rose's house."

"*Luck,*" Bernie said, "has nothing to do with it. Lily works incredibly hard." Something, I thought, was wrong with my friend's voice. It had an edge to it I'd last heard when she first met Rose's next-door neighbor, Matt Goodwill, and had taken an instant dislike to him.

"To live so close to the sea." Heather's voice was high-pitched, and she spoke almost in a singsong. "I can barely see the river from my penthouse in Manhattan. If I stand on the veranda with a pair of good binoculars on a clear day, I can get a glimpse." Her laugh was as light and carefree as the tinkle of the teacups hanging from the old oak tree.

"That is so unfortunate," Bernie said with a sad shake of her head. "I chose my house specifically for the view of the ocean from my office. It's important, I felt, to have the water close to me, as the sea plays such an important role in my book." I threw Bernie a look. She never engaged in games of one-upmanship. She might be able to see the bay from her house on an exceptionally clear day with a good pair of binoculars, but she'd been able to afford the place only because it was in such bad repair. The homeowners hadn't been able to find anyone who wanted it for a vacation rental. The last time it rained, she'd called Rose and asked if the B & B had any spare buckets lying around that she could borrow.

Heather giggled. "A top-ranked chef *and* a soon-to-be bestselling author. You're lucky to be surrounded by such talented women, Rose."

"I think so," Rose said.

My days begin before six when I start breakfast in the B & B and end long after the tearoom closes when I finish prep for the next day. Meaning twelve to fourteen hours on my feet, seven days a week. It felt so good just to be sitting down. I took the first welcome sip of the Creamy Earl Grey, rich and heady with vanilla and bergamot and just a touch of *dulce de leche* for that hint of sweetness I need at the end of a long day. "Rose tells me your family's joining you tomorrow."

Heather threw up her hands. The diamonds in the ring on her left hand flashed in the sun. "It's going to be so great! I can't wait. My gran's coming, as well as my mom and dad. You're so lucky to be able to live close to your grandmother, Lily. I adore my gran to bits, but I don't see her nearly as much as I'd like. Iowa is so far away."

"I've heard of these things called *airplanes*," Bernie said.

Heather slapped my friend's hand. "You are so funny. Isn't she a hoot, Rose?"

"Not exactly the word I'd use," my grandmother said.

"My brother and his wife are coming on our little vacation, too, and the less said about her, the better. I'm not so excited about seeing them, but we'll manage. And the kids, of course. Tyler and Amanda, my nephew and niece.

It's been ages, and I'm really looking forward to spending some time with them. I want to take them to the beach, and we're going on a whale-watching tour. I've chartered us a boat for later in the week. It's going to be so much fun." Heather beamed.

I felt myself smiling. I liked her. Her excitement was genuine and her enthusiasm infectious. Bernie clearly didn't agree. Her face was pinched with disapproval and her eyes narrow. Not exactly the picture of a *hoot*.

Cheryl appeared at my side. "I'm sorry to interrupt, Lily, but Nancy's on the phone. There's some problem with the strawberries."

"Oh, goodness," Heather laughed. "That sounds dreadfully serious. 'Some problem with the strawberries.' How dramatic!"

I didn't laugh. In my restaurant, strawberry problems are not a laughing matter. "Not again. I'll be right there." I got to my feet. "Sorry, gotta run. Nice meeting you, Heather."

She jumped up. "And it was so nice meeting you, Lily. I'll bring my family around for tea and you'll have to join us. I won't take no for an answer." She stamped her foot and crinkled her nose.

"I'd like that," I said.

"If you'll excuse me," Bernie said. "I have to be going, too. Thanks for the tea, Rose."

"So nice to meet you," Heather trilled. "Let me know when you're launching your book and I'll come!"

Bernie followed me into the kitchen. I picked up the phone. Cheryl's cousin Nancy owns a berry farm, and in my opinion, she runs her farm very badly. She'd failed to deliver my order once before, and today I simply told her that if the baskets of freshly picked strawberries weren't here tomorrow morning, I'd find a new supplier. It's important to me to use local ingredients from local farmers, whenever possible. But I have to have strawberries at this time of year."

"Isn't she a horror!" Bernie said, once I was off the phone, the Great Strawberry Crisis averted. For now.

"Nancy? I wouldn't go quite that far, although she needs to be a lot more reliable if she wants to stay in business."

"Not her. Heather."

"Heather? I thought she was sweet."

"Ha! All she talked about was herself and how much money she has."

"She actually said that?"

"Well, no. Not in so many words. But the penthouse apartment in Manhattan, the private boat she's chartered. And that gold jacket. Talk about tasteless. What do you think? Two thousand bucks?"

"I have no idea. Rose seemed to like her." No one could express disapproval better than my grandmother. I went into the pantry for my apron and hairnet and called over my shoulder, "You don't have to like her, Bernie. Besides, you're the world's worst judge of character."

"I'm nothing of the sort."

"Sure you are. Look at how much you distrusted Matt Goodwill when you met him. You practically accused him of murder. Come to think of it, you did accuse him of murder."

"That was different."

"It's always different," I said.

Cheryl ran into the kitchen. "A van's just driven up. Eight people wanting the full tea. No reservation."

I let out a long breath. It was almost closing time, but eight people were eight customers. "Do we have room?"

"I can seat them in the garden. People are starting to leave."

I did a quick mental inventory of the fridge and the pantry. "Then I can feed them. I'll have to use some of what I made for tomorrow." I reached for the fridge door. "Uh, Bernie, can you get out of the way, please."

"And that ring. Did you see that ring? Silly question, you could see that ring in outer space."

"Good-bye, Bernie," I said, giving her an affectionate push in the direction of the back door.

I didn't see Rose or her guests that evening. I worked in the tearoom for a few hours after closing, poaching chicken and boiling eggs for tomorrow's sandwiches, making scones, cupcakes, tarts, and macarons to replenish the ones I'd served to our last-minute arrivals. Despite the long hours, I always enjoy time alone in the kitchen after everyone has left. I can move at my own pace, nibble on raw cookie dough, or snatch a scone off a tray straight out of the oven, make the things I enjoy making, even though I've made them hundreds, maybe thousands, of times before. I play music from my iPad through Bose speakers and dance or sing as I work. As I inherited not one whit of musical talent from my mother, I never so much as hum if anyone's around.

By eight o'clock, the larder was once again satisfyingly full, and it was time to turn off the ovens, switch off the lights, and go home to my dog.

I might work long, hard hours at my tearoom, but my commute can't be beat. I walked down the long curving driveway toward the huge old house that is Victoria-on-Sea, my grandmother's B & B. The house had been built in 1865 as a vacation home for a Boston banker and his family. The house boasted eight guest bedrooms and suites on two floors, Rose's private apartment on the ground floor, a formal dining room, and a drawing room that was now used as a common room for visitors. The outside of the house is painted white, with a gray roof, turrets and dormer windows sticking out all over, miles of ginger-bread trim, and a wide veranda running the length of the building. The veranda, full of generously-filled flowerpots, faces east across the gardens and down the long driveway to the highway. The rear of the house faces the water, and guests are welcome to sit on the benches provided and look over the bluffs to the open waters of Cape Cod Bay. A three-car garage, painted to match the house, stands alone at the edge of the guest car park. The garage was originally the carriage house, modernized by the previous owners. We don't need space for three vehicles. Between Rose and me, we have one car. Hers. Before coming here, I'd lived my entire life in Manhattan. I can drive, if I have to, but I've never owned a car. My cousins in Iowa find that as shocking as if I'd never learned to read.

I cut across the lawn, skirted the rose garden, and slipped around the house to let myself into the small cottage overlooking the bluffs and the bay beyond.

Éclair, my Labradoodle, so named because of the streak of mocha running in a band down her stomach between her mostly cream-colored fur, ran to greet me, and I greeted her with a belly rub. I felt better knowing she hadn't been alone all day—I'd arranged for one of the B & B house-keepers to come over in the early afternoon to check her water dish and take her for a short walk.

Greetings completed, I let Éclair into the enclosed side yard while I changed out of my cook's clothes of jeans and T-shirt into shorts and another comfortable T-shirt. Then I took the leash off the hook by the door and went outside. Éclair's good enough to stay close and come when I call, so I didn't attach the leash to her collar, but I always keep it with me. Not everyone likes dogs, no matter how small or how friendly they might be, and B & B guests can usually be found enjoying the gardens or the view in the evening.

Tonight, lights shone from every upstairs room, although the parking lot wasn't full. It was still reasonably early, and most guests would have gone out for dinner. Éclair and I strolled along the path at the top of the bluffs. A few people sat on benches, looking over the bay and the lowering sun. They greeted me politely and a couple of women fussed over the dog. Éclair is always happy to be fussed over.

We enjoyed a good long walk, and I felt some of the tension of the day draining away. Back home, I fed Éclair, made myself a sandwich with some of the poached chicken I'd pinched from the tearoom, and went to bed with my book.

The exciting life of a restaurant chef in high season.

I didn't mind. This summer was all about establishing the tearoom and saving Rose's B & B from bankruptcy. A social life would have to wait.

I was asleep before it was fully dark outside, lulled by the sound of the surf crashing on the rocks below and the gentle breathing of Éclair at my side.

Chapter 3

I was up at quarter to six, as usual. I let Éclair into the yard while I had my shower, and then I gave her breakfast and dressed as she ate. At six o'clock, we walked the short distance to the rear entrance of the B & B, and I let myself into its dark, tiny, out-of-date kitchen.

The first thing I always do is put on the coffee. The initial pot isn't for the guests, but for me. That task done, I took a banana out of the big bowl on the counter and peeled it to munch on while I got the baking started. Éclair sniffed in all the corners, in case someone had been in since the last time she was here and had dropped a slice of sausage or a T-bone steak on the floor. She never finds anything, because the kitchen is normally only used to prepare breakfast, but she never gives up hope. She then settled under the Formica table to watch me work. And no doubt, to hope I'd drop something. That never happens, either.

At Victoria-on-Sea, we offer our guests a traditional full English breakfast every day, although updated to suit modern tastes and diets, along with cereal and yogurt, pastries and fruit, and a low-calorie option. In the evening, Rose leaves a note on the table telling me how many breakfasts to prepare and if there are any dietary requirements.

We had a full house today: eight rooms and suites containing sixteen adults and six children. Fortunately, no one had any special demands. Rose's note said one reservation hadn't arrived, but the guest had phoned to say their flight had been canceled and they might not get in until this morning.

I made a mental note to ensure I had extra muffins ready in case the latecomers arrived after breakfast service ended at nine. If they'd been scrambling for flights and traveling all night, they would not arrive in a good mood.

I had pork-and-sage and lower-fat turkey sausages, bought from a local butcher, frying on the stove, and bran muffins in the oven, when Edna, the breakfast assistant, arrived.

"Morning, Lily." She took her apron off the hook by the door and bent over to give Éclair a pat of greeting. "Did Rose's special guests get in?"

"I assume so, as I didn't hear otherwise."

"She's so excited about having her friends here. It's quite sweet." Edna wasn't much younger than my grandmother, and she didn't need this job, or any other. At bridge one day, Rose had overheard Edna saying she was getting bored in her retirement, and before Edna knew what was happening, she'd been hired. She put a bag on the table. Inside, glass jars tinkled. Edna made much of the jam and preserves we used in the B & B and sold in the tearoom.

I opened the bag and lifted out a jar. "Marmalade? You don't usually make marmalade."

"Oranges were on sale in the supermarket last week. Can you use them?"

"Jam's usually more popular with scones, but I have an idea. Thanks. Can I have a taste?"

"Feel free," she said. "They're yours now."

I twisted the top off one of the jars. The preserves were a brilliant orange, thick with chunks of sliced fruit and glistening jelly. I scooped up a bit with a spoon and touched the spoon to my tongue. The orange flavor was strong and tart, with exactly the right touch of sweetness. "Like eating sunshine," I said, licking the spoon.

Edna smiled and I turned back to the breakfasts.

A streak of black fur shot across the kitchen and landed on the counter next to the stove. I was so startled, I almost dropped the bowl of eggs I was beating for an egg-white frittata. Éclair leapt to her feet and let out a single sharp bark.

"Shush!" I said. "It's only Robbie." I glared at the cat. "You scared me half to death."

He gave me a look I interpreted to be a grin and then turned his attention to the sausages on the stove. I picked him up and put him on the floor, knowing that was a waste of time. He'd be back when it suited him.

Robbie coming into the kitchen wasn't unusual, but he didn't normally appear this early. That could only mean . . .

Tap tap tap came the sound of Rose's cane in the hallway.

"Good morning." My grandmother settled herself at the table and her cat leapt into her lap.

"You're up early," I said.

"Exciting day. I won't have my tea in here this morning, Edna, because I'm joining my friends for breakfast."

"That's good," said Edna, " 'cause I don't serve tea in here." She lifted a tray loaded with jugs of milk, cream, and juices and took it into the dining room.

Rose was a woman who liked color. Today, she wore an ankle-length purple dress splashed with enormous orange flowers. The dress was sleeveless, so she'd pulled it on over a bright yellow T-shirt. Long earrings made of feathers dyed purple caressed her shoulders, and she'd gone to a lot of trouble this morning with her makeup. Black liner outlined her cornflower-blue eyes, thick layers of mascara caked her lashes, rouge brought color to her cheeks, and her mouth was a slash of crimson lipstick.

Rose had lived in Iowa most of her life and I'd grown up in Manhattan, but my grandmother and I have always been close. I sometimes wonder how much of that has to do with the fact that we look so much alike. If you didn't know better, you'd think it was me smiling proudly from the silver-framed wedding picture on her nightstand. These days, her once-blond hair is a solid gray and cut into short spikes, and her fine porcelain skin is lined and folded and scattered with dark spots, but her light blue eyes still shine with intelligence and wit, and I can only hope I'll be as sharp as Rose when I reach her age. In one thing only, our appearance differs. Rose barely reaches five feet tall and is as fine-boned as a bird, whereas I get my additional eight inches of height from my father.

"Your friend arrived safely?" I asked.

"It was lovely to see Sandra again. She was tired after the trip, so we didn't get much of a chance to get caught up. I'm looking forward to doing that at breakfast."

"And the rest of the family?" I opened the oven door and checked the muffins by pressing on one of them with my finger. It felt firm, so I took the tray out of the oven.

"Sandra's come with her son, Brian McHenry, and his wife, Darlene. They're Heather's parents. Also Heather's brother, Lewis, his wife, Julie-Ann, and their two children. I told them to come down at eight for breakfast so you could join us."

"I don't—"

"So you could join us."

"I can't cook and eat at the same time."

"Why ever not? Edna can finish up in here."

Edna came into the kitchen in time to hear that. "Cooking is not in my job description."

"I believe when I hired you, I specified, '*Other* duties, as assigned.' "

"I believe when you hired me, you said, 'Please, Edna, I need you desperately. Help me and you can do your job exactly as you like.' "

"I believe," I said, "I'm the cook around here. Which means I'm in charge and I decide who does what."

As if either of them ever pays any attention to me.

"As it's still an hour until eight o'clock," Rose said, "I've changed my mind and I'll have my tea now."

"Pot's over there." Edna sat at the table to slice fresh fruit for the salad. Robbie, whose full name is Robert the Bruce in honor of my grandfather's Scottish heritage, left Rose's lap to sniff at the bananas. Edna put him on the floor. She and I exchanged glances, but we didn't say anything.

What would be the point?

I'd told Rose, more than once, that I don't want animals in my kitchen. Never mind what the health department would have to say if they saw a cat sitting on the table and sniffing at the food bowls. Rose reminded me that advertising for her B & B plainly says a cat is in residence. People who object are welcome to stay elsewhere.

I don't believe dogs belong in commercial kitchens, either, but if Rose's cat can come in, then my dog can, too. So there!

Such minor victories make up life with Rose. Everyone in my family thought I was crazy to even consider going into business with her. My mother, most of all.

I plugged in the kettle for Rose's tea. "Do they all, except for Heather, live in Iowa?"

"Yes. Brian owns some sort of a car dealership, and

Darlene, his wife, is a nurse. I'm not sure what Lewis or Julie-Ann do."

"What's the story with Heather?" The kettle boiled and I added hot water to the bags in the teapot. In the B & B, I don't bother with making individual flavors of tea or using tea leaves. I also never make scones. If people can have specialty tea and homemade scones in here, why would they come to my tearoom?

"I like her enormously. Such a fun girl. What did you think?"

"She seemed nice. She's looking forward to this family vacation. Bernie didn't warm to her, though. She thought Heather's overly keen to make sure we know she has money."

Rose shrugged. I put the teapot on the table in front of her, along with a cup and saucer and a small jug of milk. Robert the Bruce stuck his little black nose into the jug. Rose poured a splash into her saucer and he licked it up eagerly.

"Ah, yes. Money. Heather has rather a lot of it and perhaps she does like to show it off, but she has no ill intentions. She wants everyone else to share her own pleasure in it. I knew Heather when she was a teenager. She didn't get on with her parents and spent a lot of time at Sandra's house. They were difficult years, for the parents, for Sandra, for Heather. The teenage years often are, aren't they? Your mother, for example—"

I cut that line of conversation off. "Let's not go there today, Rose."

My grandmother sipped her tea. "You didn't steep the leaves long enough."

"I didn't use leaves. How did Heather manage to strike it rich?"

"She eventually settled down, after much drama and a lot of turmoil, in her mid-twenties, got her GED and went to the local community college to take some sort of business course. While there, she met a part-time teacher who was a good deal older than her."

"Hold that thought until I get back." Edna had finished the fruit salad and was about to carry the big glass bowl from which guests would serve themselves into the dining room.

"I most certainly will not," Rose said. "I'm exchanging news of my longtime friend and her family with Lily, not gossiping."

"Sounds like gossiping to me," Edna said. "And as my mother always said, 'If it sounds like gossip, it is gossip.'" Her voice faded away as she left the room.

"Who's gossiping?" Simon came into the kitchen. "Morning, all. You're up early today, Rose."

"Why does everyone keep saying that?"

"Because you're up early," I said.

Simon washed earth off his hands at the sink, then helped himself to a cup of coffee, added a generous splash of cream, and leaned against the far wall. The gardens of Victoria-on-Sea are one of the highlights of the property and one of the reasons Rose can charge as much for a night here as she does. An English country garden, particularly one on a hilltop so close to the ocean, needs a lot of work, and looking after it is Simon's job. We'd been lucky to get him. Our longtime gardener quit at the beginning of the season. As he gave his notice, while driving out of town in his new girlfriend's convertible, he also provided Rose with the number of his nephew, an experienced horticulturalist who'd recently arrived from England for a summer job, only to find the job had fallen through.

"I'm telling Lily about the granddaughter of one of my longtime friends," Rose said.

I spotted Simon eyeing the warm bran muffins. "Help

yourself. We've enough guests today, so I'm making a second batch."

He didn't need to be told twice.

"Guests arriving." Edna came back into the kitchen. "Four places, all for a full breakfast. Three with eggs over easy and the other well done."

"Well-done eggs, ugh," I said. "Might as well eat shoe leather. I'm on it. As long as you're sitting there, Rose, I need those tomatoes sliced."

"Really, love. I don't employ you so I can cook."

"If by *employ,* you mean *pay,*" I reminded her, "you don't."

Edna carried out the fruit salad, while Simon took a knife from the wood block on the counter and laid the tomatoes on a cutting board. They'd be sautéed in a splash of olive oil, along with mushrooms, to accompany the cooked breakfast. I turned the heat down on the sausages and started on the next batch of muffins. I'd get them into the oven before cooking the eggs.

"Simon understands the meaning of 'other duties, as assigned,' " Rose said.

"I understand what side my muffin's baked on," he said.

"Whatever that means," I said. "Anyway, Rose, you were telling me about Heather."

"Ah, yes. Heather. The rebellious one in her staid Midwest family. She married her part-time college teacher, who was about twenty years older than her. As well as teaching at the college, he had a small Internet start-up company. Something to do with on-time inventory for large stores. Sandra didn't understand much of it, but she understood well enough when one of the country's largest computer corporations bought his business for sixty-five million dollars."

"Wow!" I said.

"That's rather a lot," Simon said with typical English understatement.

Edna reappeared. "One for the frittata. And one who'll just have muffins and fruit."

"Heather's husband was kept on by the new owners as a consultant," Rose said, "and they moved to New York to be near the corporate offices. That happened about five years ago. They bought an apartment on the Upper East Side, as well as a house in Westchester, where he could keep his cars. He was an antique-car enthusiast, and now he had the funds to support his hobby."

"I don't suppose I dare hope she divorced him and is now looking for a handsome English gardener to be her second husband?" Simon asked as he handed me the plate of sliced tomatoes and I added them to the frying pan. I quickly cooked the eggs and served up four plates for Edna to carry out.

"She might be," Rose said. "He died not six months after they moved."

I turned around, still holding the spatula. "Oh, no. What happened?"

"Hit by a car while crossing the street outside their apartment building. Poor man. He didn't get to enjoy the fruit of his labors for long."

"That's terrible," I said. "Was that when you came to Manhattan for a visit a few years ago? I remember now. You said you'd come to be with a friend whose granddaughter had just been widowed."

Rose nodded. "Heather was estranged from her family. They hadn't approved of her marrying Norman and didn't spare any words in telling her so. They had a wedding in the registry office, and the only member of her family who attended was Sandra."

"Her parents didn't go to her wedding? How awful."

"Sandra told me Heather pretended she didn't mind, but she was badly hurt. Anyway, when Norman suddenly came into all that money, Heather's family equally suddenly wanted to kiss and make up. Heather wasn't having any of it, and she didn't want their support after he died. Sandra was worried about her for a while. She was the only one Heather wanted to see. Sandra was visiting them in New York when Norman died, and I came to the funeral to support Sandra. Which gave me a chance to visit with you and your mother."

"I'm sorry I made that crack about her being divorced," Simon said. "In light of what you've just told us, it was pretty tasteless."

Rose smiled at him over the rim of her teacup. "You didn't know, love."

"Time for me to be off, anyway," he said. "Those weeds won't kill themselves. It's supposed to be a hot one, and I've already stood around talking longer than I should have. Thanks for the coffee and muffin, Lily."

"Thanks for helping out."

When he'd gone, I turned back to my grandmother. "Heather's family is joining her on this vacation. Does that mean they've made up?"

"They're going to give it a try. It's really Sandra who Heather wants to spend time with. Sandra told her about this B and B I've bought, said she'd like to visit me here, and Heather asked if she could come, too. Somehow the rest of the family got involved."

"Heather seemed excited about it yesterday."

"Yes, she did. And I was pleased. It's been six years since she and Norman married, and four and a half since his death. Long past time to bury grievances." She studied me over the rim of her teacup with those intense blue eyes. The same eyes I saw in the mirror every morning. "Family's important, Lily. More important than anything."

I smiled at her. I didn't have to say I knew that. Family, after all, was why I was here, sweating over a hot stove in the dated kitchen of a B & B.

Edna brought in a tray of dirty dishes. "Your guests are here, Rose."

My grandmother got to her feet and picked up her pink cane. Yet another bright color to add to her purple, orange, and yellow ensemble. "This visit is important to me. Please treat my friends well."

"You mean unlike the way in which I treat the rest of our guests?" Edna said.

Rose gave her a wicked grin. "I'll have a fresh pot of tea in the dining room, Edna."

I laughed. Score one for Rose.

Chapter 4

I didn't have breakfast with Rose and her friends because I was in the kitchen cooking it, but when the final order was served and the pots stacked in the sink were almost touching the ceiling, I texted Cheryl to say I might be a bit late today. She has a key to the back door of the tearoom and could get work started if I wasn't there.

When things go well at breakfast, and I get out of the kitchen before nine, I like to take my second cup of coffee and a muffin or slice of coffee cake home to relax on my tiny porch. I sit, watching the sea come to life, enjoying a precious period of calm before leaping back into the fray of running the tearoom. We open at eleven, and I need to be in the tearoom by ten to get started on the day's baking and making sandwiches. Today, I'd skip my alone time and do my duty by my grandmother.

I poured myself a cup of coffee, put a muffin on a plate, took off my apron, told Éclair, who'd recognized the going-home signs and had run to the door, to stay, and went into the dining room to join my grandmother and her guests.

Rose sat at the head of the biggest table, the one closest

to the French doors, and a woman about her age, whom I took to be Sandra, had the foot facing the outside. The doors were thrown open, letting in the fresh sea air, the soft sound of the surf rushing to shore, and the scent of the gardens. A few other guests lingered over their tea or coffee, checking maps and guidebooks and making plans for the day.

Robert the Bruce was nestled in Rose's lap. At least he wasn't sitting on the table. My grandmother smiled when she saw me coming. The two men at the table stood up.

"Everyone, meet my granddaughter, the marvelous Lily Roberts." Rose made the introductions. Fortunately, she'd told me their names earlier, so I was able to keep them all straight: Sandra, looking every inch the proud matriarch. Her son, Brian, with a big smile full of white teeth, and an outstretched hand. His wife, Darlene, short and thin with neatly bobbed silver hair, eyeglasses with heavy black frames, comfortable clothes, and plain gold hoops through her ears. Their son, Lewis, with his wife, Julie-Ann, and their two teenage children. Heather, whom I'd met, was Brian and Darlene's daughter, and Lewis was her brother.

"You look exactly like Rose when I first met her," Sandra said. "All those many years ago."

I smiled at her. "So I've been told. Welcome."

"Hi!" Heather said. "Nice to see you again, Lily. Thank you for the lovely breakfast. You need a chair. Tyler, get the lady a chair."

"Why me?" said the teenage boy, all knees and elbows, bad skin, greasy brown hair, and overlarge Adam's apple. And attitude. Plenty of attitude.

"Because your aunt Heather told you to," said Brian, Lewis and Heather's dad, Tyler's grandfather.

The boy grumbled, but he got up and dragged a chair over from the nearest table. I thanked him and sat down.

Sandra gave me a huge smile and said, "I can not believe

we've never met before. Rose is so very fond of you." She was small and her shoulders were bent, her face a network of deep wrinkles; her white hair had been forced into tight curls and was thin enough to show patches of pink scalp beneath. She studied me with intense dark eyes.

I smiled at Rose, and then glanced around the table. Something, I thought, had happened here. Postures were stiff and people weren't looking at each other. Only Sandra and Heather continued smiling after everyone had greeted me.

"Great breakfast, Lily." Heather patted her flat stomach. "I haven't eaten so much in ages, and after that tea yesterday! They'll have to roll me into the gym when I get home."

"Please!" The woman who spoke was Julie-Ann, Heather's sister-in-law and mother of the kids. "I hope you're not going to spend the entire week complaining about how fat you are." She turned to the skinny teenage girl at the table. "It's perfectly all right to enjoy good food, Amanda. Eat in moderation is what I say, and if you do that, you don't have to worry about your weight."

"Like you'd know," the girl sneered.

Julie-Ann threw her daughter a poisonous look. She was a few years older than Heather, around the same age as her husband, Lewis. Julie-Ann wasn't fat, but she carried more weight around her waist and hips than she probably liked. Her hair was dyed a brassy blond and the red polish on her fingernails was chipped. She wore a pale blue T-shirt, beige Bermuda shorts, and practical sandals. Her face was drawn, and the bags under her eyes were deep and dark.

"That's enough of that sort of talk, Amanda," the man seated next to Julie-Ann said. "Your mother has health concerns. Which brings us back to my point. With her back, Julie-Ann shouldn't be flying economy."

"Brings us back to your point, Lewis?" Brian said. "I don't think we've ever left it. You're lucky Heather paid for your tickets. You could have taken the bus, you know."

I had no wish to be in the middle of what appeared to be an ongoing family quarrel. "What are your plans for today? The weather report's excellent. Sunny all day and in the mideighties. Should be the same for the rest of the week."

"We're going shopping, isn't that right, Aunt Heather?" Amanda said.

"I promised Amanda a small outing," Heather said.

"I'm coming with you," Julie-Ann said.

"Mom!" Amanda protested.

"I don't trust you to get suitable things. I don't trust"— Julie-Ann threw a sideways glance to Heather, dressed in a formfitting, sleeveless turquoise dress, with a deep-plunging neckline—"modern fashion when it comes to girls your age."

Amanda rolled her eyes. Heather winked at her. Julie-Ann grabbed the last muffin from the plate in the center of the table.

"I'm hoping to get some fishing in," Brian said. "I was checking out charters in the room last night before we turned in. Did you get my email with the name of the one I like, honey?" he asked Heather.

"Yes, Dad," she said.

"Great. Book it for Tyler and me for tomorrow, why don't you. You coming, Lewis?" he asked his son.

"Might as well," Lewis replied.

"Three places then," Brian said.

"Okay," Heather said.

"Thanks, honey."

"While the boys are doing that, I want a spa day," Darlene, Heather's mother, said. "Julie-Ann, why don't you come, too, and Amanda?"

Amanda looked up from an intense study of her fingernails. "Cool."

"Rose, you must know a good place," Darlene said.

"I can make a few suggestions."

"Let Heather know which is the best. We'll want a full-day package, one that includes a spa lunch."

I exchanged glances with Rose.

"It's okay to make plans," Heather said, "but don't forget I've chartered a boat to take us whale watching on Wednesday."

"That should be exciting," Darlene said.

"Hi, everyone." Bernie strode through the French doors. She leaned over and gave Rose a peck on the cheek. "Sorry I'm late, Rose, but I was working on a new scene and I got so caught up in it, I lost track of time."

"I'll forgive you," Rose said. "Everyone, this is Lily and my good friend, Bernadette. Bernie's a novelist."

"Cool," Amanda said, looking genuinely interested.

The adults all muttered some form of greeting, none of them looking even remotely genuinely interested.

Bernie dragged a chair over from another table, put it next to Rose, and sat down.

"I want to hit the beach today," Tyler said. "How do we get there?"

"Stairs leading down to the water are right outside this door," I told Tyler. "But it's not good for swimming here. It's rocky, not sandy. It's a perfect spot for walking and exploring the coastline, particularly when the tide's out and the pools are full of sea life."

"That would be great," Heather said. "The tide's going out now. Who wants a morning hike?"

"As if," Amanda mumbled.

"I'd love to go with you," Julie-Ann said, "but not with my knees. I couldn't manage those stairs."

"If you exercised now and again," Darlene said to her daughter-in-law, "you might not have so much trouble."

"Did I ask you for health advice?" Julie-Ann snapped. "I did not, but thank you so much, anyway."

"Just trying to help, dear." Darlene sipped her coffee.

"Not me," Brian said. "I want to catch the replay of the game I missed when we were in the air."

"You'll have to do that another time," Darlene said. "I'm going to the beach with Tyler and you have to drive us. It's too bad we only rented the one car." Her eyes flicked toward Heather.

"Aunt Heather has hers," Amanda said. "She can drop you on the way into town for our shopping trip."

"Heather wants to go walking this morning," Sandra said. "As for me, I plan to sit on that lovely veranda and rock back and forth and catch up with my oldest and dearest friend."

"Lily?" Heather turned to me. "Would you like to come for a walk?"

"What's that, dear?" Sandra said. "Speak up."

"Sorry, Gran. I asked Lily to come with me."

"I don't know why young people these days have to mutter all the time," Sandra muttered.

Heather gave her a fond look as I said, "I'd love to, but I don't have time. I have to get to the tearoom before opening. I'm late as it is."

"I can't wait to see your tearoom," Sandra said. "I have the most marvelous idea! We'll all meet for afternoon tea tomorrow. Can you reserve us a table for two o'clock? Rose, you'll join us, of course."

"I'd be delighted," my grandmother said.

"Can't," Brian said. "Lewis, Tyler, and I are going fishing."

"We might need to do more shopping," Amanda said. "If I don't get all the things I want today."

"Isn't tomorrow our spa day?" Julie-Ann said.

"If Gran wants to have afternoon tea tomorrow," Heather said, "then we're having afternoon tea at two o'clock tomorrow. I'll make the other bookings for the day after."

Everyone tried, with varying degrees of success, to hide their disappointment, but no one put up an argument.

"Can I go now?" Tyler had taken his phone out of his pocket and was holding it under the table, passing it from one hand to the other, like a smoker who couldn't wait to get that next shot of nicotine.

"You may." Sandra took her room key out of her pocket and handed it to the boy. "Run up and get my book, please. It's on my night table."

He leapt to his feet, snatched the key, and ran for the French doors, followed by his sister.

"I meant to ask you, Rose," Julie-Ann said, "I don't suppose you have a nicer room free? We'd love a view of the sea."

"When Heather made the booking, she said you had trouble managing the stairs, so I gave you a room on the ground floor."

"Well, yes, my knees are bad, but I can manage the stairs."

Darlene snorted. Julie-Ann ignored her. I was starting to get the feeling that Darlene wasn't overly fond of her son's wife.

"I'm fully booked this week," Rose said. "The rooms are all assigned."

"I just thought, what with Sandra being such a good friend of yours . . ."

"I would think," Sandra said sharply, "you'd not look a gift horse in the mouth, Julie-Ann."

"I was only asking."

We were the last people in the dining room. Edna puttered about, clearing tables and resetting them for tomorrow. Out of the corner of my eye, I saw a man's head pop into the room. I don't normally have anything to do with the running of the B & B, that's up to Rose, but as she was occupied with her guests, I thought I'd help him. I stood up. "Nice meeting you all. I hope you have a marvelous visit to Cape Cod. We have plenty of brochures and maps at the registration desk to help you make the most of your visit."

Bernie leapt to her feet. "Gotta run. Have a nice day."

Sandra stood up and the rest of her family scrambled to follow. Rose put Robbie on the floor.

"We'll meet in the lobby at six this evening," Sandra said, "and go out to dinner as a family."

"You'd better make a reservation, Heather," Lewis said to his sister. "I bet the nice places fill up fast in the summer."

Bernie and I headed for the lobby as the family trailed behind us. Rose and Sandra brought up the rear, talking in low voices, their gray heads close together, their sticks tapping on the floor.

"What brings you here this morning?" I whispered to Bernie.

"Rose invited me to breakfast to meet her friends. Other than the old lady, who seems nice, I'm glad I was late."

"Strange bunch," I said.

"Not at all shy about scrounging off Heather. I didn't like her much when I first met her, but now that I see the way her family treats her like their personal ATM . . ."

We went into the front hall, which serves as the main reception area. In keeping with Rose's dream of owning a stately English country house, the walls are papered in pale green and hung with reproduction eighteenth-century English portraits, and the ceramic tiles on the floor are laid in a black-and-white check pattern. A wide sweeping staircase, with scarlet runners and oak banisters, leads upstairs. A recent photo of the queen hangs over the reproduction antique desk, where neat stacks of Cape Cod tourist brochures are laid out next to a vase of fresh flowers from our garden.

A man and a woman stood in the hall, suitcases at their feet. They were both in their late fifties. He was shorter than me, and either had a basketball stuffed under his T-shirt or was considerably overweight. Red lines of rosacea crisscrossed his bulbous nose, and he wiped at beads of sweat on his forehead. She was shorter still, and softly rounded, with small dark eyes that blinked rapidly in her plump face and dyed brown hair the texture of a Brillo pad. Her T-shirt was adorned with flowers and said it was from the DESERT BOTANICAL GARDEN, PHOENIX. These must be the people who'd failed to arrive last night.

"Hi," I said in my friendly professional voice. "Can I help you?"

"We have a reservation," he said. "We were supposed to be here yesterday, but our flight was canceled. Name's French. I'm Ed, and this is my wife, Trisha."

"What the heck?"

I turned at the sound of an angry voice behind me. Brian McHenry stood in the doorway to the dining room, his family clustered behind him. His face was turning red and a vein pulsed in his neck.

"Nice to see you, too, Brian," Ed French said.

"Goodness," Julie-Ann said. "This is . . . unexpected."

"This can't be some crazy coincidence." Brian whirled around. "Heather, did you know these . . . people were coming?"

"Calm down, Dad," Heather said. "I invited them."

"Why would you do something as stupid as that?" Darlene said.

"I have to say," Trisha French said, "we didn't know

the whole miserable gang would be here. Oh, dear, not Lewis, too?"

Bernie and I looked from one person to the other. Other than Sandra's and Heather's, the faces of the McHenry family varied between shock and rage.

"Believe me," Lewis said, "I'm as happy to see you, Trisha, as you are to see me."

Heather stepped forward. If she planned to go for a walk among the tidal pools, she'd have to change those sandals. The heels were about three inches high and the straps the thickness of dental floss. She walked up to the new arrivals and gave a startled Trisha a hug and her companion a peck on the cheek. "It's been far too long," she said, "thank you both for coming." Her point made, she turned to face her family. "I wanted to spend a nice few days with my gran. Gran suggested everyone come and—"

"Actually," Sandra said, "it was more that when I mentioned our plans to Brian, he decided to join us."

"That's not what happened, Mother," Brian said. "You told us your friend Mrs. Campbell had opened a B and B. You said it would be the perfect place for a family reunion."

"And by *family reunion*," Darlene said, "we assumed you meant the *family*. Not just you and my daughter. Who— I shouldn't have to point out, but I will—hasn't bothered to come home to Iowa to visit her parents since she moved to New York. Thus the *reunion* part of *family reunion*."

"As I'm trying to get along with everyone," Heather said, "and ensure that we all enjoy a nice week here, I won't *bother* to point out that you, Mom, didn't *bother* to come to my wedding. Ed and Trisha, on the other hand, did."

Darlene had the grace to look away.

"As this trip is all about bringing the family together

and letting bygones be bygones, I invited Ed and Trisha to join us. They are part of my family. Whether you like them or not."

"Not," Darlene muttered, although I was the only one standing close enough to her to hear.

Heather spoke to Rose. "Ed was the elder brother of my late husband, Norman." Rose had told me Norman had been a good twenty years older than Heather. That would explain why his older brother was more the age of Heather's father, Brian, than her brother, Lewis. She then turned her smile on me. "If you'd be so kind as to check our new arrivals in. You'll put it on my account, of course."

"I'll take care of that." Rose settled herself at the reproduction antique reception desk. She unlocked a drawer and took out a key. "I've put Mr. and Mrs. French in room 202. Second floor. It has a lovely view over the bay."

"Hey!" Julie-Ann said. "I asked for that room."

Trisha laughed and snatched the key out of Rose's hand. "Sorry."

Julie-Ann gave Trisha a narrow-eyed glare, but she then turned to Ed with a smile. "I, for one, am pleased to see you."

"Thanks," Ed said.

Darlene glared at her daughter-in-law over the top of her glasses, but she said nothing.

Robert the Bruce came out of the dining room, stretched his body to its full length, and once he was sure he had everyone's attention, he sashayed across the room. Trisha French's round face turned pale. She visibly recoiled and said, "Oh. A cat. How . . . unfortunate."

Robbie knew when he wasn't wanted and made the most of it. He rubbed himself against Trisha's legs and purred. She threw her husband a pleading glance, but he was fully occupied in staring down Brian McHenry. I snatched Robbie up and said, "Sorry, but he has the run of the place. It says so in all our booking information. Are you allergic to cats?"

"Not allergic, no." Drops of sweat had broken out on Trisha's forehead. "I'm okay. I'm . . . not too fond of cats, that's all."

Robbie purred happily in my arms.

"This is what we have on for today," Heather said. "A walk on the beach now, then some of us are going shopping in town and others to the swimming beach. We're meeting here at six to go to dinner. A free morning tomorrow, with afternoon tea at the tearoom up by the road at two. The next day, the women are going to a spa in North Augusta and the men fishing. Whale watching on Wednesday. Doesn't that sound like fun?"

"Fun," Ed French said without a trace of enthusiasm.

"A ball of laughs," Lewis said.

"Shopping?" Trisha said. "I can do that."

Footsteps sounded on the stairs as Tyler ran down. "Here's your book, GeeGee." He tossed a thick paperback to Sandra.

"Where's your sister?" Julie-Ann asked.

He shrugged. "In our room, on the phone. She's telling Madison all the stuff she's going to buy today. Why do we have to share a room, anyway? You're not paying."

"You keep complaining," Brian said, "and you'll be sleeping in the car."

"At least we have an extra car now," Julie-Ann said. "I assume you rented one, Ed?"

"Had to get here from the airport somehow."

Sandra stamped her cane on the floor to get everyone's attention. "Now that's settled, I'm going outside for a sit. Rose, will you join me?"

"Be right there," my grandmother said.

Sandra turned and shuffled away, leaning heavily on her cane. Bernie ran ahead of her to hold open the front door. I put Robbie on the floor and shooed him away. He stalked off, tail held high. "You must be tired and hungry," I said to the new arrivals. "Breakfast is finished and we don't provide room service, but I can bring you a couple of muffins, freshly baked this morning. Every room has all the things you need to fix tea or coffee, but as you've just arrived, I'd be happy to make you something, if you'd like."

"I'd adore a cup of coffee," Trisha said. "Sleeping on an airport bench is never comfortable."

"That's why I always travel business class," Heather said. "So nice to have the use of the executive lounge."

"Nice if you can afford it," Ed said.

"And I can, lucky me. Now I'm going to change my shoes." Heather bent her leg backward and wiggled her foot. "These little darlings are perfect for clubbing in Manhattan, but not for walking on the beach."

"Coffee for you?" I asked Ed.

"I can't drink caffeinated beverages, so I always carry my own." He patted his pockets.

"I have it, dear." Trisha dug in her purse and pulled out a small plastic bag containing dry brown leaves. "Ed's special tea. Do you mind? All it needs is to steep in hot water for a couple of minutes."

"I don't mind at all." I took the bag. "You go on ahead, and I'll bring your snack up in five minutes."

I caught Bernie's eye, jerked my head, and slipped away. She followed me. When we were safely in the kitchen, I let out a long breath. Edna had finished and left, and the kitchen was once again clean and sparkling.

Chapter 5

"I'd say drama is the word of the day for that lot," Bernie said.

"You can say that again." I plugged in the kettle and got down the package of coffee beans and a single-serve French press. "What a family."

"It's almost ten," Bernie said. "You have to open the tearoom soon. I can manage two muffins and a cup of coffee, if you like."

"Thanks. I'd appreciate that." I handed her Ed French's bag of tea leaves, and she opened it and sniffed. Her face crinkled in disgust. "Smells like right after Simon's cut the lawn."

"Freshly mown grass is a wonderful smell."

"So it is. Doesn't mean I want to sit down to a plate full of the stuff. Or, even worse, drink it."

I put the beans in the coffee grinder and switched it on.

"Speaking of Simon," Bernie said over the roar of the tiny motor, "I saw him deadheading roses when I arrived. How's he working out?"

"Great. He seems to have a real knack for growing things."

"Good to know," Bernie said. "But that's not what I meant. How's he working out on the more personal front?"

"There is no 'more personal front,' as I might have mentioned more than once. He's nice, very nice, and not hard to look at, either, but neither he nor I have time to see if anything's going to develop. At the end of the summer, he'll be gone. Back to merry old England."

"You need some romance in your life, Lily. You can't work all the time."

"Truth be told, I can work all the time. And I do. But what you mean is *you* need some romance in *your* life, and you want to live it through me. Have you seen Matt lately?"

"I assume that's not a change of subject, and the answer is no."

"He's moved in smack-dab next door. His car's parked there a lot of the time, and I occasionally see lights at night. They're faint and flickering and move around, so I don't think the electricity's hooked up yet." The property next to us was as old and had once been as grand as Victoria-on-Sea, but the house had been unoccupied for many years and was falling into not-so-genteel disrepair. Matt Goodwill had recently taken up residence. He intended to do most of the work involved in fixing up the house himself, as and when time and finances allowed.

"No comment," Bernie said. "Speaking of changing the subject, are you going to work or not?"

"On my way," I said. Éclair was standing impatiently by the door. If she knew how to tap her toes, she would have.

The kettle boiled, and Bernie poured hot water into the French press and then into the teapot containing Ed's leaves. "Smells even more like grass cuttings when it's wet. I'm thinking I can save myself a lot of work thinking up dialogue for my book if I record that family's conversations and type it out. Did you think they were weird? Did you notice that Julie-Ann and Lewis, who are married, never once even looked at each other?"

"Lots of married people don't get on all that well. I didn't notice, but that might be because I was too busy dodging the verbal blows between the French and McHenry families."

"Once again, Heather had to remind us that she travels business class and goes clubbing in Manhattan. In the neighborhood I grew up in, *clubbing* meant hitting someone over the head."

"You grew up in the same neighborhood I did, and it did not. She doesn't need to remind them. They're quick enough to take her money. Not only is she picking up the bill for everyone's stay here, but she seems to have paid for their flights and car rentals. And they're expecting her to pay for all their excursions and dinners. She might have more money, a lot more money, than the rest of her family, but they could be polite about it and offer to pick up the bill for something. Anything. But what do I know? I gather she's been estranged from her family for a long time." I filled Bernie in on what Rose had told me this morning.

"Yeah, I heard that crack about none of them coming to her wedding. I wondered about that."

"This is her way of trying to repair their relationship. Good for her for wanting to."

"Okay," Bernie said. "So I now like her slightly better, knowing she was widowed so soon after her marriage. She still doesn't need to throw her money around. I get it."

"Maybe she's insecure."

"I'm insecure. I don't make a big deal of it."

I stared at my best friend. "Are you really that *un*self-aware?"

"What does that mean?"

"Nothing." A less insecure person I'd never met. When we were kids, I called Bernie "the Warrior Princess." Come to think of it, I still did. Not only because she's six feet tall, lean, and fit, with an always out-of-control mane of curly red hair, a complexion dotted with freckles, and huge green eyes, but because Bernie's the bold one, the fearless one, the adventurous one. On the other hand, I'm more hesitant, shyer, less likely to rush into things without first checking that it's safe. She encourages me to be brave, and I like to think I put the brakes on when she threatens to get too daring.

"Those late arrivals came as a shock to the others," she said. "I'd love to know what's the story there."

"Not our problem, fortunately. As long as Sandra and Rose have a nice visit, and someone pays the family's bill when they leave, and no one steals the towels, I don't care what the others get up to. They're all coming for tea tomorrow at two. You'd be welcome, as Rose's guest."

"I might just do that. More fodder for my book."

"Let's hope it doesn't come to that."

Bernie filled the coffee carafe and put it on the tray next to the cream jug and sugar bowl, teapot, and a plate with two bran muffins. "I'll practice my servant skills for using in my book. Too bad I didn't know to dress the part."

I took Éclair home, told her to have a nice day, and headed for work. Rose and Sandra were sitting on the wide veranda, which runs the length of the house. They'd pulled two white wicker chairs next to each other and their heads were close together. I called to them as I passed and they waved to me. The sound of their laughter followed me down the driveway.

Before joining Rose and her friends in the breakfast room, I'd called Cheryl and asked her to stop at the supermarket on her way into work to pick up a few oranges.

I'd recently seen a recipe for scones made with fresh orange zest, which would be served with orange marmalade rather than the usual jam. Edna's marmalade gave me a chance to try it. I tossed some grated orange zest into the dry flour mixture before cutting in the butter and then added raisins and cream. I rolled the heavy wet dough in my hands until it was the proper consistency, laid it on a flour-covered cutting board on the butcher block, kneaded the dough a couple of times to incorporate all the components, and then rolled it into one-inch thickness. I cut circles, laid them on a prewarmed baking sheet, and popped the tray into the oven. While the scones baked, I started preparing the filling for an Earl Grey Chocolate Tart.

The scones looked so beautiful when they came out of the oven, hot and fragrant, sprinkled with raisins and tinged with a touch of orange zest. I pulled one apart with my fingers and spread butter on one half. I tasted it. I almost swooned.

"Those look nice," Cheryl said.

"Try one." I spread butter on the remaining half and pointed to it.

"Don't mind if I do." She took it, broke off a piece, and tossed it into her mouth. She closed her eyes and moaned.

"My reaction exactly. They're a bit heavier than the scones I usually make, and cream is more expensive than milk, so I'm thinking of adding these to the Royal Tea rotation. They're to be served with marmalade, not jam."

"Good idea," she said. "I'd come here just to eat those. But right now, as I'm working and not dining—worse luck—I have an order for a traditional afternoon tea for two."

I was left with a whole orange minus its peel, which I put into the fridge to use for tomorrow's juice at the B & B breakfast.

The rest of the day passed uneventfully. The tearoom was full all day, both inside and on the patio. No drama. Always a bonus in any sort of restaurant.

The tearoom closes at five. By the time the last of the guests left, the kitchen was cleaned, and the dining room cleared and set for tomorrow, it was five-thirty. I planned to stay behind to get some prep done for tomorrow, but before doing that, I went into the garden to catch a breath of air and give my body a good stretch.

In the city, I'd been a keen yoga practitioner, but somehow, since arriving on the Cape and opening the tearoom, I'd fallen out of the habit.

Something about twelve- to fourteen- or sixteen-hour days, seven days a week.

I was holding my right foot in my right hand, with my left arm extended to the side, trying to keep my balance, when Simon emerged from the shed at the far end of the garden and locked the door behind him. His motorcycle was parked in its usual place at the side of the shed, and he headed for it.

By the time he drove toward the tearoom, I was standing at the garden gate, waving him down.

He came to a stop, took off his black helmet, to which he'd stuck a Union Jack decal, shook out his hair, and gave me a lopsided grin. His sandy hair was, literally, sandy. Good Cape Cod earth was trapped deep in the folds of his hands, and a streak of dirt ran down his cheek. His jeans and boots were filthy.

"Good day?" I said.

"The best," he replied. "The plants are absolutely loving all this sunshine and heat. If this weather keeps up, I'll be worried about not getting enough rain, but we're not there yet. What's up?"

"Speaking of plants, Rose's friend and her family are coming for tea tomorrow. I'd like to do something really special with the table. Whatever you can give me in terms of flowers would be great."

"Roses?"

"Perfect, but only if you can cut enough without decimating the plants."

"I think I can. I'll make sure you get something nice, Lily. You know my price."

I smiled at him. "I do. Today's bucket's by the back door." I saved coffee grounds, used tea leaves, and vegetable scraps for Simon to add to the compost or pour on the plants.

He smiled at me. I smiled back.

"Are you baking tonight?" he said. "I'd offer to give you a hand but . . . I have plans."

"Not a problem. It was a good day and I'm fully in control." Simon's mother had been a caterer and he'd grown up helping her. He knew his way around a kitchen, in particular how to make a proper English teatime scone, and had helped me in the past when I'd been in desperate straits. His father had owned a gardening business. To cook or to garden had been Simon's career choices.

"I want to get enough done tonight so I can concentrate on Rose's guests tomorrow," I said. "Have a nice evening."

"You too, Lily." He put his helmet on, twisted the controls on his bike, and the powerful engine roared to life. He sped down the driveway and turned right at the highway.

He had plans for tonight. I wondered what sort of plans those might be.

I mentally kicked myself.

Not my business.

Heather had made a reservation for the Royal Tea for eleven people for the following day at two o'clock. With Bernie, that would be twelve for tea. Our Royal Tea comes with a glass of sparkling wine and the best of my baking, and is served on our best china.

For tomorrow's guests, I decided to make the orange scones to serve with clotted cream and Edna's marvelous marmalade. The sandwiches would be Darjeeling-poached chicken, curried egg salad, cucumber with cream cheese, and thinly sliced roast beef served open-faced with fresh arugula from our garden. For sweets, I'd do pistachio macarons, strawberry tarts, mini coconut cupcakes, and slices of buttery shortbread.

I worked until almost nine, and then, satisfied with my day's labors, and the fridge and pantry full, I hung up my apron, locked the tearoom, and headed home.

The sun was setting over Cape Cod Bay in a sky the color of Edna's marmalade. A flock of birds flew overhead, heading for their nightly shelter, fast-moving black shapes against the orange sky. The garden was wrapped in long shadows. White flowers glowed in the heavy dusk, and the scent of roses filled the air. A lone figure walked slowly through the garden, stopping now and again to bend over and examine a particular plant more closely. It was Trisha French, Heather's sister-in-law. Her concentration was totally on her surroundings, and I don't think she even noticed me pass.

Rose and Sandra were sitting on the veranda. Rose had her nightly gin and tonic, and Sandra cradled a glass of wine.

"Have you two not moved from that spot all day?" I said with a laugh.

"I just got back from dinner," Sandra said. "Rose waited for me before enjoying her nightly tipple."

Rose lifted her glass in a toast.

"How was your dinner?" I asked.

"The food was marvelous, the setting equally so. A lovely place on the pier overlooking the water. The company . . ." Sandra shrugged. "I'd have preferred a quiet dinner with Rose."

"Sorry to hear that," I said.

"Families. What can you say? They bicker. I sometimes think mine bicker more than most, but then everyone says theirs is the worst, don't they?"

Rose patted her friend's arm. "True enough. But we love them, all the same."

"Tensions are compounded, of course," Sandra said with a deep sigh, "when there's such an enormous income gap in the family. I'm pleased for Heather's good fortune, I truly am. Although I shouldn't call it that. She did lose Norman far too early. If they'd stayed in Iowa, he'd still be with us." She paused for a moment and took a breath. Rose and I waited. "I was about to tell your grandmother about our evening. Lewis ordered the most expensive bottle of wine on the menu, without even consulting with the others as to what we wanted. I thought that dreadfully rude of him. He doesn't have those sorts of tastes, and I can't imagine Julie-Ann has ever had filet mignon with lobster tails in her entire life. Never mind the brandy Brian enjoyed after dinner. Surprisingly enough, the only ones who didn't go overboard enjoying Heather's hospitality were Ed and Trisha. I can't believe Heather invited them on this trip. She had to know they wouldn't exactly be received with open arms. Then again, maybe she didn't know. Even when she was a girl, Heather didn't sometimes understand what was appropriate and what was not. She could be blind to other people's opinions. And now she's surrounded by people trying to influence her with flattery and attention. That can't be good."

"What's the story with Ed and Trisha?" Rose asked.

I had little interest (more like no interest) in the feuds of the McHenry/French family, so I said, "I've had a long day. Good night."

"Good night, love," Rose said.

"Good night, dear," Sandra said. "Now, remember, we'll be having tea at your tearoom tomorrow."

"I'm looking forward to showing you my place," I said.

"At Thornecroft Castle," Rose said as I turned to leave, "Lady Frockmorton always said she and her guests were *taking* tea. I often wondered why. You *have* breakfast or dinner or supper, but *take* tea."

"One of the mysteries of life," Sandra said. "As for the French family, Ed was Norman's older brother and they were close as children, or so everyone says. But when Norman met Heather . . ."

I rounded the house and almost bumped into a woman coming the other way. We both leapt back. She let out a small squeal, and my heart sped into overdrive.

"Oh, gosh. Sorry. I didn't see you."

"I didn't see you, either." Heather was dressed in denim shorts and heavy brown hiking shoes. A thick oatmeal wool sweater shot with blue thread was thrown over her T-shirt. "I was down at the beach, enjoying a walk along the shoreline, but it's getting too dark to be out on those rocks, never mind chilly. Have you had a nice evening?"

"Me? Nice enough. I'm just finishing work."

"You've been at work? This late? I suggested we have

dinner at your place one night, but Rose told me you only do afternoon tea."

"That's right. We close at five. My staff clean up and are usually gone before six, but I like to stay and get as much prep done for the next day as I can. I stay late most nights and bake. It's my busiest time of year, so it seems as though I'm always working, but I don't mind. I like being alone in there, just me and my measuring spoons and my ingredients."

"I'll have to take your word for it. My late husband always said the best thing I made in the kitchen was reservations."

I'd heard that many times before—almost every time I told someone I was a professional cook. But I laughed, anyway.

"Good night," Heather said.

"Good night."

I let myself into my house with a sigh of relief. My cottage is small and it doesn't have much of a kitchen, which suits me fine, as I don't want to cook for myself after cooking for other people all day. I popped a supermarket-bought premade meal into the microwave, fed Éclair, and enjoyed a bit of a romp with her in the yard before settling down with my book, my rather tasteless dinner, and a glass of wine.

I didn't read for long, and before getting ready for bed, I took Éclair for a walk along the hiking trail at the top of the bluffs. It was fully dark now, and I used the flashlight attached to my key chain to guide our way. A couple of boats passed, lights blazing. More lights shone from the houses lining the cliffs, but none were on at Matt Goodwill's place and his BMW convertible wasn't parked outside. Éclair and I walked for a long time, until eventually I called to her to come back and we retraced our steps. As I approached the cottage, I heard voices coming from the side of the big house. They were low, so I couldn't hear most of the words, but the anger in them came through loud and clear.

"... and my agreement is absolutely none of your business," a man said. "Stay out of it, you interfering busybody."

None of my business, either. I called to my dog and we went to bed.

Chapter 6

"One less for the Royal Tea," Cheryl said.

"What's happened?"

"Rose says the teenage boy had a blazing row with his father and he's been confined to his room for the rest of the day."

"What was the argument about?" Marybeth asked.

Cheryl shrugged. "Teenagers. Who knows? Who cares? Anyway, the rest of them are here. Even Bernie, who looks absolutely fabulous, dressed as though she's at Buckingham Palace or Downton Abbey. Rose has also gone all out, although I don't know that the queen would approve."

"Now you've got me curious," I said.

She grinned at me.

While they talked, my assistants filled the air pots with fresh water, took down tea canisters, measured tea leaves into china pots, and got the chilled prosecco out of the fridge. In the main room, they'd pushed two of the largest tables together, covered them with a stiffly ironed white tablecloth, and set the table with crystal flutes and the dishes I'd bought specifically to match the "by the Sea" part of our name: white china, with an edge of navy blue and gold trim. Blue linen napkins were at each plate, along with sterling silver teaspoons and butter knives.

Simon had outdone himself with the flowers. The rusty hinges on the kitchen door had squeaked not long after I'd let myself into the tearoom, and he'd come in, huge grin behind an equally huge bunch of gorgeous pink and peach roses. He presented them to me with a flourish.

"Sheer perfection." I dipped into a curtsy and accepted them.

"I'm glad you think so. Hope all goes well." He took the pail of coffee grounds, sodden tea leaves, and vegetable peels waiting by the door in exchange.

The stems of the roses weren't long and their length varied, so I trimmed them and put them into a wide silver bowl that had been one of my grandparents' wedding gifts, which I'd snatched from the drawing room at Victoria-on-Sea. Before our guests arrived, I'd gone out to inspect the table, and had been truly delighted.

Of course, we had other guests to attend to, so I'd scurried back to my kitchen without waiting to greet Rose and her friends.

While Marybeth and Cheryl prepared the various teas, I arranged the food on flower-patterned three-tiered trays. "One man gave me this." Marybeth held up a small plastic bag filled with dried leaves, her mouth pinched in disapproval. "It looks like dead grass, but he said it's his own special tea. Does it matter which pot I use?"

"Kind of a gruff-looking guy? Short and big-bellied?"

Marybeth nodded.

"That's Ed, Heather's brother-in-law. He's probably never had afternoon tea in his life. Give him a pot that's not too fancy or feminine. Maybe the plain one with the green trim."

"That'll do." Marybeth took it down from the shelf,

measured Ed's tealike concoction into the pot, and then added hot water. "Smells like dead grass, too."

While Marybeth and Cheryl carried the teapots out, I finished arranging the trays and stepped back to admire my handiwork. The arrangement looked pretty darn nice, if I did say so myself. Plump orange and raisin scones in the middle, perfectly cut sandwiches on the bottom, delicious sweets on the top: a carefully controlled explosion of color, shape, and flavor.

I heard the roar of Simon's motorcycle heading down the driveway toward the highway, and I had just enough time to wonder where he was going at this time of day before an enormous crash shook the foundations of the old stone building that housed Tea by the Sea. A moment of total silence fell, and then the screaming and yelling began. Chairs scraped the floor as they were pushed back and footsteps pounded on the wide-plank old floorboards. I threw the piping bag I was using to decorate cupcakes into the sink and bolted into the dining room. Teapots and plates abandoned, people were streaming through the small vestibule heading outside. Someone shouted, "Call 911!"

The people at Rose's table had also leapt to their feet and were hurrying into the garden. As I rushed by, Rose said, "What's happening?"

Sandra got to her feet with a speed that belied her years and feeble frame. "Sounds like there's been a car accident."

I dashed across the main room, through the vestibule, out the door, onto the garden patio, and pushed my way into the excited crowd. Everyone on the patio had stood up to get a better look. Marybeth was holding a tray full of dirty dishes, openmouthed, and Cheryl had stopped laying a table. Phones were out, as some people called 911 and others snapped pictures. "Is he dead?" someone shouted.

I still didn't know what had happened. Fortunately, the crashing sound hadn't come again after that initial bang.

"I'm a doctor," the woman standing next to me said. "Let me pass."

The crowd parted for her. I fell in behind her and pushed my way through the excited, chattering onlookers and out the garden gate.

My heart stopped and I let out a gasp of horror. Simon's motorcycle had crashed into the low stone wall surrounding the tearoom patio. The big machine lay on the ground at the end of a long streak of tire marks carved through the gravel and sand of the driveway. A man lay next to it, facedown, unmoving, wearing the black helmet with the Union Jack decal on the side. Bernie crouched beside him, but she hesitated, not knowing whether or not she should turn him over. The doctor dropped to her knees next to Bernie, and I stood behind Bernie and laid my hands on her shoulders.

With a shudder of relief, my mind pulled itself out of its panic, and I realized this couldn't be Simon. It was his bike and his helmet, but the legs were too short and the body far too thin. Whoever it was wore jeans and a T-shirt and untied sneakers.

Julie-Ann ran through the gate, followed by some of the others in her party, screaming, "Tyler!"

I looked up and caught my grandmother's eye. Rose was resplendent in a long purple dress, yards of red beads wrapped around her neck, and a huge crimson hat that wasn't much smaller than the umbrellas shading the patio tables. I gestured to the woman standing next to her and mouthed, "Take Sandra inside."

Rose plucked at her friend's sleeve, but Sandra didn't

move. Her eyes were wide and she held her face in her gnarled hands.

The body on the ground twitched and then groaned. The doctor said, "Try to lie still," but the boy rolled over, sat up, and pulled the helmet off. Tyler's head popped out. He saw the circle of people watching and gave us a sheepish grin. Bernie pushed herself to her feet.

"What the heck do you think you're playing at?" Brian yelled.

"I'm okay, Granddad," Tyler said.

"Good one!" Amanda gave her brother a thumbs-up. Julie-Ann slapped the girl's hand down.

"You shouldn't move until you've been checked out," the doctor said.

Sandra gave her head a shake and turned to Rose. "You're right, as usual, Rose. Let's leave them to sort this out." The two women turned and walked away. The onlookers moved aside to let them pass.

Simon broke into the circle. "That's my bike!"

"Sorry." Tyler started to stand. His legs wobbled. The doctor grabbed his arm. Judging by the look on Simon's and Brian's faces, I thought the boy would be better to play dead. "Sorry," he said again.

Other than Rose and Sandra, no one seemed inclined to return to what they'd been doing. Brian kept yelling at Tyler, while Julie-Ann waved her hands in the air and Amanda chuckled. In the distance, a siren sounded, getting closer.

"You're not helping, Dad," Lewis said. "Let me take care of this." He started yelling at Tyler.

"I'm okay," Tyler insisted.

"Will you be quiet!" Julie-Ann shouted at Lewis. "Can't you see my boy's in shock?"

"About all I can see," Lewis shouted back, "is that you've babied him for far too long."

Brian turned and walked away with firm, angry steps.

"You might be okay," Simon said, "but my bike isn't. You're going to pay for that, mate."

I don't know much about motorcycles, but even I know the front wheel isn't supposed to be at that angle.

"Let's not worry about that now," Julie-Ann said.

"I'm going to worry about it now," Simon replied.

"What's going on here?" Matt Goodwill arrived at a run. We share part of the long driveway with his house.

"Little sod stole me bike," Simon growled. His English accent got stronger when he got angry.

"How'd he get the keys?" Matt asked.

"He must have snuck into the garden shed and taken them off the hook. I don't lock the door when I'm on the property. I will from now on."

"Hi," Bernie said to Matt.

"Hi," Matt said to Bernie. "You look, uh, nice. What's the occasion?"

"Afternoon tea." Bernie did look nice—more than nice—in a dress made of layers of ivory and gray silk that drifted softly to a couple of inches above her ankles. Gray lace trimmed the neckline and bodice, and the sleeves fell to her elbows. She wore short white gloves, a string of pearls that reached her waist, and a white fascinator with gray beads and a pert white veil.

"That's quite the outfit," I said. "Where'd you get it?"

She preened. "A little something that's been in the back of my closet for years."

As nothing more exciting seemed to be happening, a handful of people headed inside to finish their tea or resumed their seats on the patio, but a substantial crowd remained. Heather pushed her way forward. She looked beautiful and, in contrast to Bernie, very modern in a white cotton shirt cut just above her belly button and white denim shorts worn under a loose blue silk shirt that fell past her knees. Too much mixing of styles for my taste. But then again, what do I know? I'm a pastry chef, not a socialite. Her hair fell in waves around her shoulders and her long bare legs were in high-heeled sandals tied with blue ribbons up to her calves. Her blue and silver bangles tinkled as she moved. She gave Simon a smile full of brilliant white teeth. "You're the owner of the bike? I'll see you're reimbursed for the damage."

"Did you pinch it?" Simon snapped at her.

She blinked. "No."

"Then you shouldn't be paying for it, should you?"

"I just want to help," she said.

"What on earth were you thinking?" Lewis bellowed at Tyler.

"Chill, Dad. I wasn't going to take it far."

"Thank heavens, you weren't going very fast," Julie-Ann sobbed.

"I saw it all," a man said. "The dumb kid couldn't control a bike that powerful. I'm surprised he made it this far."

Tyler flushed, more offended at the insult to his motorcycle-driving skills than being caught red-handed.

An ambulance pulled up next to the tearoom and two EMTs jumped out.

"I'm not going to the hospital," Tyler said.

"It's your choice," the doctor said, "or your parents', depending on your age, but I'd advise you to get yourself checked out."

The teenager shook his head.

"In that case, I'm going inside to finish my tea." She walked away, and Lewis and Julie-Ann gathered around their son.

Julie-Ann pulled him close. "I'll go with you to the hospital."

"We don't need the expense," Lewis said. "You're sure you're okay, son?"

"I'm okay." Tyler wiggled out of his mother's arms.

"We'll need you to sign this form saying you've refused treatment," one of the EMTs said.

"Julie-Ann," Lewis said, "why don't you go inside and join Mom and Grandma and the others? Everything seems to be under control here."

"Don't tell me what to do," Julie-Ann snarled at him. "Tyler, honey? Are you sure you're okay?"

Tyler stared at his feet. Julie-Ann muttered something about knowing when she wasn't wanted and slipped away as a police car pulled up to the tearoom.

"No need to mention that he took the bike without your permission, now is there?" Lewis said to Simon. "No harm done. We'll pay for the damage."

Heather turned to the crowd and lifted her arms. "I am so sorry this silly incident interrupted your enjoyment of your lovely afternoon tea. A glass of champagne for everyone. It's on me."

People cheered.

I gulped. "Heather," I whispered to her. "I don't know that I have enough."

"No problem," she said. "I'm paying."

"Doesn't matter who pays, if I don't have it."

"Do what you can." She gave me a big smile and then sailed back into the tearoom, her long shirt flowing behind her.

People began to resume their places and their excited chatter filled the restaurant. I wasn't quite sure if they were disappointed that there had been no high drama, such as a dead body and a police take-down, or pleased that no one had been injured.

As I passed, I heard more than a few comments about

"horsewhipping," "in my day," or "ban those horrid machines."

"Lewis needs to get control over that boy," Sandra was saying as I reached the center table, "or someday he's going to get into real trouble."

"At least he had enough common sense to steal the helmet and wear it," Trisha said.

Ed reached for the white teapot with the green trim. "Maybe a night in the hospital would have been a good thing. Knock some sense into him."

"That's hardly funny," Julie-Ann said.

"I wasn't making a joke." Ed poured tea into his cup. It really did smell like grass.

The family, minus Lewis, resumed their seats.

"All's well that ends well." Sandra poured herself some tea. Judging by the rich fragrance of the scent, she'd ordered the Darjeeling.

I went into the kitchen, where Cheryl was taking crystal flutes out of the cupboard and handing them to Marybeth. "Finish serving what people ordered first," I said. "Rose's guests don't have their food yet." I stuck my head in the fridge. "Blasted Heather. Making promises I can't keep. We don't have enough wine for everyone. I'll have to make a run into town."

"Bit of excitement to liven our day." Cheryl lifted two food trays by the handles at the top.

"Excitement I don't need," I said.

The back door opened and Simon and Matt came in. "I could use a cuppa," Simon said.

"Then you've come to the right place. Are you okay?"

"I'm madder than a wet chicken—" Simon said.

"*Wet hen*," Matt interrupted.

"What?"

"The saying is 'madder than a wet hen.' Not *chicken*. I don't know why, but that's what it is."

"I'm trying out my Americanisms, trying to fit in, like."

"Never mind the state of damp fowl," I said. "Back to the original question. Are you okay, Simon?"

"Yeah, I'm okay. Thanks. I didn't want to, but only because these people are Rose's guests and I don't want to give her any grief, I told the police no harm done. I've been promised the boy's family'll pay to have my bike fixed."

"Kid should be sent up the river," Matt said. "I sense a life of crime that needs to be nipped in the bud. I don't want to be writing about this boy someday." Matt was a true-crime writer, successful enough to have been able to buy his family property when his father wanted to sell it, but not successful enough to be able to pay for all the renovations it needed. He was a lean, trim six-two, with dark hair and dark eyes and a square jaw. Very New England spoiled-rich-kid preppy-looking, which might be part of the reason Bernie had disliked him on sight. But we'd come to learn, he was anything but.

"Maybe Tyler got a scare," I said.

"Scared straight," Marybeth said. "Do you have to stand right there, Matt, in front of that platter?"

Matt looked around. "I don't see anywhere else to stand."

"My point exactly," she said.

Matt tried to make himself smaller. It didn't help. My kitchen was crowded when I was the only one in it.

"I've called a repair shop," Simon said, "and someone's coming to pick the bike up. Miserable little sod."

"As you're okay," I said, "I need a run to the liquor store. Say, ten bottles of prosecco. Cold if you can get it. As well as the thirsty hordes out there, I need to have some on stock in case we have more people coming in for Royal Tea today."

"Allow me to point out," Simon said, "that I don't have a mode of transportation."

"I'll go." Matt dodged Marybeth and her tray. "As my presence doesn't seem to be needed here."

"You can say that again," Marybeth said.

"Before I do that," Matt said, "I'm thinking of having a tea party at my house one day next week. Do you do that sort of thing, Lily?"

"Catering? No, I simply don't have the time." I took prebaked tart shells out of the fridge and prepared to add strawberry filling and decorate them with fresh cream and one perfect red berry. "How many people will be coming to your party?"

"Two."

"Two?" I looked up.

"Bernie looks so fabulous in that outfit, I thought she'd enjoy another chance to wear it." He gave me a wink and left.

"Do I have to make my own tea?" Simon asked.

"Yes," I said, "you do."

Matt successfully completed his errand and the Great Prosecco Crisis was resolved. Sandra and Heather sent their compliments to the chef into the kitchen, and Heather paid for the tea with a handsome tip. A truck came for Simon's motorcycle, and I didn't see Tyler again that day. He was wise to stay well out of Simon's way.

"How'd it go?" I asked Bernie when she came into the kitchen to say good-bye.

"Good. The food was great, and everyone enjoyed it. The snide cracks and backbiting were kept to a minimum, although Trisha did suggest that maybe Julie-Ann's a bit overindulgent with her children, and Julie-Ann replied that at least her children came on vacation with their parents rather than make an excuse to stay home."

"Ouch."

"Ouch, yes. Amanda wasn't served any prosecco, so she

grabbed Darlene's when Darlene wasn't looking, and Rose snatched it out of her hand. Heather thought that was dreadfully funny. She made sure we all knew she was leaving a *huge* tip because your staff were *so* inconvenienced by Tyler's little *escapade*." Bernie wiggled her fingers and made fluttering signs in the air with her hands.

Marybeth paused emptying the dishwasher to laugh. "Yeah, that's the way she talks. Love your dress, by the way."

"Thanks," Bernie said. "I found it at the vintage-clothing store in town. Lily and Rose taught me that afternoon tea is an occasion. An indulgence. And so I dressed the part."

"You impressed Matt Goodwill," I said.

She grinned. "I did?"

"So much so, he wants me to cater a tea for just the two of you."

"He does?"

"Don't get too excited. I told him I don't do catering."

"I'm not excited." Her eyes danced.

"Coulda fooled me," I said.

I decided to rest on my laurels and take the evening off. At five-thirty, I locked the tearoom behind Cheryl and Marybeth and went home.

It had been a good day, and I was pleased with myself.

A good day, other than the stolen motorcycle incident, that is, but Tyler was unharmed and Simon's bike could be fixed. I gave Bernie a call as I walked across the lawn. "I'm finished work. Feel like coming around for dinner tonight?"

"Yeah, that'd be good. I got some great ideas down for an afternoon tea scene in the book. Rose's mother puts on a tea party, and it descends into an argument about women's suffrage."

"Does this scene fit the trajectory of the book?" I asked.

Bernie had a tendency to get distracted by the latest shiny object that flashed in front of her.

"No, but I'm thinking it will help establish the dynamic between Rose and her family."

"Haven't you done that already?"

"It needs embellishing."

"If you say so. As you're coming this way, anyway, will you stop at the supermarket for a ready-made chicken and ingredients to make a salad?"

"The only reason I'm not going to complain about being invited to dinner and then asked to bring it is because you fed me so well once today already. See you soon."

"A bottle of wine would be nice, too."

"Don't push your luck."

A handful of guests were admiring the gardens, and Rose and Sandra had taken their usual places on the veranda. They waved at me, and I trotted over to say hello. "How's Tyler?"

"A few bruises, his mother tells me," Sandra said with a shake of her head, "but otherwise, none the worse for wear. A couple of weeks in a full-body cast might have taught him the error of his ways."

"What are your plans for this evening?"

"None of us need much for dinner," Sandra said, "because of your beautiful tea, so we're going out for something light. I asked your grandmother to join us, but—"

"But I've had enough of the pleasure of your family's company for one day," Rose said. "As charming as they all are."

"Sarcasm does not become you, dear," Sandra said. "Frankly, I'd prefer to sit here all evening, but I'm a big believer in family togetherness. No matter what."

Lewis, Julie-Ann, Amanda, and Tyler stepped onto the veranda. Tyler avoided his great-grandmother's eyes and hurried down the steps. I was pleased to see that he limped ever so slightly.

"*Soooo* childish," Amanda said. She descended the stairs gracefully and then took off like a shot to the parking lot. "I want shotgun!"

"Are you ready to go, Grandma?" Lewis asked Sandra.

"Are your parents coming?"

"I knocked on their door and they said they'd be right with us," Julie-Ann said. Her eyes were tinged red, as though she'd been crying, and I assumed delayed shock had set in over her son's brush with death. She still wore the ill-fitting white capris and plain blue T-shirt she'd had on at tea.

"I'll wait for them," Sandra said.

"We'll go on ahead then," Lewis said. "You can get a ride with Heather."

They left, and I turned to Rose and Sandra to once again say good night. Before I could do that, Heather came outside with Brian, Darlene, and Trisha.

"I'm not sure," Trisha was saying. "Maybe I should stay."

"Good idea," Darlene said.

"Nonsense," Heather said. "He'll be fine. Men always overreact to the slightest illness."

"I suppose you're right," Trisha said.

"What's the matter?" Sandra asked. "Where's Ed?"

"He's not feeling too good," Trisha said. "He doesn't want dinner."

"No reason for you to miss your meal." Sandra started to stand, and Brian offered her his arm. "Men don't need constant fussing over, do they, son?"

"Do what I say, not what I do," Darlene muttered. "If Brian has so much as a sniffle, you're at our house with your chicken soup and tucking his blankets around him."

"Chicken soup," Sandra said, "has preventative properties, I always say. Better to nip a cold in the bud than let it fester." She clung to her son's arm as she descended the steps.

"There's a story there," I said to Rose when the family was out of earshot, "but I don't want to hear it."

"I'm afraid my friend can be rather possessive of her only child, even though Brian is now a grandfather of his own. When it comes to her family, Sandra is what they refer to these days as a *control freak*."

I eyed my own grandmother and made no further comment.

The door opened once again, and more guests spilled out. Rose greeted them, and I made my escape.

Bernie and I enjoyed a dinner of chicken salad, and then I found a DVD of one of our beloved bad romantic comedies and we settled in with a glass of wine to shout our favorite lines in sync with the actors. Once the movie was over and the wine finished, we took Éclair out for her nightly walk. Bernie noticed a light burning in the windows of Rose's suite on the ground floor of the main building. "It's late, but it looks like Rose is still up. I'll pop in and say good night."

"I'll come with you. She might have locked the front door." The parking area was full, meaning the guests had returned for the night. Lights still shone from many of the guest bedrooms and the drawing room. The front door was locked, Rose's last task of the day, and I let us in. The door opens onto the hallway and the reception area. The dining room is across the hall facing west over the bay, and the drawing room looks across the veranda and the gardens to the tearoom and the main road. The sweeping oak staircase, banisters wide enough for mischievous children to slide on, leads upstairs from behind the reception desk, and a closet for the dining-room linens is tucked underneath.

We heard voices coming from the drawing room and Éclair ran in to say hello.

"I'm calling an ambulance," Trisha said.

"Are you sure? Maybe you should wait to see how he is in the morning," Brian said.

"Of course, I'm sure. I know—"

I popped my head in. "Sorry to interrupt. Is it Tyler? Is he having delayed problems because of the crash this afternoon?"

"It's my husband, Ed," Trisha said. "He's not well. He's feeling sick."

"Do what you want, Trisha," Brian said. "I really don't care. I've had enough drama for one day."

"I hardly think it's our fault your fool of a grandson stole a motorcycle," Trisha said.

"I don't think we want to get into that now," Heather said. "I agree with Brian. Let's wait until morning. Oh, is that your dog, Lily? So cute. What's his name?" She crouched down, holding out her hand, palm up, and clicked her tongue. Éclair's little tail wiggled in ecstasy as she accepted the attention.

"I don't need anyone's approval." Trisha pulled her phone out of her pocket. "I'm calling an ambulance."

"I'm going to bed," Brian said. "Wake me if something important happens. Darlene, are you coming?"

"Be right there."

Brian walked past us, shaking his head. "Much ado about nothing," he muttered as he went up the stairs. "Guy ate something that didn't agree with him. Wimp."

He passed Julie-Ann, coming down.

Trisha stood in the center of the drawing room, phone in hand. She glanced between one person and another, clearly undecided on what course of action to take.

"He's been sick again," Julie-Ann said. "And he's in pain. I have some prescription painkillers in my bag that I could give him. I'm prone to terrible headaches," she added quickly.

"Worth a try." Heather didn't look up as she played with Éclair.

"Sharing prescription medicine is not a good idea," I said. "Trisha, if you're unsure, make the call. Better to be safe than sorry."

"I, uh . . ." She glanced at the faces around her, looking for someone to tell her what to do.

Bernie obliged, and she crossed the room in three long strides. She snatched the phone out of Trisha's hand and punched in the emergency number. She gave Trisha back the phone as the operator said, "Police, fire, or ambulance?"

"Uh . . . ambulance? It's my husband. He's taken very ill. We're at . . . Where are we?"

"Victoria-on-Sea B and B outside North Augusta," Bernie said.

"I'm going upstairs," Julie-Ann said. "I'll wait with Ed until they arrive."

It was nice, I thought, of Julie-Ann to forget family differences and step in to help when she was needed. I jerked my head at Bernie and called to Éclair, who came reluctantly as Heather wiggled her fingers at the dog and said, "Bye-bye." We slipped into the hallway and went down the corridor to Rose's rooms. I knocked and she called, "Come in."

My grandmother was in her sitting room with Sandra. Two mugs of tea rested on the table between them. Rose's suite is also used as the B & B office. The main room's neatly divided in two. One half for B & B business, with a desk, a large-screen computer, filing cabinets, and notices and calendars pinned to a corkboard; the other half for relaxing, with a rose-colored damask chair and matching love seat, masses of family portraits in silver frames, china figurines and hand-painted plates on delicate little piecrust tables.

"They've called an ambulance for Ed," Bernie said.

"Glad to hear it," Rose said. "They should have taken him to the hospital before this. Instead, they all trooped out to dinner and left the poor man alone."

"People get all in a fuss over the smallest things these days. It's nothing but a tummy upset." Sandra looked at me quickly. "Nothing to do with your lovely tea, dear, I'm sure. Although I couldn't help but notice the way he plowed through the selection as though the entire tray was for him alone."

"Is someone with him now?" Rose asked.

"Julie-Ann's upstairs with him," I said. "Trisha's in the drawing room dithering."

"As could be expected," Sandra said. "Trisha to dither and Julie-Ann to rush to Ed's side in his hour of need."

"There's a story there," Bernie said.

"Not mine to tell, dear." Sandra sipped her tea.

I was in the kitchen the next morning, putting the day's muffins into the oven, when Rose came in. I knew right away the news wasn't good. She was still wearing her long white cotton nightgown under a tattered purple dressing gown. Half of her hair stood in spikes and the other half was flattened against her head. Without her makeup, her face was pale, drawn, and heavily wrinkled, and her eyes were weary.

She dropped into a chair. Even Robbie seemed to be down in the dumps this morning, with less of a bounce in his leap onto her lap than usual.

Edna took one look at Rose and said, "Why don't I put the kettle on."

I crouched in front of my grandmother and looked into her eyes. "Ed French?"

She nodded. "Sandra just called me. Trisha phoned her from the hospital. Ed died a short time ago."

I took Rose's hands in mine. "I'm so sorry to hear that. Do they have any idea what happened?"

"Not that Sandra told me. I said I'd bring a cup of tea up to her."

"Let me do that," Edna said.

Rose smiled sadly at her. "Thank you. They weren't at all close, Sandra and Ed, but it is still most upsetting."

"You go to Sandra," I said. "I'll come with you. She's going to be devastated, and—"

"You have other guests to take care of," Rose said. "They'll be wanting their breakfasts."

"But I want to help. Everyone's going to be in a state of shock. I know I am, and he wasn't even someone I knew. The guests can wait."

"If I couldn't manage to console my longtime friend by myself, love, I'd tell you. But I can. You get yourself back to work."

I pushed myself to my feet. I took a breath and considered what Rose had said as Edna prepared the tea. I pushed my own shock and sorrow aside and said, "Okay, Rose. Even the French and McHenry families will need to eat." I chuckled without mirth. "Tyler certainly will. As for their rooms . . . I hate to sound so mercenary, but we should find out what's going to happen. Heather's group's supposed to be staying until Thursday. Do you think they'll leave early?"

"If I have to hazard a guess, I'd say no," Rose said. "Heather invited Ed and Trisha, but the others didn't seem all that pleased to see them. They're unlikely to cut their holiday short because of Ed's death. Heather might, though. And here the poor dear was only trying to get the family together again. I assume Trisha will want to stay until arrangements can be made. I have no idea how long that can take."

"Whatever they decide is fine with us. The poor man. His poor wife." I started as Éclair leapt to her feet with a sharp bark. Seconds later, a firm rap sounded at the door to the outside. Without waiting for me to answer, the door flew open. Detective Chuck Williams, of the North Augusta Police Department, stood there.

He glowered at me.

I was about to ask what he wanted when I heard heavy footsteps coming down the hallway. I whirled around to see Detective Amy Redmond walking into the kitchen, a bank of stern-faced uniformed officers behind her.

Robbie leapt to his feet. He arched his back, his long black fur stood on end, and he hissed. Éclair continued barking.

"Rose Campbell and Lily Roberts," Williams said. "I have a warrant to search the restaurant named Tea by the Sea and everything in it."

Chapter 7

I watched men and women in white suits, hairnets, blue booties, and thin gloves carry the fruits of my labor out of the tearoom. They took not only my baking, but many of my raw ingredients, and even yesterday's garbage.

How many of those cookies, tarts, and scones, I wondered, would see the inside of an evidence locker? Many of them, I suspected, would end up being shared around the police station lunchroom.

Simon, Bernie, and Matt were at a table in the tearoom garden with me. Rose was up at the house, trying to explain to our guests why there'd be no breakfast this morning. She'd earlier called the North Augusta Diner and asked them to accept vouchers for breakfast.

That would set us back a pretty penny. Money we didn't have to waste. The only reason Rose had turned her home into a B & B was to help pay the upkeep and expenses of the grand old house. After three years of barely keeping her head above water, she'd finally convinced me to come and help her by cooking the breakfasts and turning the unused cottage on the property into a tearoom. This was my first season, and the busy summer months had to provide enough income to get us over the long, cold winter when tourists were scarce.

When Williams and Redmond invaded the B & B kitchen, I'd held out my hand. Williams slapped the warrant into it. A malicious spark glinted in his eyes, and he'd barely been able to contain his smirk. He and I had business before—his, not mine. I'd outwitted him (more like tripped over the solution to his case) and he clearly hadn't gotten over it yet.

The warrant said the police were authorized to search Tea by the Sea for any potentially dangerous consumables. I'd demanded to know what that meant, and Williams had merely smirked again and ordered me to unlock the tearoom.

Simon and Matt came running when they saw the police activity, and Bernie appeared without me quite knowing how she knew what was going on. A call from Rose, probably.

In complete contrast to my mood, it was an exceptionally beautiful morning. Birds chirped from the trees, fluffy white clouds drifted lazily overhead, the rising sun threw warm rays onto my not-smiling face, and the china cups hanging from the branches of the ancient oak tinkled softly in the light, fresh breeze.

"They must suspect he was poisoned," Bernie said in a low voice.

"That can't have happened here!" I wailed. "I don't serve poison! No one else got sick."

"Then you've nothing to worry about," Simon said. "It's probably just routine."

"It's not," Matt pointed out. "They have to have a reason to . . ." He noticed Bernie's not-subtle-enough shake of the head and quickly said, "Yup, just routine."

Williams and Redmond came out of the tearoom. Williams ignored us, clambered into a waiting cruiser, and drove the two hundred feet up the driveway to the house. Redmond approached me and my friends. She was young and pretty, but no one would ever mistake her for anything but a cop. Her eyes moved constantly, taking everything in, sizing everyone up. Her tall, lean body always looked as though it was ready to leap into action at any moment.

"I know this must be difficult for you, Lily," she said, "and I'm sorry, but it has to be done."

"Why?" Bernie asked. "What happened to Ed French? Was he poisoned?"

"The doctor believes he consumed something that made him ill, yes."

"Well, he didn't eat it here," I said. "We had a full house yesterday from opening until closing. No one else has fallen sick, have they?"

"Not that we're aware of at this time," Redmond admitted. "No one has presented with similar symptoms at North Augusta Hospital, and we've put the word out to neighboring hospitals and clinics to advise us if anyone comes in."

"So there," Bernie said firmly. "It can't have been something he ate here. I was with him and the rest of the group, I ate the same things he did, and I'm not sick." She held her arms out to her side and smiled at Redmond. "See?"

"I see," Redmond said.

"I will also point out," Bernie said, "that there was a total of"—she counted quickly on her fingers—"eleven people at our table, including two elderly ladies. I haven't seen Mrs. McHenry this morning, but I spoke to Rose Campbell on the phone not long ago and she assured me she feels perfectly normal."

"Drop it, Bernie," Matt said. "We get the point."

"Just making sure we're all on the same page here."

"Would you prefer we wait until there's an epidemic before investigating further?" Redmond asked.

"No," I said.

"No," Bernie admitted.

"Glad to hear it." Redmond turned to walk away.

"But"—Bernie never was one to let anyone else have the last word—"bear in mind, Detective, that the food was served communally. We ate off the same trays. No one had an individual serving of anything. That's the way you do things here, right, Lily?"

"Usually, yes," I said. "But in this case, Ed French did have something no one else did."

The detective swung around. "Is that so? What?"

"Tea. He brought his own personal tea. Scented leaves, anyway. Something noncaffeinated."

"Yes!" Bernie said. "I remember. He asked Marybeth to make it for him. He didn't hand her the tea himself. His wife had it in her purse and she gave it to Marybeth."

"Guests choose what tea they want from our tea menu and we serve it in individual pots," I said. "But Ed had brought his own mixture for us to use."

"Mrs. French told us about this tea when we spoke to her at the hospital," Redmond said. "Thank you for confirming it, Lily. You were at the table, Bernie. Did anyone else try it? Anyone accidently pour from Mr. French's pot?"

Bernie shuddered. "Not as far as I know. It smelled like wet, rotting grass. Simply dreadful. Hard to mistake that sludge for a proper pot of tea."

"When can I reopen?" I asked.

"When we've learned all we're going to learn," Redmond said.

"You do realize this tearoom is my livelihood?"

Redmond studied my face. I shifted uncomfortably. "I am aware of that, yes," she said finally.

"What happens now?" Matt asked.

"Trisha French told us she and her husband are here for a family reunion. We'll be talking to the others. She said neither she nor her husband had met you or your grand-mother before their arrival yesterday, Lily. Is that correct?"

"Yes."

"Then you can be reasonably confident your grand-mother won't be a suspect. This time." She walked away.

"That's good to know," Bernie said.

My phone rang. "Inspector Williams has returned to speak to the family," Rose said when I answered.

"It's Detective Williams, as you are well aware, and, yeah, I know. He's just left here. He got a lift. Too lazy to walk up the driveway."

Unlike Detective Redmond, Detective Williams was not tall and fit. More like short and dumpy, and rather than looking as though he was on the alert for trouble at all times, he gave the impression he was excessively eager for quitting time to arrive.

"Most of the non–McHenry family guests have left clutching their breakfast vouchers, and Heather and her group are in the dining room. Edna's serving coffee. I told Inspector Williams he can use the drawing room to inter-view them."

"That's good."

"Shall I assume you have baking in the freezer here?"

"Some muffins and a coffee cake, in case we have an un-expected rush one breakfast or I'm late getting in. Why?"

"I'll have Edna serve that. It'll help keep the police in place, in case Inspector Williams gets the foolish idea of going elsewhere to talk."

"I see what you're getting at, Rose, but this doesn't have anything to do with us. We don't want to get involved."

Three sets of eyes watched me. I turned away, not that that would prevent my friends from listening in.

"Are the police presently combing through your clotted cream, poking your pastry with their fat fingers, sniffing your sugar?" Rose asked.

"Yes, but—"

"Is your place of business closed until further notice? Are people, even as we speak, slowing down as they pass to have a look at what's going on?"

I couldn't see the main road from here, but I could hear cars, and, yes, some were slowing. A few heads even popped over the garden gate, to be chased away by the police officer guarding what they would, no doubt, label as "the scene of the crime."

"Someone from the newspaper was poking around a few minutes ago," I said. "He took a picture of the tearoom sign. I told him to go away." He hadn't appeared inclined to do what I asked, not until Simon stood up and Matt growled. The reporter then hightailed it out of here mighty fast. Perhaps I'd been too polite.

"Therefore," Rose said, "it has a great deal to do with us, whether we want it to or not."

As much as I hated to admit it, my grandmother was right. As she usually is. "On my way." I hung up and pushed myself to my feet. "Rose needs me. I'm going to the house to see what's happening. Can you keep an eye out here, and call me if I need to know anything or if the cops want to speak to me?"

Simon started to stand. "I'll come with you."

"No," I said, more sharply than I'd intended. "I mean, no thanks. I need you here."

"I'll stay," Bernie said. "I can work in my head." She turned to Matt. "Do you do that, too? When you're writing, I mean."

"I'm always writing," he said.

"Me too," she replied.

"If you two are so busy writing, I need Simon to do the

watching-the-police part." I took off before he could argue with me.

I ran through the gate, down the gravel driveway, past the rose garden, which was just coming into glorious bloom; past the tall, swaying pampas grass that separates parts of our property from Matt's; across the emerald lawn, around the ancient oak tree and the hosta beds beneath, and past the sign directing people to the car park. I took the four steps to the veranda, two at a time, and sprinted across the wide-planked boards past the iron urns planted with white and red geraniums, fountain grasses, and trailing vines. I threw open the door and burst into the front hall of Victoria-on-Sea.

Detective Redmond had arrived only moments before me. She spun around and said, "What brings you here in such a hurry?"

"Nothing," I panted.

She gave me a suspicious look, but said no more.

"I asked Lily to come and give me a hand." My grandmother had taken a seat behind the reception desk. Robbie was stretched out across it to his full length, allowing her to stroke his belly. "I'm sure you and your people would like to take some light refreshment."

"That's not necessary," Redmond said.

"No, but it is polite," Rose said. "Even before I joined the household at Thornecroft Castle, my mother taught me that one always offers refreshment to guests." Rose had been a kitchen maid in her youth, and she was raised with a broad, down-to-earth Yorkshire accent. Over the years—too many episodes of *Upstairs, Downstairs* and *Downton Abbey*, perhaps—she'd refined her accent and could do snobby when she wanted. She wanted to now.

"We're not your guests," Redmond said.

Rose smiled at her. "But I insist."

"In that case, thank you." Redmond gave up the argument and went into the dining room, where a babble of voices greeted her.

"Quiet, everyone!" she bellowed.

The babble stopped instantly.

Rose and I exchanged glances and pricked up our ears.

"Thank you," Detective Williams said. "Now that I have your attention, I'll need to talk to each of you in turn."

"I don't see what any of this has to do with us," Darlene whined. "Until this week, I hadn't had anything to do with Ed French for years. I want to go to my room. I'm very upset."

"We're all upset," Heather said. "But I'm happy to help the police with whatever they need. We all should be, as I'm sure even you'll agree, Mom. You can speak to me first, Detective. This holiday was my idea."

"And you are?" Redmond asked.

"Heather French. Of New York City. Edward French was the brother of my late husband. I was formerly Heather McHenry. Darlene and Brian are my parents, and Lewis is my brother."

"Where's Trisha, anyway?" Julie-Ann asked. "Shouldn't you be talking to her first? Isn't the widow always the prime suspect?"

"Julie-Ann!" Lewis said. "That was totally uncalled for."

"It's true, isn't it? Aren't we here to tell the truth?"

"The truth as it pertains to our relationship with Ed," Heather said, "not what you've seen on *CSI: Miami*."

"We spoke to Trisha French at the hospital," Redmond said.

"She's upstairs," Amanda said. "GeeGee's with her."

"Amanda means my grandmother," Heather said. "Sandra McHenry."

While I kept one ear open to the chatter in the dining room, Rose and I put our heads close together.

"I'll help Edna with refreshments, love," my grandmother said. "You can monitor the conversation."

"If I must," I said.

"You must," she replied.

Rose stood up and assumed her post at the door to the dining room. Robbie rolled over, stretched, jumped off the desk, and strolled into the dining room in search of further attention. Rose checked no one was coming and gave me a sharp nod to indicate that the coast was clear.

Inside the dining room, voices rose and fell as people continued squabbling. Williams and Redmond remained quiet, no doubt hoping someone would accidently confess. Darlene said, "Oh, there's that darling cat," and made clucking noises.

I glanced up and down the hallway and checked the stairs. No one was coming, and I slipped into the linen closet. This house had been used as a B & B by the previous owners, but they hadn't lived on the premises. When Rose bought it, she'd had the necessary renovations done in order to create a private apartment for her own use, and at the same time, the workers had knocked down a few walls to make a larger guest suite out of a couple of minuscule bedrooms. The blueprints had revealed a secret room tucked under the staircase, accessible from the linen closet. Rose showed me the room when I came to live here, but only she and I knew about it. We'd never told anyone on staff or even Bernie. We'd been nothing more than mildly amused about it, until recently when a man died on our property and Rose had been accused of murder.

That's when we realized the secret room was an excellent place from which to hear everything that went on in the drawing room. Such had obviously been the intention of whoever'd built the secret room, as the wall between it and the drawing room was not only exceptionally thin, but small holes had been driven through the wall, and then covered by a painting of an eighteenth-century sailing ship battling storm-tossed seas.

I moved a stack of tablecloths and napkins off the two bottom shelves of the linen closet, dumped them on the floor, and carefully lifted the shelves out of place. I rested them against the wall and pulled the now-exposed lever. Sucking in my stomach, I shut the closet door behind me, bent low, duck-walked under the upper shelf, and emerged into the tiny space. It was completely dark, but I know my way around well enough that my fingers soon found the small desk lamp and I switched it on. We'd figured why not eavesdrop in comfort, so we'd fitted up our secret room with a comfortable chair, small table, and a lamp.

The main purpose of serving coffee and muffins to our "guests" was not to be polite, as Rose had said, but to keep Detective Williams from deciding to take everyone down to the police station to talk to them there. Once I was out of sight of anyone who might wander past, Rose would go to the kitchen and help Edna prepare the refreshments. That's a rare occurrence, indeed. My grandmother's perfectly capable of playing hostess to a house full of people, but after spending her youth as a kitchen maid in one of the stately homes of England, followed by fifty married years of cooking, cleaning, raising five children, and helping my grandfather, Eric, run his business, Rose had declared that part of her life to be over when her husband died. She hired Edna and, nominally, me to serve the guests, and women from town to do the cleaning. On the rare occasion she entertained friends, she reheated a frozen meal and left the dishes for the kitchen staff (again meaning Edna and me) to take care of in the morning.

*   *   *

I was making myself comfortable in the chair when I heard the door to the drawing room open and then Williams's plodding tread, the heavy boots of a uniformed officer, and the steps of a woman in light shoes.

"Please," Williams said, "have a seat."

"Thank you," Heather replied.

Briefly and concisely, Heather told Detective Williams that she'd originally planned a few days' vacation in North Augusta with her grandmother, Sandra McHenry, at the B & B of Sandra's longtime friend, Rose Campbell. When her father heard about the plan, he decided to come, too, and before Heather could stop him, he'd also invited Heather's brother and his family. She laughed lightly. "As long as my vacation was turning into a family reunion, at my grandmother's suggestion, I asked Ed and Trisha to join us. I haven't seen them for ages and thought it would be nice to get caught up."

"You haven't seen your brother-in-law and his wife for some time. Why not?"

Heather explained that she now lived in New York City and the rest of the family lived in Grand Lake, Iowa. She hadn't been home since moving East. "People drift apart, even close families. Once Norman died, well . . ." Her voice trailed off.

Williams gave her a moment to collect herself and then he said, "What about Rose Campbell?"

"What about her?"

"What's her relationship with the deceased?"

If I hadn't been in hiding, I would have stormed through the thin wall. Surely, Williams wasn't planning on again concentrating on Rose to the exclusion of other, better suspects?

"You'll have to ask her," Heather said. "Grand Lake's a small town. Everyone knows everyone else."

"And her granddaughter, Lily Roberts? Does she know everyone?"

"I can't say," Heather answered. "I'd never met her before Saturday. Doesn't mean the others hadn't."

I was disappointed that Amy Redmond had been excluded from the conversation, but not surprised. The two detectives had a difficult relationship. Williams was old-school, local-boy, longtime cop. Redmond was from the big city, new, eager. He was drifting toward retirement; she was out to prove herself.

He was an incompetent idiot. She was not.

It didn't make for a comfortable partnership.

"At your little tea party yesterday afternoon, Edward French drank a specially made pot of tea," Williams said.

"That's right. Trisha had the tea in her bag, and she handed it to the waitress and asked her to prepare it for Ed. She, the waitress, served it in its own pot. All the tea was served in individual pots."

"Did anyone else drink from Mr. French's pot?"

"Not that I noticed," Heather said.

There was a light tapping at the door. Williams called, "Come in."

"Mrs. Campbell thought you might like some coffee, Detective," Edna said. I heard the tinkle of china and a thump as she put the tray on the table. "And a couple of Lily's homemade muffins. We have tea, if you'd prefer."

"Never been a tea man," he grunted. "Thanks."

The door closed behind Edna. Williams's chair creaked as he stood up. Cream splashed into the mug, sugar was stirred in. The chair protested his weight as he sat down and resumed his questioning. Around a mouthful of muffin, he asked Heather what they'd had to eat at the tea. She replied that the food wasn't served for each person individually, but came to the table on trays from which everyone helped themselves. She didn't notice who ate what. She hadn't had any of the desserts, she said. Although, come to think of it, Ed consumed far more than his share of the strawberry tarts.

Williams munched and sipped happily away and didn't ask a single question about the relationship between Ed French and the McHenry family. Heather gave the impression they were here for a fun gathering at the seaside and he swallowed it.

"Thank you for your time, Mrs. French. I'm afraid I'm going to have to ask you and your party to remain in North Augusta for a few days."

I heard the shrug in Heather's voice. "Not a problem. Will it be necessary for me to contact my lawyers in New York City?"

"That would be up to you, Mrs. French," he said, "but I see no reason."

Heather was dismissed, the officer told to bring in the next person.

One by one, they all, except for Trisha, were questioned. No one mentioned any tension between the McHenry and French families. According to them, all was sweetness and light.

Even Julie-Ann backtracked on her earlier declaration that Trisha might have been responsible for the death of her husband. "I wasn't thinking straight," she said with a nervous laugh. "My husband says I watch too much TV."

She was dismissed, and the officer went to fetch Lewis.

A scratching began at the door to the linen closet: Robbie, wondering what I was doing in here, and had I found any mice? Drat that cat! If someone opened the door to let him in, they'd see the pile of linens on the floor and the shelves out of place.

"What are you after, you naughty boy?" came Julie-Ann's voice. "Whatever's in there, I'm sure it's not for you. Silly thing." She laughed. "Why don't you come with me? Trisha doesn't like cats, but I'm sure she'd *love* a visit from you."

Robbie meowed, and I heard Julie-Ann walk away, chuckling at her own cleverness.

"I hope this isn't going to take too long." Lewis's voice came from the drawing room. "I don't know anything about what happened to Ed, and I don't know why you're making such a fuss about it. Have you seen the man? Heart attack looking for a place to happen. My wife and I work hard all year, and right now, we want to continue with our vacation."

"Pardon me for inconveniencing you," Williams said. "Have a seat."

Lewis muttered something about the waste of time, but I heard the squeaking of the chair as he sat.

When questioned, everyone said they all ate from the same platters of food at the tea and no one had shared Ed's brought-from-home tea concoction.

The only line of questioning that deviated from the events of yesterday was directed at Lewis. Williams asked Lewis what Ed did for a living, and Lewis said he owned a computer company. "They sell computers, computer parts, and accessories. Install and make repairs to computers for small businesses and at people's homes. That sort of thing. I don't know for sure, but I think he does okay."

"What about you? What do you do?"

"I own a Toyota dealership."

"Tough competition in that business?" Williams asked.

"Oh, yeah," Lewis said. "It's brutal. Our town's not doing too bad, not as bad as some, but people don't have a lot of money to spend on new cars or even good used ones."

"Anyone else from Grand Lake on the Cape this week?" Williams asked.

"What?"

"Did you see anyone you recognized since you arrived here?"

"No. I mean, I don't think so."

"Give it some thought," Williams said. "Okay?"

"Yeah, sure. I'll do that."

Oh, dear. Detective Williams was hoping to find that someone had followed Ed French from Iowa and killed him. He was no doubt also hoping the killer had gone home again, and thus the case could be handed over to the Grand Lake police.

He seems to have not bothered to wonder how this person could get unseen into Tea by the Sea and close enough to Ed to poison his tea.

I was jerked out of my thoughts by the sound of my name. "Lily Roberts next," Williams said.

The door to the drawing room opened and the sound of the cop's boots crossed the floor.

Oops.

I didn't dare leave the secret room without Rose telling me it was safe. I'd put my phone on silent, and while I'd been hiding, I received a string of texts from Bernie telling me what was going on up at the tearoom. Simon had gone back to work, and Matt had headed for his house. They'd both told her to call if there was any change in the police activity. Watching the police coming and going was, she told me, giving her some great ideas for her book.

I sent Rose a text: **Cops are looking for me.**

Rose: **Wait.**

I waited. While I waited, I heard Williams on the phone asking for the results of a record search on Edward French, Brian McHenry, and Lewis McHenry. Unfortunately, he didn't repeat what he heard, just muttered a lot.

Noticeably, he didn't ask about the women in the group. And that, I thought, was a big mistake.

"Everything all right here, Constable?" Rose's voice came from outside the linen closet.

"Perfectly all right, ma'am," the uniformed officer replied politely.

"It's so comforting," she said, "knowing you're standing guard right here in the hallway." She took the English accent up a notch, probably thinking it made her sound more important. Or maybe more like a dotty old lady.

"My pleasure, ma'am," he said. "I've been asked to get your granddaughter, but she isn't in the dining room or the kitchen. Do you know—"

"I . . . I . . ." Rose's voice wavered. "Oh, my goodness. I don't feel so well all of a sudden. I . . . I . . ."

"Whoa!" he cried. "I got you. Careful there, ma'am. You need to sit down. Let me—"

"No! Not there. I wouldn't want to be in anyone's way. I'll take a seat in the dining room. Oh, dear. Everything is swimming. If you could help me to a chair. No one else seems to be around at the moment."

"Do you need me to call a doctor, ma'am?"

"That won't be necessary. These spells come over me now and again. I'll be fine after a few minutes of peace and quiet."

Their voices faded as the young officer helped Rose into the dining room. I crawled out of the secret room and slipped out of the closet. I was rearranging table linens when the drawing-room door opened and Chuck Williams stuck his head out. "Where the heck is . . ."

I smiled him.

"Oh," he said, "there you are. Where'd Officer LeBlanc get to? Never mind. You're next. Come in."

I took a seat on Rose's favorite damask-covered wingback chair. I crossed my legs at my ankles, my hands in my lap, and smiled sweetly at Detective Williams.

The drawing room at Victoria-on-Sea, like the guest bedrooms and other public areas, is intended to put our visitors in mind of a stately English home, as though one had been invited by the Countess of Grantham for a stay at Downton Abbey. The room was papered in blue, flecked with gold leaf; the carpet a rich cream with blue accents; velvet sashes tied the heavy blue drapes back from the wide windows overlooking the expansive gardens. Inset bookshelves, painted white, were crammed with well-used paperbacks and a selection of board games. The reproduction antique desk beneath the windows was a match to the one in the hallway. Prints of eighteenth-century British paintings hung on the walls, and couches of well-worn brown leather studded with brass hobnobs were on either side of the working fireplace, which, rather than a fire at this time of year, contained a silver vase full of yellow roses.

The door flew open and the young cop came in. "I can't find . . . Oh, there you are. Never mind."

I smiled at him and then turned my attention back to Detective Williams.

Who, try as he might, couldn't get me to confess that I'd poisoned Ed French's tea or that I was careless when handling food. I repeated that I'd never met Ed or anyone else in his party before this week. I had no reason to kill him and no knowledge of why anyone else might. His wife had given his bag of leaves to Marybeth, and Marybeth had added them to a pot of boiling water. That was all.

"Are you positive he was killed by whatever he ate or drank?" I asked.

"The autopsy will say for sure, but at the moment, I'm acting on that assumption. The doctor who treated Mr. French when he came in last night was pretty sure it was something he'd recently consumed. His wife told us about this special tea of his, and she gave us what she had left of it. We'll be having it analyzed. Mrs. French said his tea was made for him at your place, so I've sent Detective Redmond to speak to your staff."

"The teapot was left unattended for several minutes," I said.

He cocked his head and studied my face. "What does that mean?"

"It means the teapot was left unattended for several minutes. Darlene and Brian told you . . . I mean, I assume someone told you about the motorcycle incident."

"Yeah. The kid stole your gardener's motorcycle and crashed it. He was lucky he wasn't hurt. I had a word with him about that."

"I'm sure you did."

"He says Heather French is going to pay for the damage. Why would she do that and not his own father?"

"You know Heather has the money in this family, right?"

"She does?"

"She does. But that's not what I'm trying to tell you. Tyler crashed Simon's bike and everyone in the tearoom ran outside to see what was going on. This was after the tea was served, but before the food was brought out. Which means the teapots were left on the table unattended."

"Everyone went outside?"

"I believe so. It was quite a mad rush, and, of course, we had other customers besides the French party. We were full, both inside and outside on the patio."

He stroked his chin. I tried not to fidget. He'd missed a spot on his lower right jaw when shaving this morning. I tried not to point that out.

"You can go," he said at last.

I stood up. "When can I open my tearoom?"

"I'll let you know."

"Detective, it's obvious Mr. French wasn't killed by my

food. No one else has taken ill or has the slightest symptoms, including two elderly ladies."

"I'll be in touch," he said.

The uniformed officer edged toward me. I stood my ground. "My tearoom is important to the tourist business of North Augusta. It's the beginning of the season. I'm sure my good friend the mayor will have something to say about this. And if not, Lincoln Goodwill will."

I'd met Mayor Susan Powers once or twice, so by no stretch of the imagination could be she called my good friend. Town patriarch Lincoln Goodwill, father of my next-door neighbor, Matt, couldn't care less one way or the other what happened to my little business. But Chuck Williams knew who held the reins of what might be called power in our town, and he cared more about that than he should.

"I'll see what I can do," he said.

"Thank you," I replied.

Officer LeBlanc escorted me out.

Chapter 8

When I emerged from the drawing room, the house was quiet. I peeked into the dining room, but it was empty. The coffee cups and side plates had been cleared away and the tables were freshly laid for tomorrow's breakfast.

I found Rose and Sandra ensconced in their chairs on the veranda. I perched on the railing, and we watched Detective Williams and Officer LeBlanc drive up to the tearoom. Williams got out of the car, went through the gate, and approached Bernie, still at her post.

"Bad business," I said.

Rose and Sandra nodded.

"How are you holding up, Sandra? This has been such a shock."

She gave me a tight smile. "Thank you for asking, dear. I'll be fine. We old Midwestern biddies are a lot tougher than most people think. Isn't that right, Rose? It's sad, of course, and dreadful for Ed's family, but I must confess that I haven't had much to do with anyone in the French family, other than Heather, of course, for many long years."

"I hope you don't mind my asking, but yesterday at the tea when we all went outside to see what Tyler was up to, I don't suppose either of you saw anyone interfering with Ed's drink?"

"I assumed that was what Williams was trying to ask us, without coming right out and saying it," Rose said. "Man's a blasted fool. Ask the blasted question already, don't let us dance around the subject. He sent Amy Redmond into town to speak to Marybeth and Cheryl. He should have sent a uniform to do that and let Redmond ask the important questions, such as 'Did you kill Edward French?' "

"I can't accept that someone in my family killed a man," Sandra said. "I won't accept it. He was substantially overweight, wasn't he? He must have had a bad heart. Poor man."

Rose patted her friend's hand.

"The teapot?" I prompted.

Rose and Sandra exchanged glances.

"I don't remember," Sandra said. "We were settling down to enjoy ourselves and then we heard that crash. It was all so confusing."

"Everyone leapt to their feet and was milling about," Rose said. "We went outside along with the others to see what was going on. Much ado about nothing."

"That's right," Sandra said. "When we saw Tyler was unharmed, we returned to our table."

"Yes," Rose said, "but we went to the ladies' room first."

"Did we?" Sandra asked.

"The ladies' was occupied," Rose said, "so I went into the men's room and left Sandra on guard outside. You really should have two ladies' rooms and one for the gentlemen, love."

"Right. With all the empty space we have," I said.

"The point being," Rose said, "we did not see anyone interfering with Ed's tea. Or anything else."

Sandra nodded in agreement.

"Where's everyone now?" I asked.

"Trisha's in her room resting," Rose said. "She shouldn't be alone, but she insisted she wants to be. Julie-Ann brought Robbie up to her room, supposedly to comfort her, but Trisha made quite a fuss and ordered her to get Robbie out. Not everyone is as fond of cats as I am."

"Julie-Ann," Sandra sniffed in disapproval, "is not always sensitive to the feelings of others."

"I told Trisha I'll be here all day," Rose said, "if she needs anything. The others have carried on with their plans. Brian, Lewis, and Tyler have gone fishing, and Heather, Amanda, and Julie-Ann are about to leave for the spa." Rose also sniffed.

"Don't judge them, Rose," Sandra said. "No one in my family was at all close to Edward or Norman, his brother."

"Except for Heather," I said.

"My granddaughter doesn't ever need to explain herself to me," Sandra said, "but she told me a day at the spa will help her deal with her grief better than sitting alone in her room."

I pushed myself away from the veranda. "I'm going up to the tearoom to see what's happening."

The two women waved me off.

The forensic van and two cruisers were still parked at the side of the tearoom, fully visible from the highway. Not good advertising for either the restaurant or the B & B.

Williams had gone inside by the time I reached the tearoom, and Bernie was typing on her phone. She looked up when I came through the gate and put her phone away.

"How'd it go? Dare I hope someone confessed?"

I dropped into a chair. "Sadly, no. Williams spoke to you?"

"More like growled at me and ordered me to confess. When I failed to do so, he went inside the tearoom. Before she left, Redmond asked what I saw here yesterday afternoon. I saw nothing and told her so. I also told her I didn't know Ed French or any of the people who had tea with him, other than Rose, of course, so I can't be of any help. What do you think happened, Lily?"

"I'm not saying anyone poisoned Ed's private stash of so-called tea, but that seems to be the assumption the police are working on, and that's probably the right thing to do. No one else has taken ill. Not that we know of, anyway. His entire batch of tea might have been poisoned, which would point to his wife as the killer, I guess. Or someone who had access to their room or her purse."

"The rooms all have locks on the doors, don't they?"

"They do, but not everyone uses them. Some guests assume that anyone who can afford to stay here isn't going to be the sort to rifle through other people's rooms. Not always a safe assumption."

"As I know from my former job. You wouldn't believe the petty crimes some of my firm's most important clients were accused of. Hey, that might be an interesting angle for the book. Rose and Tessa are able to trap a top criminal mastermind because his son . . ."

Bernie, like Rose, is perfectly capable of holding and contemplating two totally different thoughts in her mind at the same time. I sometimes have trouble walking while chewing gum. "Can we return to the matter at hand, please?"

"Sorry. Go ahead."

"Trisha gave the police Ed's unused tea, and Williams told me they'll be testing it. If the whole batch wasn't poisoned, it's possible that whatever substance was used had been put into the teapot after the leaves were steeping. Which means after Marybeth made Ed's tea. If that is what happened, then almost anyone who'd been in the tearoom at that time could have done it. But they would've needed to be unobserved, and this is a busy place . . ."

"Busy. Except when everyone ran outside."

"Precisely what I'm thinking. Tyler stole Simon's bike and got as far as the tearoom before crashing it."

"He was darn lucky he didn't get to the highway."

"That he was. Whereupon everyone in the tearoom, including me, ran out to see what was going on. You were with him when I got there, as I recall."

"That's right," Bernie said. "I heard a scream from the garden and then a crash. I figured right away there'd been an accident—the whole building shook. I ran outside. I think I was the first. People came behind me, but I can't place anyone in particular. I got to Tyler, but I didn't know what to do. He wasn't moving. Then you and the doctor arrived."

I leaned back in my chair and thought. I tried to draw up a mental image of who was where when, but it was all a blur. The only person I could place until everyone trooped back inside the tearoom was Lewis, who'd stayed with his son until the police arrived. Lewis, and Tyler, of course. Then again, I hadn't noticed when Lewis left the restaurant. I didn't remember seeing Ed or Trisha at all. Even Sandra couldn't be accounted for the entire time. Rose said she left Sandra guarding the door to the men's room.

Meaning anyone of them might have had the opportunity to poison Ed's tea. It would be no more than a matter of seconds to ensure no one was watching, then open the teapot and drop in . . . something.

"Ed might not have been the intended victim," Bernie said.

"What do you mean?"

"Maybe someone got the teapots mixed up."

"That would depend on what was used, I guess. Most of our teas are subtly flavored. It would be noticeable if anything was added."

"If it had a strong taste," Bernie said. "Not everyone's a regular drinker of fine tea. They might not know if something was obviously out of place."

"True. I don't suppose the police will tell us what they find."

"Highly unlikely."

"He might not have been murdered, you know. Maybe it was an accident. Maybe his tea was bad, or something."

At that moment, a car pulled up and Amy Redmond got out. She saw us watching and gave us a nod. She went into the tearoom the back way.

"I absolutely hate this," I said. "Sitting outside, helpless, while they destroy my business."

"If it makes you feel any better," Bernie said, "I don't think they're destroying anything. I don't hear the sound of roof beams being shattered or floors dug up."

"I've been avoiding it, but I'd better check the tearoom voice mail."

I'd left a message on Tea by the Sea's number to say we were closed for an emergency. I called up the voice mail and soon wished I hadn't. It was filled with cancelations, some stretching into next week.

"It's hit the news," Bernie said. "This place was mentioned by name. Don't look at Twitter if you want to keep your blood pressure down."

I next accessed the online reservations system. More cancelations.

"This isn't good," I said.

"Nope."

"I wonder if the same thing's happening at the B and B."

"I didn't see Victoria-on-Sea mentioned on social media, so you might be safe there."

A car drove slowly past. The man in the front passenger seat rolled down his window, leaned out, and took a picture. I refrained from sticking out my tongue.

Amy Redmond came out of the tearoom. She put her sunglasses on as she walked toward us. "We're finished here, Lily," she said. "For now."

I brightened up. "So I can open tomorrow?"

"You'll remain closed until we tell you otherwise."

I deflated. "Can I go inside?"

"Yes."

"Can I bake?"

"Yes, but you can't serve customers. You might want to visit the supermarket first. We've had to take some of your supplies."

"That's good, isn't it, Lily?" Bernie said. "Baking is Lily's happy place, Detective. My happy place is the swim-up bar at a luxury resort on a Caribbean island, but each to her own. What about you? Do you have a happy place?"

Redmond peered at her over the top of her sunglasses.

Bernie threw the detective a big smile. "Just being friendly."

The forensic van drove away, followed by one of the two cruisers. I was happy to see them go.

"When's the autopsy?" Bernie asked.

"Tomorrow morning," Redmond said. "First thing."

"You'll let us know what you find out." Bernie phrased her sentence so it wasn't a question. Redmond didn't bother to reply.

"Thanks," Bernie said, as though the detective had agreed.

I cleared my throat. "In case it wasn't made clear, you need to know there was some tension between the French and McHenry families."

"Why would you think it wasn't made clear?" Redmond asked.

"No reason." The always-helpful citizen, I smiled at her. She didn't return the smile.

"Wouldn't the people involved tell the police that?" Bernie said.

"Maybe they didn't want to speak ill of the dead," I said. "If that's what happened, I mean. That it wasn't made clear. Not that I overheard anything like that. Or anything at all."

"Are you trying to tell me something, Lily?" Redmond asked.

"Nope. Just trying to be helpful. As a good citizen should."

"What sort of tension are we talking about?"

"The McHenrys were not happy when Ed and Trisha showed up here. More than not happy—they were angry. It sounds like a minor thing, but Julie-Ann McHenry took Rose's cat to Trisha French's room, knowing Trisha doesn't like cats. You'll have to ask them why."

"I'll do that," she said, then added under her breath, "if I'm allowed to ask anyone anything."

Chapter 9

"I bet her happy place is the basement of the police station before a suspect's lawyer arrives," Bernie said as we watched Redmond drive away. "Williams's is the La-Z-Boy in his living room with a beer in one hand and a bag of chips in the other."

"You're probably right about him," I said. "But not her. I trust her."

"You're too trusting for your own good, Lily."

"Maybe. But I like it that way."

"Which is why you need me to protect you from yourself."

"Whether I want you to or not."

"Right." She hopped to her feet. "I'm off. While I've been waiting ever so patiently here, watching the police activity, I've had some great ideas. I want to get them down while they're fresh in my mind. You will call me if anything happens, if you need anything?"

"Of course," I said.

She wrapped me in a hug. "Try not to worry."

I returned the hug, and I thought, but didn't say, *Easier said than done.*

I went into my tearoom. It was, as Bernie had said, my happy place. My pride and joy. I'd been a pastry chef in Manhattan. I'd worked at several bakeries and then at a Michelin-starred restaurant and I'd always dreamed of having my own place one day.

I might not have always dreamed of being in business with my grandmother, or cooking the breakfasts at a B & B, but we have to make compromises sometimes. So far, Tea by the Sea was turning into everything I'd dreamed of.

Except for the not insignificant matter of people dying after drinking tea prepared in my kitchen and my place being closed by the cops.

To my relief, the restaurant didn't look as though it had been tossed. In the vestibule, the long, high-backed wooden bench and the small antique dresser displaying our menu were undisturbed. The tables in the main room and the quiet alcoves were set with crisp white tablecloths, linen napkins, and silver cutlery. A bowl or vase of beautiful fresh flowers picked by Simon himself graced every table. A small side room near the kitchen is devoted to things we offer for sale: locally made jams and preserves and chutneys, collectable teapots and cups, a few souvenirs of Cape Cod. Everything there, I was pleased to see, was untouched.

I went into the kitchen.

It was not untouched.

Canisters of tea, flour, sugar, had been opened and the contents scooped out. The fridge was almost empty—not only of ingredients such as eggs, cream, butter, or berries, but of premade sandwiches, tarts, and cupcakes. The freezer was the same. Not a single scone remained.

I let out a long breath and reminded myself that nothing was irreplaceable. I'd simply make more. I took out my phone and started on a shopping list. As I typed, I decided to look on the bright side. Maybe I could get enough baking done before the tearoom reopened that I could treat myself to a half-day vacation. I hadn't so much as had time to go to the beach since I'd arrived in Cape Cod over the winter and started work renovating the decaying stone cottage to turn it into my tearoom.

A knock on the back door. A loose floorboard squeaked as I crossed the room to open the door.

"Everything okay?" Simon said. "I saw the last of the cops leave."

"Okay as can be. I have to go to the store. I can use my kitchen, even if I don't have any customers to serve."

He glanced around the room, at the open canisters and the bare shelves. "They took my compost bin."

"They did what?"

"Took the compost. I hope they get some use out of it."

"Looking for the remains of Ed French's tea, I suppose."

"Good luck with that. First thing this morning, I came around to get what you'd left for me last night. I dumped yesterday's offerings into the composter and gave it all a big stir to get the older stuff aerated."

Simon turns our kitchen scraps, coffee grounds, and used tea leaves into rich compost to feed his plants. In return, they provide us with beautiful flowers. A perfect relationship, and one that never ceases to give me joy and amazement.

His eyes darkened. "What do you think happened, Lily?"

I ran my fingers over the butcher block. "The police seem to think something deadly was in Ed French's personal supply of tea. No one else got sick, not even any of the people at his table, but I guess they searched in here in case it was something he ate. Something I fed him. If it turns out that's what happened, I'll be ruined. No one will ever want to eat my food again." I swallowed heavily and felt tears welling up behind my eyes.

Simon gave me a soft smile. "You're worrying for nothing, Lily. You didn't poison him, accidently or otherwise. Speaking of accidents, maybe he picked the . . . whatever it was . . . himself without knowing it was deadly. Gardens are full of lethal substances, if one knows where to look." His mouth twisted in amusement. "I didn't bother to point out to the coppers, as they hauled away my compost, that I do know where to look."

I smiled back at him. For a long moment, neither of us made a move. We just stood there, smiling.

"I don't suppose they'll bother to return it," he said at last.

"Return what?"

"My compost. Black gold. I could sue to get it back, but by the time the case winds its way through the courts, it'll probably be thrown on a refuse heap somewhere."

"You'd have to be able to identify your compost from the common and garden dirt at the back of the police station."

"DNA tests might help," he said. "You buy all your eggs from Willowbay Farm, right? And you crush the shells and throw them in with the vegetable scraps. We can order DNA testing on my compost and compare that to Willowbay's chickens."

I laughed at the absurdity of it and realized I felt a lot better. Simon's bantering words had blown away the clouds gathering above my head. "I don't know if you can get identifiable chicken DNA off the inside of an eggshell."

"I'll ask Matt and Bernie to look into it. Give them something to do they can call research."

We smiled at each other some more until at last he said,

"Better get back at it. If you need any help, give me a shout." He touched his finger to his forehead and left.

I let out a long breath and returned my attention to my shopping list.

When I got back from the supermarket, I baked for the rest of the day and that went a long way toward putting me in a better mood. Not knowing when we'd be allowed to reopen, I made things that would keep in the freezer until needed.

By six o'clock, I had a healthy supply of tart shells, two types of scones, cupcakes, and shortbread, as well as chocolate chip cookies for the children's tea all neatly stacked in the industrial-sized freezer next to the pantry.

I untied my apron, checked the ovens were off, switched off the lights, locked the door, and went home. Guests were strolling in the gardens or sitting on the veranda with their books and an evening glass of wine. We exchanged greetings as I passed, but no one stopped me to ask about the earlier police activity. I assumed Rose had done all she could to fill people in as to what was going on. When she wanted to, which wasn't often, Rose was an expert at English understatement. She would have done a good job of downplaying the visit from the police.

I took my dog for a long walk, reheated a frozen meal in the microwave, and was in bed with my book by ten o'clock. The late afternoon and evening had passed so peacefully and uneventfully, I dared to hope that the worst of the trouble was over and the police would soon solve the case and life would be able to return to normal.

But nothing is ever normal at Victoria-on-Sea.

"Has the paper learned anything more about what happened here?" I asked Edna the next morning. I was mixing batter for a coffee cake, and Edna was peeling fruit and chopping ingredients for the breakfast salad. Edna's husband, Frank, is the editor in chief of the *North Augusta Times*.

"Not that I've heard," she said. "Frank read Ilana's story before it went to print and he ordered her to cut the line about being rushed to the hospital after eating at Tea by the Sea."

"Thank heavens. Thank him from me."

"I don't need to," Edna said. "Frank's been in this business long enough to know about unfounded accusations and deliberate misstatements. At the moment, no link has been established between that man eating at your place and dying several hours later, but . . ."

"But if there is, the paper will report it. Fair enough. There won't be." In the bright light of early morning, some of last night's optimism had faded, and I spoke with more confidence than I felt.

Edna glanced at the clock on the wall. "The autopsy should be under way by now. Hopefully, that'll tell the police more." She put down her knife and carried the finished fruit salad into the dining room. I used a thin wooden skewer to gently swirl the coffee mixture into the center of the cake to create a nice marbleized effect and then popped the cake into the oven. I took sausages out of the fridge and a package of bacon out of the freezer. We normally serve sausages *and* bacon only on Sunday, but I decided that today I'd offer our guests a small treat. They deserved something for not fleeing at the arrival of a full forensic team on the property.

The McHenry party and Trisha French were due to leave tomorrow. I wondered if their plans would change. I assumed Trisha would want to stay until her husband's body was released, but I didn't know how long that might be, and she might prefer to be at home with her family in the meantime.

The noise level coming from the dining room told me it was full, the frying pan was sizzling with a second batch of sausages, and the cake was warm from the oven and sliced for serving when Bernie came in. "Morning."

"This is a surprise," I said. "What brings you here so early?"

"I thought there might be developments. Are there?" She reached for a slice of coffee cake.

"Hands off," I said.

She snatched it, anyway, and bit into it before I could snatch it back. "Sorry, I didn't have breakfast."

"Nothing's happened that I know of," I said, "except for the theft of one piece of cake. I might report that next time the police are here."

She munched happily. "Umm. This is good. Nice crunchy cinnamon topping. I like that. Has Rose come in yet?"

"Not yet. It's still early."

"She called me and suggested I come over in case we have work to do." She held the cake—missing one enormous bite—up. "Thus I need sustenance." She poured herself a cup of coffee.

"What sort of work?" I asked, although I probably didn't want to know.

Bernie didn't answer. Instead, she took her coffee and cake and left.

"Keep your secrets," I called after her.

"Table of four wanting the full breakfast," Edna said. "Rose's friend, Sandra, will have that also, but the younger woman with her wants only fruit and yogurt."

"That's probably Heather. Any sign of the others?"

"They're all down. Even the teenagers. I've served them

already. Two fried eggs over easy, and two sunny-side up. Sandra wants hers poached."

I cracked eggs into the hot fat, and while they cooked, I laid sausages and bacon, grilled tomatoes and mushrooms, onto plates. When the fried eggs were ready, I plated them. As Edna carried the breakfasts into the dining room, I put the poaching water on the boil.

"That's the last of them." Edna came back as I carefully slipped one perfect farm-fresh egg into the hot water.

"Glad to hear it." I leaned backward to give my back a good stretch, and then reached for my own coffee cup.

Tap tap tap. Rose, Robert the Bruce, and Bernie came into the kitchen as I was carefully removing the poached egg from the hot water.

"We've been summoned," Rose said. She'd dressed for the day in an orange, pink, and purple ensemble that put me in mind of a sunset.

"We've what?" I asked.

"Inspector Williams has just called me. He requests that the friends and family of Edward French be gathered in the drawing room in ten minutes."

"Did he say why?"

"No."

"He's probably going to do his Lord Peter Wimsey impersonation," Bernie said. "Too bad for him, he's not an English lord. Or smart."

"It has to be to give us the autopsy results," Rose said.

"Let me find out from Frank if that's finished." Edna pulled her phone out of her apron pocket.

"If it's not, shouldn't Williams be at it?" Bernie asked.

"Detective Williams likes to get out of anything that might be at all unpleasant," Edna said. "He always has."

"Why did he become a cop, then?" Bernie asked.

"He didn't have much choice. His father was chief of police for many years, and Chuck was expected to follow in those distinguished footsteps. He would have been a lot happier if he'd become a kindergarten teacher."

"A terrible thing to do to innocent little children," Rose said.

"Instead, the innocent little citizens of North Augusta have to suffer," Edna said as she called her husband. "Hi, honey, it's me. I'm still at Rose's place. Any news?" She paused for a moment, nodding her head, as Frank filled her in. "Thanks, hon." She put her phone away. "Autopsy's over. Results have not been released to the press." She picked up Sandra's breakfast plate and carried it into the dining room.

Rose caught my eye. She tilted her head slightly to the right and opened her eyes very wide. She was asking me if I wanted to go into the secret room.

In answer, I took off my apron. "As everyone's been summoned as though we're in a Lord Peter Wimsey novel and he's about to make an accusation, I'll join you."

"No refreshments this time," Rose said. "We want this to be as short and to the point as possible."

Éclair had come out from under the table to greet Rose and she recognized the sign of me removing my apron. Stubby tail wagging, ears up, she ran for the door.

"Sorry," I said. "We're not leaving yet." I pointed to the floor under the table. "Stay!"

Her ears dropped, her face crumbled, her tail drooped. Slowly, ever so slowly, she crawled under the table and sat down. She let out a mighty sigh and stared at me through enormous liquid brown eyes.

"Drama queen," I said as I bent over and reached under the table to give her an affectionate pat.

I left Edna to finish cleaning up and followed Rose and Bernie into the dining room. Sandra and Heather occupied a table for two. Darlene, Brian, Lewis, and Julie-Ann sat together, and Amanda and Tyler were at a separate table, heads down, fingers flying over their phones. There was no sign of Trisha.

"Would you go and get Trisha, please, love," Rose whispered to me. "Room 202. Tell her the police want to speak to her. I'll tell the others we're needed in the drawing room."

"Will do," I said.

Rose crossed the room and whispered in Brian's ear. He looked up sharply, but nodded. Other guests were still lingering over their breakfasts and Rose didn't want to disturb them.

I ran upstairs and knocked on the door of room 202.

"Who is it?" answered a muffled voice.

"Lily Roberts. Rose's granddaughter."

"Just a minute."

I heard the bed creaking, the sound of shuffling, and then the turning of the lock. The door opened and Trisha French's head popped out. Her eyes were red and her nose swollen. Her hair stood on end and she was still dressed in her pajamas, which, patterned as they were with brightly colored cartoon characters, looked so out of place on a woman recently widowed.

"I'm sorry to disturb you," I said. "The police are on their way. They want you . . . They want everyone in the drawing room."

She blew her nose with a tattered scrap of tissue. "Must I?"

"I'm sorry, but I'm only delivering the message. Do you want me to make your excuses?"

"No. I'll come down." She lifted her chin and looked into my face. "I can face her. I can face them all."

Her? "Who do you mean? Has Amy Redmond said something to you?"

But the door had shut in my face.

*   *   *

I arrived at the bottom of the stairs in time to see Detectives Williams and Redmond coming into the house.

"Hi," I said. "I mean . . . hello. I won't say you're welcome, but come on in. Looks like the gang's all here. Except Trisha. She's on her way down, should be here shortly."

I turned at the creak of a stair. Trisha had pulled a sweater over her pajama top and put on a pair of track pants. She twisted a tattered tissue between her fingers.

"Good morning, Mrs. French," Redmond said.

Trisha muttered something and blew her nose.

The drawing room did look like a scene out of a Lord Peter Wimsey novel. Rose was in her favorite chair, with Robert the Bruce curled in her lap glaring malevolently at everyone. Sandra sat in the matching wingback chair next to the bookshelves. Brian and Darlene were on one leather couch. Lewis and Julie-Ann had taken the other couch, but rather than reaching for each other for comfort or encouragement, they sat about as far apart as was possible, facing straight ahead, their backs stiff. Bernie leaned against the wall, Amanda had taken a window seat, Tyler stood behind his grandfather, and Heather was perched on the edge of the desk chair. Detective Williams leaned against the mantel of the fireplace scowling. His expression, I couldn't help but think, was a lot like Robbie's.

All that was missing was the monocle and cigar.

Trisha hesitated in the doorway, glancing from one person to the other.

No one said a word. Finally Heather stood up. "Here," she said, "you need to sit down."

"Thank you," Trisha said in a low voice. She crossed the room and took the offered seat. I went to stand next to Bernie, who waggled her eyebrows at me.

"Gang's all here," Tyler said.

"Be quiet," Brian snapped.

Detective Williams cleared his throat. He puffed up his chest and spread his feet a bit wider. I glanced at Amy Redmond. She kept her face impassive, but looked quickly away when she saw me watching her.

"I'm sure you're wondering why I've called you all here," Williams said, when every eye was on him.

"That goes without saying," Sandra said. "Get on with it, man. What do you have to tell us about Ed? I hope you're here to say you've apprehended his killer and we can go home."

"What about our whale-watching trip?" Tyler said. "We're going to miss the boat if we don't leave soon."

"Will you be quiet," Brian said. "That's hardly the most important thing at the moment. Have you done the autopsy, Detective?"

Trisha wept into her tissue. Heather rested her hand on Trisha's shoulder.

"Sorry," Brian muttered.

"Don't be," Sandra said. "It's what we all want to know. Spit it out, Detective."

"We have ... uh ... yes ... completed the autopsy on Mr. French. The pathologist is reasonably confident that he died as a result of something he ate or drank Monday during the afternoon to early evening."

People murmured to each other. Trisha continued sobbing. Brian put his arm around his wife's shoulder and Darlene nestled closer to him. Julie-Ann and Lewis didn't look at each other. Heather bent over and whispered something into Trisha's ear. Rose stroked Robbie, and Sandra sat stiffly in her chair, her cane by her side.

"That is so awful," Amanda said with a dramatic shudder.

"I've been told," Williams said, "that Mr. French didn't go to dinner with the rest of you Monday evening because he wasn't feeling well and that nothing was taken to him in his room. Therefore, I have to conclude that he consumed . . . uh . . . whatever did him in . . ."

"That's one way of putting it," Lewis muttered, "although not exactly tactful."

". . . at the tearoom."

"Good thing I wasn't there," Tyler said. "You can't accuse me of doing it."

"I've had about enough of you," Brian growled.

"Whatever," Tyler mumbled.

"Leave him alone," Julie-Ann said. "We're all on edge."

Tyler didn't bother to hide the smirk he threw at his grandfather. Brian didn't try to hide the glare he threw at Julie-Ann.

As Williams spoke, Redmond was studying the people in the room. I avoided her eyes. I knew I hadn't killed Ed French, but even so, I felt compelled to look away.

"Have any of you thought of anything you might have forgotten to tell me yesterday?" Williams asked.

No one spoke.

I heard footsteps on the stairs and voices in the hallway as our other guests went about their day. Outside, people strolled in the gardens, and cars drove down the long driveway. Simon was deadheading the geraniums on the window boxes lining the veranda.

"The food served at the Monday tea was not prepared for individuals, and everyone ate from communal trays," Williams said. "Or so you all say."

I pulled my attention back to the room. "That's the way it's always done at afternoon tea. If needed, I can accommodate special diets, such as gluten-free or vegan, but that didn't happen on Monday."

"Gluten-free," Williams said. "My wife put me on that last year. More like flavor-free if you ask me."

"Which is neither here nor there," Redmond said. "Mr.

French drank tea served only to him. I"—she glanced at Williams—"I mean, we pointed that out to the pathologist."

"Yeah," Williams said. "Traces of green stuff were still in French's stomach, and—"

Trisha let out a low moan. Tyler laughed.

Amanda said, "Ew! Gross," and Brian snapped, "Have some delicacy, please, Detective. My mother is present."

"Don't mind me," Sandra said.

Redmond cleared her throat. "What Detective Williams is trying to say is that a toxicology analysis is currently being done. When the lab people know what they're looking at and for, it speeds things up considerably. We're hoping to have a complete chemical analysis shortly. We're also analyzing the unused tea that was in Trisha French's possession, as well as what we can find from the tearoom trash. In the meantime—"

"It had to have been an accident." Lewis looked directly at me. "Carelessness on the part of the restaurant staff."

I blinked, not quite sure what he was saying.

Rose was quicker than me to react. "Let me assure you, Lewis, my granddaughter and her employees are not *careless* in the least."

"A busy place," he said. "A lot of pressure. Things happen."

I found my voice. "That's preposterous. We boiled the water for Ed's own supply of tea. That's all."

"Maybe, maybe not," Lewis said. "You might want to see if you have grounds for a lawsuit, Trisha."

"What! I . . . I . . . ," I sputtered.

Sandra pounded her cane on the floor. "Not another word, Lewis, or I'll cut you out of my will. Lily's a highly responsible cook and restaurateur. Ed, I'll remind you all, provided his own tea. I'd be more interested in where that came from than accusing the people who work at the tea-room. Trisha, what do you have to say about that? Trisha!"

Trisha lifted her head and blinked. "What?"

"Where did Brian get that foul mess he grandly called tea?"

"His tea? We brought it from home. I buy it at a health food store in Grand Lake. It's supposed to be good for—"

"You will instruct the Grand Lake police to remove this tea from the store's shelves," Sandra ordered Detective Williams.

"We've been in touch with them," Redmond said. "In the meantime, in light of this development, we're asking you to remain in North Augusta until further notice. Any questions? No? Thank you for your time." She took a step toward the door, but wasn't quick enough.

Lewis leapt to his feet. "What do you mean we have to remain in North Augusta? I can't stay here. I have a business to run. Our return tickets are for tomorrow. Do you know what it costs to change flights at the last minute?"

"For heaven's sake, Lewis," Heather said. "Is money all you can think about?"

"Easy for you to say," Julie-Ann said. "Some of us weren't lucky enough to fall headfirst into a mountain of money."

"I would hardly call the death of my husband lucky," Heather said.

"Julie-Ann didn't mean it that way," Lewis said.

"Of course, she did," Heather replied. "Julie-Ann's so green with envy she puts Kermit the Frog to shame."

"Stop that!" Sandra yelled. "Do I have to remind you squabbling children that a man has died and the police are asking for our help? Which we will be happy to provide as and when we can."

Lewis had the grace to duck his head. Julie-Ann and Heather glowered at each other. Heather turned away first. "As for the cost," she said, "it's not your problem, anyway, brother dear. I bought your tickets in the first place, so I guess I'm the one who's going to be out of pocket to replace them."

"Business class would be a nice gesture," Julie-Ann said, "seeing how traumatized we all are by recent events."

Heather ignored her.

"Don't you people get it?" Tyler said. "The police are saying Ed was murdered, and that means someone in this room killed him."

"Well, it wasn't me!" Amanda said.

I expected Williams or Redmond to object. Instead, they remained quiet, letting the drama play out. Rose and Bernie watched everyone. Robert the Bruce washed his whiskers.

Brian leapt to his feet. "I've had enough of you, Tyler. You've caused nothing but trouble on this trip. That's a preposterous idea. I suggest you keep your mouth shut from now on."

"But it did happen." Trisha's voice began to rise. "My husband is dead, and someone killed him. You McHenrys always had it in for Ed. Are you happy now, Brian?"

Brian glared at her.

"Watch your mouth, Trisha," Sandra said. "The McHenry and French families have had our differences over the years, but no one in my family had any reason to kill Ed."

"I bet it was a random killer. Like a serial killer or something," a wide-eyed Amanda said, not at all helpfully. "Waiting for a chance to poison someone and get away with it. You should check the national police databases for similar cases. I bet you'll find something."

"This is preposterous," Brian said. "You're all making something out of nothing. The man was a walking heart attack. Sorry, Trisha, but it had to happen one day. And you," he said to Williams, "are a small-town cop trying to play at solving what you want to be a murder so you can get your picture in the paper."

Williams turned red. He sputtered. Redmond made no further move for the door; she simply looked from one person to another, taking in the family dynamics.

Amanda stood up, pulling her phone out of her pocket. "Can I go now? I'm sorry Mr. French died, but I didn't know him."

"Me neither," Tyler said.

Williams hesitated. They took that as approval and bolted for the door. "I cannot wait," Amanda said to her brother, "to call Madison. Imagine. I was right there, at the same table. If he'd offered me some of his tea, I might be dead now! When they catch the killer, maybe the papers'll want to interview me about my close escape from the Tearoom Killer."

That was not a phrase I ever wanted to hear repeated.

Sandra was next to get to her feet. "Thank you for coming all this way to tell us personally, Detectives. It's what we were expecting to hear, but upsetting nonetheless. I'm very tired and need to retire to my room." She leaned heavily on her cane and walked slowly across the room.

Lewis turned to his wife. "Will you see Grandma upstairs? Please."

Julie-Ann sighed mightily, but started to stand.

While everyone had been talking, Trisha had sat quietly, pulled in on herself, sobbing steadily and tearing at the tissue in her hands. Now she looked up. Her eyes blazed and she lifted one hand. She pointed directly at Julie-Ann. "Don't you dare leave this room. You think I didn't know you've been trying to get back with Ed? Sending him messages at night, asking to meet behind my back."

Julie-Ann's mouth dropped open. She glanced around the room. "That's not true. I never . . . I mean, Ed and I had business to talk over."

Trisha stood up. A vein pulsed in her neck, and her eyes were wild. "You always were a horrid, selfish woman. You couldn't bear it, could you, knowing he didn't want to be with you again? So you killed him. Detective, I demand you arrest that woman. She murdered my husband."

Chapter 10

"You're out of your tiny mind," Julie-Ann shouted. "Can you hear yourself?" She turned to Detective Williams. "Trisha might not hear herself, but we all heard her loud and clear. She thought her husband was interested in me, but I can assure you such was no longer the case. Ed and I had some business transactions, that's natural enough. We live in the same small town. You must have mistaken me for someone else, Trisha. Was he having an affair? I wonder who that person might have been, but it doesn't matter now, does it? Maybe you killed Ed, fearing he was about to leave you?"

"How dare you?" Trisha said. "That's a vile accusation."

Sandra had stopped halfway to the door. She pounded her cane on the carpet. "That's enough!"

No one paid her any attention.

Williams and Redmond watched silently as Julie-Ann continued the attack. "If you thought Ed was still interested in me, Trisha, why did you agree to come on this little vacation, anyway? Seems a funny way of keeping him away from me."

"I didn't know you were going to be here, did I? She didn't tell us the whole miserable lot of you had been invited, but I should have known. Miss High-and-Mighty, with her secrets and her money, playing people like they're pieces on a chessboard."

"I assume that jab's aimed at me," Heather said. "Pardon me for trying to get everyone together for a reunion."

"I knew not to trust you one bit, but not Ed," Trisha said. "Ed was always too kind for his own good. 'Let bygones be bygones,' he said. Look where that got him." She burst into tears and ran from the room.

No one tried to stop her. Lewis grabbed Julie-Ann's wrist and pulled her onto the couch beside him. "Not one more word," he snarled at her.

"I'm only telling the truth," she said. "Someone has to."

"I hope," Sandra said, "you'll forget that unpleasantness, Detectives. We are all naturally very upset. Saying things we don't mean." She threw a look at Julie-Ann that could have melted the delicate porcelain statue on the table next to her.

The chances, I thought, *of the detectives forgetting what's been said are mighty slim.*

"If that is all, I'll be resting in my room." Sandra lifted her head, straightened her back, gripped her cane, and proudly, although slowly, walked out of the room.

"Anyone else got any confessions or accusations to make?" Williams said.

No one spoke.

"Mrs. McHenry," Redmond said to Julie-Ann. "I'll need to talk to you privately."

"No," Brian said.

"I beg your pardon?"

"My daughter-in-law is . . . confused. She didn't mean what she said. I'd prefer it if you didn't take the matter any further."

"I don't much care," Redmond said, "what you'd prefer."

"It's all right. I'll do all I can to help." A slight smile touched the edges of Julie-Ann's mouth. It put me in mind of a cat playing with a mouse.

"And then," Redmond said, "I'll have a private chat with Trisha French and get her side of the story."

Julie-Ann's smile died.

"What a waste of time." Darlene spoke for the first time since we'd gathered. "You should be searching for whoever killed Ed, not harassing my family."

"Harassing?" Redmond's eyebrows arched. "Mr. French was deliberately poisoned. And, in light of the circumstances surrounding that poisoning, it's clear that someone in this house was responsible."

"That was interesting," Bernie said.

"It would have been interesting if it had been on TV," Rose said. "In my house, it was not interesting—it was potentially disastrous."

We were back in the kitchen. The McHenry family had been ordered out of the drawing room so Redmond could talk privately first to Julie-Ann and then to Trisha. Williams had been about to settle himself into a vacated chair, but Redmond suggested maybe he should guard the door to prevent people from trying to listen in.

Unfortunately, that meant I wouldn't be able to sneak into the secret room.

Once we were all standing in the hall, I gave Williams a broad smile. "You're making great progress, Detective. Good job. With your permission, I should be able to open for business in a couple of hours."

"Huh?"

"My tearoom? I assume I can reopen?"

"No."

"No what?"

"No, you cannot reopen. Not until I say so. And I am not saying so."

"But you said the poison was in Ed French's tea. As we didn't provide the tea, he brought it himself, we can't be considered to have been at fault in any way."

"When we have the tox reports, I'll decide. Not before."

"But—"

"No buts, Ms. Roberts." He peered at me from under his overgrown eyebrows in a look he no doubt intended to be intimidating. I wasn't intimidated, but I recognized the signs. Any further attempts by me to press the point would only have him digging in his heels further.

Rose put her hand on my arm. "I feel in need of a restorative cuppa, love. Let's see what's left of this morning's coffee cake."

"Coffee and cake would be good," Williams said.

I refrained from asking if he wasn't afraid it had been poisoned and let Rose drag me away. I put the kettle and coffeepot on as Bernie rummaged in the B & B fridge for leftover baked goods. "No coffee cake, but there are some nice-looking muffins in here."

"Wait while I find the box of arsenic to sprinkle on Williams's," I said. "It must be in here somewhere."

"Don't joke," Rose said. "He's not here, but the walls have ears."

"As we know," I said.

"What does that mean?" Bernie asked.

"Nothing," Rose and I chorused.

My friend gave us a suspicious look.

The kettle began to boil, and I poured water over tea bags in a small pot. I put the pot and a cup in front of Rose and took a jug of milk out of the fridge. I then poured three mugs of coffee: one for Bernie, one for Williams, and one for me.

"Not a word until I get back," Bernie said. "We need to come up with a plan of attack." She carried a tray containing the mug of coffee and a muffin—unpoisoned—out to Detective Williams.

I sat at the table and put my head in my hands. Éclair wiggled her muzzle onto my lap and I automatically stroked it. "This is a disaster, all right," I moaned.

"Potentially so, yes." Rose stirred milk into her tea. Robbie put his front paws on the milk jug and tried to stick his nose into it. I snatched it away. He pretended not to mind.

"He's not happy cooling his heels in the hallway," Bernie said when she returned. "He's standing in front of the drawing-room door all puffed up with importance, snarling at anyone who walks by to keep on moving and attempting not to look like he's getting ear strain from trying to hear what's being said inside."

"Is there such a thing as ear strain?" Rose asked.

"If there isn't, there should be."

"Interesting about Julie-Ann and Ed," Bernie said. "I wonder if there's anything to Trisha's accusations."

"It does make things look bad for the both of them. A secret lover. A wronged wife. The stuff classic detective novels are made of."

"Did you notice," Rose said, "how they referred to any relationship between Ed and Julie-Ann with words like *still interested* and *again*. Something lies in their past. Whether or not that something also existed in the present is the point right now."

"If it was up to Williams," Bernie said, "they'd never get to the bottom of it. But Redmond seems competent."

"Detective Redmond quite niftily took over the questioning," Rose said. "Williams was outside facing a closed door before he knew he'd been dismissed."

"We can't count on that happening all the time," Bernie

said. "Now that he's been outmaneuvered once, he'll be on his guard."

"If there's one good thing about this mess," I said, "at least he's not considering you, Rose, to be a suspect this time."

"Oh, I'm sure he'll remember me eventually." She sipped daintily at her tea. She'd added a splash of milk to her saucer and Robert the Bruce was on the table, licking it up. If the health inspectors saw a cat eating on the table, they'd shut us down fast enough.

That, I'd worry about another day. I had enough to worry about at the moment. "I don't know how long I can stay closed without going under. It's coming up to what I expect to be the busiest time of the year, when I need to make enough money to see us through the winter. The longer I'm closed, the more it will look as though the police have ordered me closed for a reason. I might not get many customers when I do reopen. And even if I do, I'll have lost my staff by then. Cheryl and Marybeth can't go long without being paid, and I can't pay them if I don't have any income." I rubbed Éclair's nose and she snuffled happily. "Have any of the other guests complained about the police storming around in here?"

"No," Rose said. "Some of them seem to think it dreadfully exciting. All fine and good when you're not involved. Fortunately, the name of the B and B has been kept out of the press, unlike last time, so I haven't had any abrupt cancelations."

"People aren't afraid they'll be murdered between their two-hundred-thread-count sheets with their heads resting on the feather pillows and covered with the embroidered white lace duvets?" Bernie asked.

"Not this time," Rose said dryly. "However, we have another problem."

"Oh, good," I said. "More to worry about. Don't tell me."

Rose sipped her tea. I drank my coffee and tried to bite my tongue. Eventually I gave in, as she knew I would. "I guess I need to know. What now?"

"We're fully booked beginning Friday, which is the day after tomorrow, right through the next two weeks."

"That's a problem because . . . ?" Bernie said.

"The police have asked the French family and Trisha not to leave North Augusta," I said. "You'll have to tell them to find another hotel, Rose."

"I can't throw one of my oldest friends into the street, never mind her family."

"You'll have to," I said. "We can't cancel guests with less than forty-eight hours' notice. They won't be able to find other accommodations, not this weekend, and our reputation will be ruined, probably permanently." Visions of irate online comments and plunging satisfaction ratings flew across my eyes.

"If they can't find other accommodations, neither can Sandra and her family."

"They can pitch a tent on the lawn, for all I care," I said.

"Amanda and Tyler can do that," Bernie said. "I don't see Heather sleeping in a tent."

"Sandra can move into my place," I said. "I'll stay with Bernie. One of the others can have my couch."

Rose shook her head. "Thank you, love. But that still doesn't account for them all. Maybe we'll be lucky and the police will solve the case by tomorrow and they can go home."

"Trisha might want to leave," I said. "If she thinks Julie-Ann or someone else in that lot killed her husband, she won't want to stay under the same roof."

"I don't know what she believes," Rose said. "She

spoke in anger. They all did. It's a hard thing to think someone you know would have hated a man enough to murder him in cold blood."

"And poisoning his tea, if that's what happened," Bernie said, "is mighty cold."

"Indeed. Easier to accept it was an accident. Something added incorrectly to the so-called tea at its point of origin."

"Maybe we'll be lucky," I said, "and that's what they'll find. That the whole lot of tea was off, not just what Ed drank on Monday."

"Regardless of the sleeping arrangements," Bernie said, "I'm not trusting to luck, and certainly not to Detective Williams's investigative skills. You know what this means, Rose?"

"Yes," my grandmother said, "I do." She put down her cup and lifted Robbie off her lap. "Time to get to work. I'll start with the unsuitably named Grand Lake, Iowa."

"Why is that unsuitable?" I asked.

"The lake outside of town is what they call in other parts of the world a puddle ," Rose said.

"I get it," Bernie said. "The townspeople have delusions of grandeur. I'll dig deep into the finances."

"What are you two talking about?" I said. "Are you going to Iowa, Rose? Isn't this rather a bad time? I need you here. Whose finances, Bernie?"

Bernie and Rose exchanged knowing glances. A bad feeling began to creep over me. "Oh, no. Don't tell me . . ."

"Someone needs to move this investigation along," Rose said, "before you and I are both in the workhouse. And do it quickly. It's up to Bernie and me to do our part."

"I don't think that's a good idea," I said. "Remember what happened last time? Your amateur investigating almost got me killed."

"But it didn't, did it?" Bernie said cheerfully. "And here you sit before us now, still hale and hearty."

Rose smiled at me. I didn't trust that smile.

I'm Rose's granddaughter, physically an almost spitting image of her in her youth. But other than looks, Bernie's far more like my mother's mother than I am.

Whenever I think of Rose and Bernie, I remember an expedition to Central Park when we were in fifth grade. We'd been caught by a sudden rainstorm, and while Mom and I cowered in the shelter of the Metropolitan Museum of Art, Rose and Bernie danced in the rain and splashed, roaring with laughter, through the puddles.

I let out a world-weary sigh. "Okay, what do you want me to do?"

They gave me identical patronizing smiles.

"You bake, love," Rose said.

"It's what you do best," Bernie said.

"We'll let you know if we need you." Rose checked her watch. "Shall we reconvene at six to report on our findings?"

Bernie stood up. "Sounds good to me." She disappeared through the back door without another word.

Rose headed for the hallway. "There is one thing you can do, love."

"What?"

"Have dinner ready for us, please. We private investigators need plenty of feeding."

Grumbling, I cleared up the dishes.

I was in my happy place—making pistachio macarons—but not feeling at all happy about life, when a knock sounded on the back door.

"It's open," I called. "Come on in."

The old hinges and the loose floorboard squeaked as Amy Redmond entered.

"If you're not here to tell me I can reopen, you're not welcome," I said.

What might have been a trace of a smile tugged at the corners of her mouth. "Then I'm safe. What are you making?"

"Pistachio macarons. I just finished a batch of toasted hazelnut and chocolate. Would you like one?"

"I would. Thank you."

I opened the fridge. Redmond let out a low whistle when she saw the contents. "Wow, you have been busy."

"I have to do something. This is my livelihood, you know." I took out the tray of macarons and put two onto a plate. "Would you like tea?"

"No, thanks. I don't want to take up too much of your time. I'm here to tell you that you can reopen tomorrow." She accepted the offered plate.

I let out a long sigh. Happy, once again. "That's great. Thanks. What's happened? Did you find the killer?"

"No. Not yet. But we will. Have you had many people poking around today? Scene-of-the-crime groupies, I mean?"

"That's a thing?"

"Sadly, yes."

"A couple. Someone was on the patio when I arrived this morning, taking a picture of the front door. She had the grace to scurry away when I told her we were closed."

"You shouldn't get many more bothering you. They have a limited attention span. Once we've left and taken down our tape, they go on to the next thing. Is your gardener still around?"

"Simon? I think so. I didn't hear his bike go by."

She tossed a macaron into her mouth and chewed. Judging by the look on her face, she was enjoying it. A lot. "That is quite simply," she said when she could speak again, "possibly the single best thing I have ever eaten."

"Wait until you have one of the pistachio ones," I said, feeling ridiculously pleased at the praise.

She snatched the second pastry up, as though afraid I'd change my mind and take it back. "Can you take a break?"

"Your timing's good. These have to sit for about half an hour or so before I bake them."

"Why do you do that?"

"They need to dry out before being baked to get a nice crispy shell." I washed my hands in the sink. "Where are we going?"

"I need to talk to Simon and I might as well fill you in at the same time."

We crossed the lawn together, heading for the garden shed at the far corner of the property. Simon kept his own hours, coming and going as he liked, but his motorcycle was parked by the shed and the door was open, so he hadn't left yet. His bike had been returned this morning, as good as new. As we approached, he came out of the shed, carrying a saw with a lethal-looking set of razor-sharp teeth.

"Hey," he said. "What's up?" He glanced between Redmond and me.

"I have an initial toxicology report," she said, "and a couple of questions for you. I know Lily's interested, so I invited her to tag along."

"Happy to be of help," he said.

"Only because I'm the nervous sort"—she gestured at the saw—"can you put that down first, please?"

He grinned at her. "Come into my office."

We stepped inside. The shed was clean and neatly organized. Rakes, brooms, spades, and pitchforks hung from hooks on the walls; vessels of all sizes and materials were stacked on shelves; bags of mulch and potting soil were piled on the floor. The enclosed space was warm from the sun hitting the roof. It smelled of the good clean earth of Massachusetts, and I breathed in deeply.

Simon hung the saw on an empty hook and said, "I can't offer you chairs. Sorry."

A single ray of sunlight poured through the small window facing west and lit up Redmond's spiky, cropped blond hair as though her head were surrounded by a halo. Other than that, there was nothing at all saintly about her. She'd showed some signs of friendship toward me in the past, but I knew better than to regard her as anything but a cop. Not when she was working. And, I suspected, Detective Redmond was always working.

"Not a problem," she said. "I'm a city girl, born and raised in the suburbs of Boston. My parents had a house with a small garden that was mostly weedy grass with a few impatiens stuck here and there for color. When I moved away from home, I went into a college dorm and then an apartment. Why I'm telling you all this is so you understand that I know absolutely nothing about gardening."

"Okay," Simon said.

"Edward French died because of an overdose of digitalis."

"Foxglove," Simon said.

"So the pathologist suspects."

"What's that mean?" I asked. "I've heard of digitalis. It's a heart medication. But isn't foxglove a flower?"

"Yes, on both accounts," Simon said. "Digitalis, which is a commonly prescribed heart medication, is an extract of foxglove, which is a popular garden plant. They're tall and highly attractive and quite striking lining a border, so people like to have them in their gardens. As I said the other day, the average backyard garden's full of poisonous plants. Foxglove's one of the most dangerous."

"Simon's right," Redmond said.

"I assume," Simon said, "you want to ask me if we have foxglove growing here because you can't distinguish it from a petunia."

"That's about it. Although I have seen pictures."

"No. We don't. Grow foxglove, I mean. As you know, I've only been working here a short while, but I know the garden pretty well by now. No foxglove. No oleander, either, or anything else I'd say is dangerous. My uncle Gerald worked this garden for a long time. He probably planted most of the things here. The garden's open to the public, B and B guests, tearoom guests, anyone who wants to have a look 'round. People bring their kids here. You'd be asking for trouble to have poisonous plants on the premises."

"What about other properties in and around North Augusta?"

Simon shrugged. "Likely quite a few of them have foxglove. As I said, it's attractive and popular and grows well at Zone 7a."

"What's that mean?" Redmond asked.

"That's the gardening zone for Cape Cod. Geographic zones are based on climate to help ascertain what plants do well where. As for foxglove, I can't say I've noticed any in particular around here. I've joined an Internet chat room that discusses gardening in the northern Cape. A group of other professionals, gardeners who work at the hotels or for the towns, plus keen amateurs. I can ask about foxglove, if you like."

"Thanks," she said. "I'd appreciate that, but only if you can do it without saying why you want to know."

"I'll tell them I'm thinking of putting some in. They know I'm not from around here, so I've been asking a lot of basic questions."

She smiled at him. He smiled back. I felt a sudden, unexpected jolt of jealousy. Redmond was an attractive woman, slightly taller than me, slightly shorter than Simon, with smooth olive skin and deep dark eyes, and hair dyed a pale blond. She was thin, but the fit of her classically cut jacket and trousers indicated that she was a runner. She probably put in a couple of miles every morning before breakfast. Whereas I tried not to recall when I'd last been to yoga class or the gym. She was close to my age, but the stresses of her job, and no doubt the things she'd seen, were carved into the delicate skin around her mouth and eyes.

"So," I said, perhaps in a harsher tone than I intended, "what does this mean for me? You said I can reopen."

"I did. An analysis of Ed French's supply of unconsumed tea provided to us by his wife, Trisha, showed that it contains nothing out of the ordinary. I might not want to drink that muck myself, but doing so wouldn't kill me or even upset my tummy. But the lab found traces of foxglove in his stomach contents, among the tea sludge and in the compost we removed from here. The compost Simon told us contained kitchen residue from the tearoom."

"So you are saying the poison came from my kitchen!"

"Relax, Lily. The only foxglove in the compost was mixed in with the residue from Ed's tea."

"Someone actually went through all that compost and located individual particles?" Simon said. "Wow, I am impressed. Not a job I'd want to do, though."

"We were helped by the fact that Ed's tea leaves weren't nearly as finely ground as the tea Lily uses. They weren't that difficult to find."

"Can I have my compost back?" Simon asked.

I glanced at him. The twinkle in his eye indicted he wasn't entirely serious.

"Put in a claim," Redmond replied with a grin. "In light of all that, I can conclude you served nothing deadly in your restaurant, Lily. Nothing other than what the deceased provided for himself. So you can reopen tomorrow."

Relief washed over me, but I couldn't forget that a man

had died in my tearoom. "If Ed French's dry tea doesn't contain foxglove," I said, "but the tea in his pot did . . ."

"Then someone added the foxglove after the tea was handed to your waitress." Redmond's smile had disappeared. "She says she took the bag containing the leaves into the kitchen, put a spoonful into a teapot, added boiling water, and put the pot on the table next to Ed French's place. At the same time, she gave Trisha French back the bag of dry tea, in which a few spoonfuls remained. I've been assured that neither Cheryl nor Marybeth are anything other than the North Augusta mother-and-daughter team they appear to be."

"Meaning they're not killers for hire," Simon said. "Always good to know."

"We're acting on the assumption that the foxglove was added to Ed's pot when everyone was outside seeing to the motorcycle accident."

"Don't remind me," Simon muttered.

"I see it parked outside," Redmond said. "Is it fixed?"

"Yes. Heather French picked up the bill."

"Was it a coincidence, do you think, that the tea was poisoned at the same time the bike was stolen?" I asked. "Or were there two people acting together? Although, that would mean Tyler's involved, and I can't see him keeping something like that to himself for long."

"We've checked into him," Redmond said. "He's never come to the attention of the police in Grand Lake. He doesn't run with a bad crowd, what there is of one in that town, anyway. More likely, a case of the killer waiting for the right moment. And it conveniently presented itself. Enough foxglove to kill a man would easily fit into a pocket or small purse. I have to ask you again, Lily, did you see anyone paying any undue attention to Ed's teapot?"

"No," I said firmly. "I did not."

"They must have been one mighty cool customer," Simon said. "To walk around with that in their pocket, waiting for a chance to use it."

Despite the warmth of the tiny room, I shivered.

"What happens now?" Simon asked.

"We keep investigating. Will you let me know what, if anything, you find out about foxglove in gardens around here?"

"Sure," he said.

"Are you going to tell the family what you've told us?" I asked.

"Yes. I'm heading up to the house next. I wanted to ask Simon if the plant grew on this particular property before I did that."

"Does it make a difference?" I asked. "If it had been growing here?"

"Malice aforethought," she said. "As there isn't foxglove readily at hand, our killer picked it ahead of time and brought it with them. Yes, that makes a difference."

Chapter 11

On my way back to my macarons, I sent Bernie and Rose a text: **Tox analysis done. Foxglove in Ed's tea. Redmond on way to the house with the news.**

Rose: **I'll be with Sandra.**

Bernie: **Good to know. See you at six.**

"As no one broke down and confessed," Rose said, settling herself comfortably at the kitchen table, "our work continues. What did you bring for our supper, love?"

Robbie had followed her in. He perched on the countertop next to the fridge and eyed Éclair, sitting at my feet. Éclair eyed Robbie. They weren't exactly enemies, but they did live in a state of mutual distrust.

"You're lucky I brought anything at all," I said. "I found a chicken in the freezer and a loaf of bread only slightly past its best date. We're having toasted chicken sandwiches." I put the chicken, which I'd thawed over the afternoon, on the counter, took a butcher's knife out of the drawer, and set to carving the thing up. I'd separate the breasts and grill them for our dinner. The rest of the bird would go back to the tearoom to be poached in Darjeeling liquid to make tea sandwiches.

"I'm opening tomorrow. Business as usual. I called all the people who'd left messages asking about reservations to let them know, and I reopened the web page to accept online reservations. I phoned Marybeth and Cheryl to tell them to come in and to expect a regular day."

Marybeth had pretended to be disappointed at not getting another day's vacation, but I knew she needed the money and I was glad for their sakes I could tell them their jobs were safe.

While my macaron shells were baking, I'd checked Twitter and Facebook and had seen that the social media references to Tea by the Sea being the site of a *brutal murder* and *deadly poison in the tea* were down considerably. As Redmond had said, public interest moves on. "You're not having any B and B cancelations because of Ed's death, so this is no longer any concern of ours. You can leave it in the capable hands of the police and we can enjoy our dinner—"

"As plain as it is," Rose said.

"—and talk about other things."

Bernie snorted. "Capable, indeed. Williams obviously checked the contents of Heather's bank account and is now tripping all over himself, tugging his forelock and saying he's sorry to inconvenience her. Man's a fool."

"So he is, but Amy Redmond is not." I separated the two breasts from the chicken and sprinkled salt and pepper over them. I switched the oven broiler on, and while it heated, I took a sip of the wine Bernie had brought. "Were you there when the police told the family the results of the tox reports?"

"Williams came to the house while Redmond was talking to you and Simon." Rose had brought her nightly gin and tonic with her and sipped at it. "He spoke to Sandra as though she was addled. Talking *slooooowly* and *carefullllly* and taking great pains to explain what digitalis is." If Rose wasn't a lady of a certain age, and if she wasn't in her own house, she would have spit on the floor. "As though anyone our age isn't thoroughly acquainted with digitalis. Sandra's husband had a heart condition, that's what he died of. The drug would have been in their house while he was alive."

"What about the rest of them?" Bernie asked.

"Only Sandra and Trisha were here. The others had gone out. Whale watching, I believe. They were able to reschedule the departure, as Heather had booked an entire boat for their party. I was with Sandra when Williams told her, but I wasn't allowed to come to Trisha's room with him." She sniffed in disapproval. "Thus the rest of the group learned it second- or thirdhand. Sandra phoned Brian, and he would have told the others. Not a good thing for analyzing people's reactions."

"As for giving up our investigation," Bernie said, "not going to happen, Lily. I've learned quite a lot since we last spoke, and I don't think that information should go to waste. Unless you want to forget about it, Rose?"

"Perish the thought," my grandmother said. "Do you want to go first?"

"Why not?" Bernie took a sip of her wine, then put the glass on the table and opened the iPad she'd brought with her.

I laid the seasoned chicken breasts on a tray and put them in the oven. Once those two got an idea in their heads, nothing on earth—certainly not my feeble protests—would move them.

They were determined to involve themselves in the police investigation, and all I could do would be to listen politely and hope they wouldn't try to rope me into helping.

"As we know," Bernie began, "Heather's husband, Norman French, made a lot of money when he sold his Internet start-up five years ago. Heather and Norman moved to New York City, and he died a few months after."

"Remind me how he died," Rose said. "Something about being hit by a car, as I recall."

"He was a pedestrian. Stepped into a busy intersection on the Upper East Side directly in front of a cab. No indication of foul play. The cabbie stopped on the spot and told police the man suddenly appeared in front of him and he didn't have time to avoid him. He was quite shaken up about it."

"Happens all the time in Manhattan," I said. "Even worse now that people are paying more attention to their phones than to oncoming traffic."

"Right." Bernie said. "The one thing of interest I found is that Norman's brother, Edward—"

"The late Edward French, the reason we are gathered here," Rose said.

"The very one. Ed had threatened to sue his brother before Norman died."

"That is interesting," Rose said.

Bernie was a forensic accountant. Until recently, she'd worked for a big Manhattan criminal law firm and she had an extensive network of contacts in the financial world to tap into, as well as an uncanny ability to dig through vast amounts of data in search of one small salient detail. She'd been a computer whiz in high school and college, and I sometimes wondered if her data-gathering efforts were entirely aboveboard. I thought it better not to ask.

"Sue him?" I said. "On what grounds?"

"Ed claimed that he'd worked alongside Norman in the development of Norman's software product, albeit unofficially. Meaning he wasn't on the payroll. But even though Norman officially owned the business, as the two men were brothers, Ed believed they were partners."

"A foolish assumption," Rose said. "Nothing destroys families faster than money."

"To be fair, when they started, no one could have guessed Norman would get sixty-five million bucks for his idea."

"Ed should have." Rose stroked Robbie. Robbie yawned. Éclair was sniffing around the floor between the fridge and the stove, hoping to find some previously undiscovered scraps.

"How far did this lawsuit get?" I asked.

"Not far enough," Bernie said. "It was prepared by a lawyer, but never filed. Norman died, and according to his will, his widow, Heather, got it all."

"Ed didn't try to go after Heather for his share? Or what he thought of as his share? Just because he claimed to have helped develop the product doesn't mean he did. Although Ed's in the computer business, someone told me his business in Iowa was selling and servicing computers. Did he provide any evidence he worked alongside his brother?"

"I have no way of knowing," Bernie said. "I couldn't see the actual details of the proposed suit."

"Fancy that," I said.

Bernie gave me a look. "Even I have my limitations. The suit was never filed, meaning it's not a matter of public record."

"Probably irrelevant," Rose said. "Edward thought he had a case, and that's all that mattered. He didn't try to get money out of Heather after his brother's death?"

"Not that I can find. No more was said. Legally speaking, anyway. He might have spoken to her directly, meaning there's no legal trail to follow. But as he doesn't appear to have come into money, I'd say nothing came of it."

"Heather invited Ed and his wife on this trip," I said. "Do you think she was trying to make up with him?"

"Could be. Let bygones be bygones, and all that. It's entirely possible Ed felt bad at Norman's death and decided not to harass the young widow. And so he let it go."

"Was there any suggestion Ed might have had a hand in his brother's death?" Rose asked.

"Not a whisper. Ed was in Iowa at the time."

"That's all interesting," I said, "but I don't see that it has anything to do with Ed's death. He and Heather made up. The financial affairs of the French family would have had nothing to do with the McHenry family."

"And that's where I come in," Rose said.

"Do tell," Bernie said.

I got up to take the chicken out of the oven. I sliced the breasts into strips, dumped them into a bowl along with chopped onion, celery, chives, salt and pepper, mayonnaise, and a sprinkle of paprika. While I fixed the sandwiches, Rose said, "I have more than a few good friends back home in Grand Lake. I made a few phone calls today. Just catching up, you know. In many cases, I didn't even have to say more than 'hello' before my friends demanded to know what had happened to Ed French."

"Are they a well-known family?" Bernie asked.

"Very. They're longtime residents and are involved in several local businesses. Norman and Ed's mother, now deceased, was a fund-raising force to be reckoned with. I remember more than once ducking down alleys and side streets when I saw her marching determinedly in my direction. And that was before Norman made all that money and became even more the talk of the town."

I laid the sandwiches on a platter, put the platter on the table, and sat down.

Bernie helped herself, but Rose looked around. "This is it?"

"Your dinner? Yes, this is it," I said. "I've been cooking all day. You invited us, remember?"

"I thought at least a bowl of soup to accompany a chicken sandwich."

"Did you make soup, Rose? No? Then we have no soup."

" 'No soup for you,' " Bernie quoted.

"You know I don't cook, love," Rose said. "That's why I employ you."

I opened my mouth to point out once again that Rose might think she employed me to help around the B & B, but considering she didn't actually pay me a wage, that concept was nebulous at best. I stuffed a sandwich into it, instead. What was the point?

"It's a hot night," Bernie said, "and I don't mind not having soup, as long as there's something fabulous for dessert. What did you make, Lily?"

"I don't know which one of you is worse," I growled around a mouthful of chicken sandwich. It was too bland. I should have added some curry powder.

"I guess that means no dessert, either," Bernie said. "Back to the goings-on, according to the gossip mills of small-town Iowa."

"That the French brothers fell out when Norman sold his company is well-known," Rose said. "I heard about it myself at the time. Norman moved away, and then he died. Heather stayed in New York, and as far as the locals were concerned, that was the end of that. I didn't know until today about any pending lawsuit, so perhaps Ed had the good taste to keep it under wraps. Their mother would not have been happy to see her sons fighting."

"What happened to her?" Bernie asked.

"She moved to Arizona at the same time Norman and Heather went to New York. I heard they bought her a house. She died two or three years later."

"What about the McHenry family?" Bernie asked. "Are they also prominent citizens?"

"Again, yes. Sandra's husband was the mayor for many years. Sandra was also a force to be reckoned with in charitable circles, and many people said she was the motivation behind her husband's political career. It was rumored for some years that he had ambitions at the federal level. Nothing came of that, and people said those ambitions were more hers than his. Which I can believe. Sandra and I were friends, but many people didn't like her."

"Why not?"

"They consider her to be overly full of herself. Sandra enjoys being a big fish in the small pond that is Grand Lake, Iowa. At one time, her son, Brian, owned several new and used car dealerships, but he sold all but one over the years. Lewis now manages that, I believe. All of which is background. However, I did hear something of interest that I didn't know." My grandmother's eyes glittered with excitement. She smiled at Bernie and me.

I turned to Bernie. "As there's no dessert, do you feel like going into town for ice cream after?"

"Sure," Bernie said. "That would be good. I've hit a sticky plot point in the book I want to run by you. Do you think Rose—my Rose—and Tessa need to bring a man into their detecting agency?"

"Are you thinking that would give it more historical accuracy? Maybe they should. He could go places they can't and—"

"Most amusing," Rose said. "Do you want to hear what I learned or not?"

"Clearly, you want to tell us," I said, "so go ahead."

"When you're ready," Bernie said.

Rose huffed. "You heard Trisha accuse Julie-Ann of wanting to get back with Ed?"

"Everyone heard that," I said. "But so much was going on, it slipped my mind."

"Didn't slip mine," Bernie said.

"Like old sins, good gossip is never forgotten," Rose said. "All it needs is new developments for everyone to bring it up again. Julie-Ann was engaged to Ed French at one time. Ed unceremoniously dumped her when he met Trisha, so everyone says. Julie-Ann married Lewis on the rebound."

I got up, took the bottle out of the fridge, and poured Bernie and me another glass of wine. "So, what? That had to have been decades ago. Lewis and Julie-Ann have teenage children."

"It might have been decades ago," Rose said, "but obviously the matter remains fresh in Trisha's mind."

"Why? In the battle for Ed French, Trisha was the winner. Why would she hold a grudge?"

Rose grinned. "Because the battle, it would appear, had recently reopened on a new front. Julie-Ann told one of her friends that she regretted marrying Lewis, and Ed regretted marrying Trisha. Only days before her wedding to Lewis, Ed spoke to her. He said he was sorry, he'd made a mistake and he hoped they could get back together. But by that time, Ed and Trisha had started a family, and Julie-Ann was pregnant with Amanda, and so she reluctantly turned Ed down and went ahead with the wedding to Lewis."

"Rubbish," I said. "You can't seriously be suggesting that sixteen-year-old gossip is relevant to a murder."

"It can be highly relevant," Bernie said, "if the people still have those feelings all these years later."

"Some friend," I said. "I assume this friend Julie-Ann confided in, in the strictest of confidence, told everyone in town."

"Something like that," Rose said. "There's not a lot to do in an Iowa farming community in the winter. The gossip, however, is not sixteen years old, but much more recent. Julie-Ann said this quite recently."

"I wonder if Lewis, Julie-Ann's husband, knows," Rose said.

"What if he does? This isn't Victorian times. People get divorced all the time. They don't have to kill to"—I made quotations marks in the air with my fingers—"be free."

"True, but people still get jealous. And vengeful," Rose said.

"Even when there isn't a lot of money involved," Bernie said. "Although maybe there is money involved if Ed was still wanting a cut of what his late brother did him out of. Maybe that's why Julie-Ann wanted to get back with him."

"And why," Rose said, "Trisha might have objected to any divorce."

"You two," I said. "Each one of you is as bad as the other."

"Someone did kill Ed French, love," Rose said. "We didn't make that up."

"I guess not," I admitted.

Rose took the last bite of her sandwich and then finished her gin and tonic. "An ice cream sounds nice. Get the taste of that bland chicken out of my mouth. But before we go, I learned one other thing of interest in my telephonic trawl of Grand Lake, Iowa. Brian McHenry and Ed French had once been in business together. They owned several car dealerships. Ed, so I've been told, was a mostly silent partner, while Brian ran the day-to-day. Their partnership ended badly when Brian accused Ed of cheating him. He sued, but the case was thrown out of court because Brian couldn't prove his claim. Brian accused Ed of bribing his lawyer to fumble the case. Again, that's something I vaguely remember from when I lived in town, but I've been reminded that the bad blood lingers. Only a few short months ago, Brian and Darlene walked out of a friend's retirement party when Ed and Trisha arrived. That, as you can imagine, had the phone lines humming for days."

"They weren't happy to see the Frenches checking in here on Sunday," I said.

"Why do you suppose Heather invited them here?" Bernie asked. "Considering how much they don't get on?"

"I suspect," Rose said, "she simply didn't know the old animosities still lingered. Remember, Heather hasn't been home for several years."

"Heather's pretty self-absorbed," I said. "I doubt she spends a lot of time worrying about other people's feelings."

Rose tapped her lips with a paper napkin. "Now I, for one, am ready for ice cream. I'll see if Sandra would like to come with us."

Bernie and I waited at the bottom of the stairs while Rose went up to get Sandra.

"Isn't this investigating taking time you'd be better spending on your book?" I said.

"This is important. Rose needs my help. You know I'd do anything for Rose." Bernie paused. "Well, almost anything."

I decided it was a good thing that Rose didn't seem to need *my* help. "Be careful, please. Things could have gone badly wrong last time, you know."

"But they didn't, did they?" Bernie punched me in the

arm and gave me that giant Warrior Princess grin. "All we'll do is hand whatever we learn over to the police. You have to admit it's possible—likely even—the origins of this case are to be found in Grand Lake, Iowa. Rose knows people there and she can use her phone to tap into the town memory, as well as her own. The North Augusta police cannot."

"Okay," I admitted. "I suppose you have a point, but please don't lead Rose down any dark alleys."

"You can count on me," she said.

I gave her a grin in return. I knew I could. Bernie was always there for me. I hoped I'd always be there for her.

Sandra and Rose carefully descended the stairs. Sandra came first, holding the banister for support with one hand and gripping her cane in the other. Rose followed closely behind her, her eyes fixed on her friend and her arms ready to move if Sandra faltered. I leapt forward and ran up the stairs. I held my arm out to Sandra, and Rose gave me a smile of thanks.

"I can manage perfectly well, dear," Sandra said. "Not that old yet." But she took my arm and we descended the rest of the stairs.

"I'm pleased you can join us," I said.

"The family's gone out to dinner, but I decided not to go with them. I've had more than enough high drama to last for the rest of my lifetime. Julie-Ann has always been a drama queen. As far as Julie-Ann's concerned, everything in life is about Julie-Ann, and the foolish girl's milking this unfortunate business for all it's worth. As for Trisha thinking Julie-Ann would leave Lewis for Ed French, of all people, the very idea's preposterous. Brian's totally exasperated by Tyler at the best of times, and I fear Tyler's playing that up to get a rise—as you young people say—out of his grandfather."

"Families," Rose said. "I could tell you some stories about drama queens." I assumed that was a dig at my mother, so I didn't respond.

"Don't leave without me," came a voice from the top of the stairs, and I looked up to see Heather hurrying toward us. She was casually dressed in beige capris and a loose blue linen shirt. Sneakers were on her feet and a woolen oatmeal sweater tossed over her shoulders.

"You didn't go out to dinner with the family?" I asked her.

Heather shook her head. "I've had enough of them for today, but a walk on the pier sounds lovely."

"Trisha will be joining us also," Rose said. "She wasn't invited to dinner with the others, and she didn't want to come with us now, but Sandra knocked on her door and told her she wouldn't take no for an answer."

"The poor thing needs to pull herself together and get her mind off what happened," Sandra said.

"She just lost her husband," Bernie pointed out. "Surely, she's allowed to think about it."

"I am aware of that dear, but watching TV and weeping does no one any good, now does it?"

"I guess not," Bernie said.

"As it's a lovely evening, why don't we wait for Trisha outside?" Rose said.

"I told her not to dawdle." Sandra headed for the door.

We took seats on the veranda while we waited. A car came down the Goodwill driveway, and a few minutes later, Matt loped across the lawn.

"Thought I saw your car," he said to Bernie. "How's everyone this fine evening?"

"We're going into town for ice cream on the pier," Rose said. "You can come with us." She made it sound like a command, not an invitation.

He blinked. "Uh, okay. If that's okay with you, Bernie? I mean Bernie and Lily."

As though he cared about my opinion.

"The more the merrier," my friend said as color rushed into her cheeks. With that red hair and pale skin and those freckles, Bernie never could hide her feelings. Much to her chagrin.

Matt grinned at her. Bernie studied the contents of the nearest tub of flowers. The red geraniums, I couldn't help but notice, were about the same color as her cheeks.

Trisha stepped out of the house. Her eyes were blood-shot and her nose red and puffy, and she clutched a tissue in her hand. But she'd combed her hair and washed her face and she'd pulled on a pair of jeans and a T-shirt under a light gray sweater. She smiled weakly at us. "I'm ready."

Matt stepped forward and put out his hand. "Hi. I'm Matt Goodwill. I live next door."

She accepted it and they shook. "Trisha French."

"I'm sorry for your loss," he said.

"Thank you," she replied in a low voice.

As there were so many of us, we had to go in two cars. Bernie took Matt and Trisha in hers, and I got Rose's aging Ford Focus station wagon out of the garage for her, Sandra, and Heather. Éclair would have enjoyed the out-ing, but I didn't think the others would want her jumping around on their laps. Éclair loved to ride in the car and never sat still.

The town of North Augusta is a small but thriving tourist town facing west over Cape Cod Bay toward the mainland. On this pleasant, warm evening in late June, both tourists and locals were out in force. Crowds were strolling on the sandy stretch of beach or the long pier, watching boats returning to the small sheltered harbor, having dinner in the restaurants lining the seafront, popping in and out of the charming shops, or enjoying an ice cream.

I was lucky enough to snag a parking spot near the waterfront, but Bernie had to go around the block in ever-increasing circles. She eventually found us waiting on benches outside the candy store, watching people streaming in and then coming out again, happily licking towering cones or scooping up caramel sauce with tiny wooden spoons.

"What would you like?" I asked Rose and Sandra when the others had joined us.

Rose stood up. "I won't know until I see what they have, now will I?"

Matt held out his arm, and she took it with a smile. Heather walked with Sandra. Bernie, Trisha, and I brought up the rear, and we joined the line waiting to be served.

"Reminds me of holidays at the seaside when I was a girl," Rose said. "Not that we had many holidays. My father didn't have money for what he called frivolities, and the postwar years were hard for everyone. I particularly recall one week in Scarborough the summer before I went into service at Thornecroft Castle. The rain never let up. Mother never stopped saying, 'Isn't this delightful?' and Father never stopped complaining at the cost of a cup of tea and a biscuit. My sister Violet fell off a swing and broke her arm, which cut our holiday short." She sighed happily. "Ah, memories."

"Sounds like a laugh riot," Bernie said to me.

"Are all the women in your family named after flowers?" Matt asked. "Rose. Violet. Lily."

"We three sisters were Violet, the youngest, me in the middle, and Poppy, the eldest. My mother's name was Petunia. I named my only daughter in honor of my mother."

"She did?" Bernie whispered to me. "Your mom's name's Tina, isn't it?"

"Nope. It's actually Petunia, and don't you dare call her that." Mom hated the family flower names, Petunia above all, and hadn't wanted to call me Lily. But Rose suggested it and my dad liked the name, and in those days, all Mom wanted was to make my dad happy. So Lily I am.

My half sister, daughter of Mom and her second husband, is named Christine.

While we moved steadily up the line, we dithered over the selection. That's to say, the others dithered. I always know what I like. Plain old French vanilla. That might say something about my personality, but why would I try something new when I know what I like?

Matt ordered a triple chocolate peanut butter and told the clerk he'd pay for us all. Heather protested, but he insisted. Bernie asked for bubble gum flavor, which I thought must taste as lurid as it looked, while Rose had maple walnut, Sandra strawberry, Heather chocolate chunk, and Trisha ordered a butter pecan.

Once we were all served and licking contentedly, we went for a stroll along the pier. Night was closing behind us, the sun sinking into the bay. Lights lining the pier, bobbing on boats rising and falling with the gentle swell of the ocean, and shining in town gave everything a warm glow.

Matt fell back to walk next to Bernie, and her laughter drifted on the soft air. I liked Matt, and I was pleased that he and my best friend were finding each other after a very rocky start.

"Rose. How nice to run into you. How are you, dear?" A woman walking toward us stopped directly in front of my grandmother. Her long, thick brown-and-gray hair was gathered up behind her head and her smile was enormous.

Rose's eyes darted about the pier, seeking escape. Trisha went to stand at the railing, where she stood still, looking out to sea. Heather walked with Sandra, but I stayed with my grandmother. Seeing that rescue was not forthcoming, Rose said, "Linda. I'm well, thank you, and you?"

"Perfectly fine. Isn't it a lovely evening?"

"It is. I'm sorry, but I can't stop to chat. My friends are ready to leave."

Linda was maybe a few years younger than my grandmother, and she held the arm of a man, who I guessed was her son. He nodded politely at us.

"I must apologize for missing bridge so much this spring," Linda said.

"No need."

"I've been so busy. It's the height of the gardening season, you know. My place has been chosen for this year's garden tour and that means I have so much to do to get everything absolutely perfect."

"I'm sure you have competent help." Rose began to edge away. I kept my smile locked in place and edged with her.

"You can be sure of that," Linda said. "At my age, I can't do everything myself, but staff need constant supervision." She turned to me. "I don't believe we've met."

"I'm sorry. Linda, this is my granddaughter, Lily Roberts." Rose's eyes flicked longingly down the pier to where the rest of our party was disappearing among the crowd.

"The tearoom lady," Linda said. "I'm pleased to meet you. I have family arriving next week, and one of the things I want to do is treat them to afternoon tea."

"You'd be very welcome," I said.

"I'm one of your closest neighbors. My house is on Bayshore Road, which, despite its name, is not on the bay. It would be nice to be on the sea, as you are, but growing conditions are so much better farther away. Rose, Lily, this is my son, Howard."

Howard muttered something that might have been "nice to meet you." He studied the slats of the pier and ground his right toe into the wood.

"I heard about the murder at your place." Linda's bun wobbled as she shook her head. "I can't imagine what North Augusta's coming to."

"The police haven't confirmed it was a murder," Rose said. That wasn't entirely true: They'd told the family, but hadn't released the information to the media. Yet. "The man was substantially overweight." That was a safe comment to make to these two. Linda and her son looked as though they had trouble staying upright in a strong wind. "I've been told he had a bad heart."

Linda was not to be dissuaded. "They keep telling us tourism's good for the town, but I don't know. I suppose it is for some"—she gestured to our almost-finished cones—"but all these city people coming here and making trouble. We're better off without them, I always say."

"So you do," Rose replied.

All around us, people laughed and chatted, ate ice cream or sipped icy drinks, rushed to the railings to watch the seals playing in the cool waters below, or called to racing children to take care. City people enjoying a break at the seaside. Just like me.

"Did you hear about that ruckus in town last week?" Linda went on. "Garbage cans overturned on Main Street in the middle of the night. It made quite the mess." ·

"Wasn't that kids from North Augusta High?" I said.

"My point exactly," Linda said triumphantly. "The bad influences of the city are affecting our young people."

"Enjoy your evening." Rose tugged at my arm.

"Nice to meet you," I said.

"And then to have an intruder in my own garden! I tell you, Rose, I was frightened out of my life. I called 911, but by the time the police arrived, he was gone. They told me it was probably someone looking for a lost cat or who wanted to admire my garden. But really, who wanders onto private property at night to look at the flowers? No one who's up to any good, let me tell you."

"When did this happen?" I asked.

"Sunday. I know it was Sunday because I always phone my daughter who lives in Boston on Sunday evening before turning in. I'd only just hung up and was getting ready for bed when I heard a noise in the garden. I looked out and saw a . . . person . . . standing there. Right beside the perennial beds at the front of the house. Gave me the fright of my life, I tell you. Fortunately, my bedroom's on the second floor, so I could open my window and yell that the police were on their way. They ran off fast enough."

"Terribly frightening for you. I hope to see you at bridge soon." Rose yanked at my arm.

I resisted the yank. "You have an extensive garden, do you?"

Linda lifted her chin. "Not large, nothing like you have at Victoria-on-Sea, but it's one of the finest private gardens in North Augusta, if I do say so myself. And I do. I started it when we bought the property all those years ago. It's been the labor of a lifetime. I can't do the heavy work myself anymore, but I still supervise the placing of every plant and the trimming of every bush. I've had a wonderful idea! Tea and flowers. You should approach the garden club about making your tearoom a stop on the tour."

Howard continued to study the patterns in the wood at his feet as his mother's words washed over him.

"That's a brilliant idea," Rose said. "We'll think about it. Come on, Lily. The others are ready to leave." She pulled my arm so hard, I was almost jerked off my feet.

I stood my ground. "Do you have a lot of flowers in your garden, Linda?"

"Oh, yes. Perennials are my specialty. Annuals are nice for spots of color when placed strategically or in pots on a deck or patio, but there's nothing like perennials. I regard them as I would old friends, returning to the Cape after wintering away. Are you interested in gardening yourself?"

"I would be if I had more time. My mother was a keen gardener—"

That took Rose by surprise. She opened her mouth to say, "Are you kidding?" but I silenced her with a look.

"—and she particularly loved foxglove. Do you have foxglove?"

Linda clapped her hands. "Masses of them. I adore foxglove. I particularly love plants that, as well as providing us with stunning beauty, do good. Foxglove is used in heart medication. Did you know that? I also grow—"

"I see our friends waving at us," I said. "We'd better catch up to them. Nice to meet you Linda, Howard."

"Feel free to come by anytime and have a look at the garden, dear. No need to wait for the tour. Bring your mother."

"Thanks. We might just do that." I allowed my grandmother to drag me away. Despite her age, Rose had a heck of a strong grip.

"That is the most boring woman in North Augusta," Rose said when we were sure we were out of earshot, "if not the entire eastern seaboard. Her son's perfectly capable of stringing a sentence together, but he learned long ago not to bother. That you pretended interest in her garden can only be because you believe there's something significant about her intruder. Normally, I'd say Linda was making something out of nothing. She has a tendency to do that. Her so-called intruder may have been nothing more threatening than a deer or a fox. But I didn't fail to miss the mention of foxglove. You think that's related to what happened in the tearoom on Monday?"

"It's worth considering," I said. "We don't grow foxglove in our garden, but a near neighbor does? Someone was creeping around her garden the night before foxglove was added to Ed French's tea?"

The others were waiting for us at the end of the pier. Bernie and Matt stood close together at the railing, looking out over the darkening bay. The sky was streaked in a multitude of shades of purple and gray, but the sun had dipped below the horizon. We'd missed watching it set.

"Are you going to tell Sandra and her family what you learned?" Rose asked me in a low voice.

"I'm only guessing. No need for anyone else to know. You go and join the others. I'll call Detective Redmond."

Rose walked away, her long skirts, a match for the colors in the sky, swirling around her ankles. She carried her pink cane loosely in her right hand, but she didn't need it on the smooth, flat surface of the pier. "Sorry," I heard her say. "Ran into a dear friend."

"You missed the sunset," Sandra said.

"There will be other sunsets."

I turned my back to the group to make the call. Amy Redmond answered her phone on the first ring. I heard the hum of voices and the sound of dishes clattering in the background. "Sorry to bother you, Detective," I said. "But I've learned something I thought you might want to know. About the Ed French case, I mean."

"You're not bothering me." The background noise faded as she sought privacy. "What's up?"

I told her about the intruder in Linda's yard and the presence of foxglove.

"What's this woman's last name and her address?"

"Oh. I . . . uh . . . didn't get that. Bayshore Road, I think she said. Sorry." Here I was, so proud of my detecting prowess, and I'd forgotten to ask for the most important details.

"Not a problem. You say this happened Sunday night. If she called 911 and a car was sent, there'll be a record. It might not mean anything, but . . ."

"But it might," I said.

"Thanks for this. Good work."

I hung up, feeling extremely pleased with myself. I had been of help to the police.

Yay, me!

Chapter 12

My tip didn't finger the killer, but it did have one result: The police showed up the next morning to confiscate everyone's electronic devices.

I heard the yelling from the kitchen.

"What's happening out there?" I asked Edna as she came in with a stack of dirty plates and more breakfast orders.

"Detective Williams has arrived with two uniforms. They're demanding everyone in the French and McHenry parties hand over their cell phones and tablets."

I turned off the burners on the stove, wiped my hands on my apron, and hurried into the dining room. Brian McHenry was on his feet, legs apart, hands on hips, red-faced, glaring at Detective Williams. The uniformed cops stood behind Williams, glancing around the room and waiting for someone to tell them what to do.

The dining room was full. Sandra and Heather had taken a table for two, as had Amanda and Tyler. The rest of the McHenrys occupied the big table in the center of the room. Trisha sat on her own, an outcast at a small table close to the door. She had an iPad propped up in front of her and scrolled through the screen with one hand as she scooped eggs into her mouth with the other.

The guests who were not part of Heather's group openly stared.

"I'm not explaining myself to you," Williams was saying as I came in. He caught sight of me hurrying across the room. "Oh, there you are, Ms. Roberts. We're acting on your tip."

Brian threw me a poisonous look. "Is this your doing?"

"Uh. No. What's going on?"

"I need the friends and family of Ed French to give me their cell phones and other electronic devices," Williams said. "*Now.*"

"Can we not talk about this here?" I said. "Our guests are enjoying their breakfasts. Maybe we can gather in the drawing room?" So far, Rose had not appeared this morning.

"I'm not giving up my phone!" Amanda wailed. "I might as well die."

"That can be arranged," her brother said.

"Will you be quiet!" Julie-Ann snapped.

"Nothing to talk about," Williams said. "I want those phones. All of you, follow me." He walked out of the room, gesturing to the officers to ensure the others followed. I ran after him.

"Where's Detective Redmond?"

"Busy."

"Busy at what? If this is because of what I told her last night, she should be here."

He turned to face me. "I decide the appropriate allocation of resources in my department, Lily. Not you."

"I didn't mean—"

My protest was drowned out by the babble of voices spilling out of the dining room into the hall.

". . . outrageous . . ."

". . . my lawyer . . ."

". . . treating us like suspects . . ."

". . . I'm sure they have a reason . . ."

"I'm on call with my employees back at home," Lewis said. "I can't be without my phone."

"Do you have a landline in this house, Ms. Roberts?" Williams asked me.

"Yes. Yes, we do."

"Then I'm sure you'll allow anyone who needs to place a call to use it. Everyone, give your phones and tablets to this officer. He'll bag them and write your name on the bag. We'll return them when we're done with them."

"You still haven't shown me your warrant," Brian said.

Williams pulled a piece of paper out of his pocket and slapped it into Brian's hand. "As you can see, the warrant is to be executed immediately. To prevent the possible destruction of evidence."

"I'm more than happy to be of whatever assistance I can." Sandra stepped forward. She placed her phone on the reception desk. It was a flip phone. Probably ten years old. The young cop eyed it as though he'd never seen such a thing before, but he put it in an evidence bag and asked Sandra for her name. "There," she said. "That wasn't so difficult, was it? The rest of you, hurry up now."

"I resent being treated like a suspect in this nasty business," Julie-Ann said. "I need to go home tomorrow. I have an important meeting of the hospital volunteer committee Saturday morning."

"Then someone else will have to organize the bake sale, won't they?" Sandra said. "Get on with it, Julie-Ann. I don't have all day."

Julie-Ann lifted her chin, ignored her grandmother-in-law, and pointedly looked around the hallway. "Where's

Trisha? If you should be taking anyone's phone, Detective, it should be hers."

"I'm here," Trisha came out of the dining room, her iPad in her hand. "I've got nothing to hide. As for being treated like a suspect, Julie-Ann, maybe they're treating you like a suspect because you are one." She studied the faces of the group, one at a time. "All of you are. One of you killed my husband."

"Not me," Tyler said. "I wasn't even there when you had your fancy tea. Hey, Detective! That means you don't need my phone, right?"

"Hand it over," Williams said.

Tyler grumbled, but he did so.

A couple came down the stairs. They hesitated on the bottom step and glanced nervously at the uniformed officers.

"The breakfast room's open." I gave them a welcoming smile. "Please go on in."

They slipped through the crowd. I shut the door behind them, cutting out the excited voices as the other diners speculated as to what might be going on.

"Don't try to deflect blame by throwing it on me, Trisha," Julie-Ann said. "Are you aware, Detective, that Ed was about to divorce Trisha?"

"Julie-Ann!" Lewis said. "Stop that. Wild rumors and common gossip aren't helping."

"I am not gossiping," she replied. "I am doing my civic duty. The police need to know these things."

"I have no idea what makes you think Ed and I were having problems. Other than wishful thinking, that is." Trisha pulled her phone out of the pocket of her jeans and put it and the iPad on the desk.

Julie-Ann opened her mouth to respond, but Lewis

grabbed her arm. "No more," he said in a low, warning voice. She yanked her arm out of his grip and threw him a glare, but she pressed her lips tightly together and said no more.

"I agree with Brian," Darlene said. "This is an insult, pure and simple. It's sad that poor Ed died, but it has nothing whatsoever to do with us." She threw her phone onto the table. "When will I get this back?"

"When I'm ready to give it back," Williams said. "And not before."

"Is there an Internet café anywhere?" Amanda said. "I have to text Madison right away and tell her what's going on."

"You can't text from a computer, dummy," Tyler said.

"I'm sure we can find one," Julie-Ann said. "I have to contact the hospital volunteer committee to let them know I've been delayed."

"At least no one from home's likely to see me," Amanda said, "in an Internet café. Like some loser who doesn't even have her own phone."

Heather had kept quiet, standing at the back of the crowd, watching the others bicker and complain. She was the next to step up to the reception desk. "I expect to have this back by this evening, tomorrow morning at the latest, and in the condition in which I'm giving it to you. Or my lawyers will have something to say about it."

"I'm sure we can do that, Mrs. French," Williams said.

"How come my daughter's getting hers back, but the rest of us have to wait?" Brian said. "Wouldn't have anything to do with a donation to the Police Benevolent Association, would it?"

"Go ahead and accuse the police of accepting bribes, Brian," Sandra said. "That will make them inclined to view you favorably."

"I don't want them to view me favorably," he replied. "Just fairly."

"What did you say?" Sandra snapped. "I missed it."

"Nothing, Mother," Brian said.

"Now," Williams ordered, "your iPads, tablets, and other devices, please."

"I left it upstairs," Brian said.

"Officer LeBlanc will accompany you to get it."

Brian grumbled, but he led the way to his room.

"Anyone have a device you're not telling me about?" Williams asked.

Heads shook and people muttered, "No."

"If I find you've been holding back, it will not go well for you."

"We all want to cooperate, Detective," Heather said. "No need to make threats."

"Not a threat, ma'am, simply an observation."

"Sounded like a threat to me," Tyler whispered to his sister.

It sounded like a threat to me, too, but I didn't say so.

"If we're done here," Julie-Ann said, "Amanda and I are going into town. We'll need the car. Who has the keys?"

They wandered away, leaving Sandra and me with the police.

"Where's Rose?" Sandra asked.

"Probably hiding," I said.

"In that case," Sandra said, "I'll leave her in peace." She climbed the stairs, slowly, carefully, clinging to the banister.

Edna's head popped out of the dining room. "Lily, I've got a ton of breakfast orders. I'm offering muffins and coffee cake, but there's not a lot of those left and people are starting to mutter."

"Be right there," I said. "Can I help you with anything else, Detective Williams? If not, I'm very busy . . ."

"We'll be taking that computer." He pointed to the one on the reception desk.

"What! Why?"

"Computers with public access are mentioned in my warrant. Do you have any others for the use of your guests?"

"No. You can't take that. We use it to run our business."

"Sorry. Bag it," he said to the remaining officer.

The front door flew open and Bernie fell in. "What's going on? Are you making an arrest?"

Williams ignored her.

She looked at me and opened her eyes wide in a question. I shrugged in return.

"What's the password on this computer?" the cop said. "So I can shut it down properly."

"Thornecroft." I spelled it out. "With a capital *T*." He punched the word in, powered off the computer, and then began pulling out plugs to disconnect the keyboard, mouse, and monitor.

"That's a terrible password," Bernie said. "Anyone who knows Rose will be able to guess that. You want one with a mixture of numbers and upper-case letters and even some symbols."

"Such as two capital *N*'s and a capital *B* for *Not Now, Bernie*?"

"Just trying to be helpful with security around here."

"She's right," the cop said, hoisting our computer into his arms. "You can't be too careful these days."

Officer LeBlanc came back with Brian's iPad in an evidence bag.

"We're outa here," Williams said.

My phone was a lump deep in the pocket of my capris. I decided not to point out to the detective that he hadn't asked for it. "I'd appreciate it if you could get that back to us as soon as possible."

"You'll get it when I'm ready to give it back," he said, "and—"

"And not before, thank you."

They left, carrying a computer and a pile of phones and tablets.

"What's going on?" Bernie said. "What was all that about?"

"What are you doing here? I have to get back to work. You can tell me in the kitchen." I headed down the hallway, Bernie trotting along behind.

"Rose called. She said the police had arrived, and she needed me to find out what was going on. What was going on?"

"Why didn't she ask me? Or better still, come out and handle it herself."

"Keeping a low profile, maybe."

"Like that's ever happened. Call her now and tell her they've left."

Six sausages sat in congealing fat on the cold stove. I switched the burner on and tried to remember what Edna's last order of eggs had been. Two over easy and one poached. Or was it one over easy and two poached? I stirred the pan of mushrooms and tomatoes and put them on low heat to warm up.

Edna came into the kitchen. "We didn't lose anyone. I suspect they were hoping to hear gunshots and screams coming from the hallway."

"I've forgotten the last order."

"Table of three. One scrambled eggs, one sunny-side up, and one over easy."

"Good thing I didn't try to remember." I cracked eggs into a bowl to scramble with a splash of cream, salt and pepper, a handful of cheddar cheese, green onions, and fresh-from-our-garden herbs.

"What did Williams want?" Edna asked.

Bernie poured herself a cup of coffee. "That's my question. What did the police want?"

"I found out something interesting. I didn't get a chance to tell you yesterday." I poured the eggs into a pan of sizzling butter.

When we got back to Victoria-on-Sea after our walk on the pier last night, Bernie hadn't come into the house. She dropped Trisha at the B & B and then took Matt home. I'd considered calling her, but thought she might not appreciate a ringing phone if she and Matt were . . . uh . . . getting to know each other better.

"How'd it go last night, anyway? After you left here, I mean. With Matt?"

"You were out with Matt?" Edna waggled her eyebrows. "Do tell."

"Nothing to tell," Bernie said. "I dropped him at his house, but I didn't get out of the car. We didn't so much as shake hands good night. Don't change the subject. What did you not have a chance to tell me?"

I dished up the scrambled eggs and put the sausages and accompaniments on the plates while the other eggs sizzled in the frying pan. When they were ready, Edna balanced the three plates on her arms. "You can fill me in when I get back," she said as she carried them out.

I topped up my coffee cup and dropped into a chair at the table. "Last night at the pier, Rose ran into someone she knows. This woman apparently has a small but nice garden, good enough to be on the garden tour. She lives near here and had an intruder on Sunday night. She called the police, but when they arrived, the intruder was gone."

"So?"

"She grows foxglove."

Bernie grinned. "Foxglove. And she lives near here?"

"Yup. I called Redmond and told her. She obviously told Williams. I'm not sure why he wanted everyone's phone, though. Never mind our reception computer."

"That's obvious," Bernie said. "Remember what Redmond said about malice aforethought? Our killer had to get the foxglove somewhere, assuming they didn't bring it from home. You said this woman's house is on the garden tour?" She pulled her own phone out and began typing.

"What are you looking for?"

"Information about gardens in North Augusta. I see yours is listed as number one on Tripadvisor. That's nice. Good shot of the tearoom in the background, too. And a link to it. Did you know Tea by the Sea is the number two tearoom in North Augusta? That's odd, as you're the only tearoom in North Augusta."

"I'll worry about my ranking later. You mean the killer might have searched online to find out who in the area grows foxglove? Surely, people don't list every plant they have in their gardens?"

"No, but there are pictures." She held the small screen close to her face and squinted. She turned it sideways and expanded the image with her fingers. "Kinda hard to tell on the phone."

"What's that got to do with our computer? I hope Williams isn't thinking Rose was the one searching for foxglove."

"It's in a public place. With an easily guessable password."

"Not that easily guessable," I said.

"Sandra would know how important Thornecroft is to Rose."

"You don't think Sandra—"

"I don't think anything about anyone, Lily. I'm speculating. It's what we detectives do."

"Spare me," I said.

"That's the last of them coming in now." Edna brought a stack of dirty dishes into the kitchen. "They're going to help themselves to muffins and coffee in take-out cups and be on their way."

"Did anyone in the McHenry group come back?" I asked.

"The teenage boy's now plowing his way through the muffins and most of a fresh box of cereal. That's after having the full English earlier."

"Oh, to have the appetite of a teenage boy," Bernie said dreamily. "And the metabolism to go with it."

I stuck a fork in the single lonely sausage now congealing in the frying pan and held it up. "Want this?" I asked Bernie.

"No thanks. I was finishing up my own breakfast when Rose called."

"Speaking of Rose . . ." I put the sausage on the cutting board and sliced it into pieces. Guessing my intentions, Éclair hurried out from under the table, sat politely at my feet, and smiled up at me as her whole body quivered in anticipation. I placed two slices of sausage on the floor and told her to have at it. She dove in. I'd mix the rest of the meat with her dinner tonight. "Someone needs to fill Rose in on everything that happened. Seeing how we're late getting breakfast finished, since I was helping the police in the absence of the homeowner, you can do it, Bernie. I have to take Éclair home and go to the tearoom."

"What are you going to do about kicking Heather and her lot into the street tomorrow?" Bernie asked.

"Fortunately, that's not my problem. Oh, be sure to tell Rose the police took the main computer. She'll have to use the one in her rooms until we get it back. Fortunately, all the B and B data's kept in the cloud."

"Does she know how to access it?"

"She knows better than I do."

I called to Éclair and we left the kitchen. It was time to get up to the tearoom and start my second job. Once again, I'd have to miss my brief morning recharging time.

* * *

A few B & B guests were walking along the top of the bluffs, enjoying the fresh sea air and the magnificent view or heading for the steep stairs that led down to the rocky beach. Sandra McHenry leaned against the fence, staring out over the water. She turned abruptly and walked across the lawn and into the dining room, her head down, her steps firm. I don't think she even saw me.

Farther along, a lone figure sat on a bench. I considered leaving her alone, but Éclair ran over to say hi and I followed.

Trisha bent over to give my dog a scratch on the top of her head. Éclair wiggled in delight. "This is a cute dog. What's her name?"

"Éclair, like the pastry."

"A suitable name. I never did get the chance to thank you for the lovely tea we had on Monday. Not your fault it . . . ended badly."

"Thank you," I said.

She slid over on the bench. "Please have a seat."

I sat.

"It must be nice," she said, "to live here, to be able to enjoy this view every day. To own your own business."

"It is. I'm so sorry about what happened."

She ducked her head and muttered, "Thank you." She twisted the ever-present tattered tissue between her fingers. Her nails were bitten to the quick and a ripped hangnail marked her right thumb.

"Is there anyone you can call?" I said. "To be with you? I know the McHenrys aren't being much support."

"To put it mildly. The French and McHenry families have never been the best of friends. I told Ed I didn't think we should come on this trip, but he wanted to let bygones be bygones. I can't imagine what Heather had been thinking to figure it was a good idea to get us all together. She's moved on from Grand Lake. I suppose she thought the rest of us had, too. Not always easy to do. Where did you grow up, Lily?"

"Manhattan. About the furthest thing from a small town there is."

"It's kind of you to think of me, but I'll be fine here until I"—she paused and took a deep breath—"can take Ed home. Our daughter wanted to come, but she's just started her summer job. It's at a lake resort and I don't want her to leave when the season's getting under way. She'll be a senior in high school next year, and she's hoping to go into hotel management, and this job's an important step toward that."

"Is she okay? Your daughter?"

"My brother and his wife went around to the house to be with the kids when I broke the news. They'll stay with them until I get home. My sister and I are close, and she said she'd come if I needed her. But she can't afford to take the time off work, even if I pay for the flight and then a hotel. Speaking of hotels, I've been trying to find one. I don't want to stay here, as nice as it is. Not with her—with them—around. Everything in my price range is fully booked for the weekend."

"Her?" I said. "Who do you mean?"

"Julie-Ann. I'm sure you noticed that Julie-Ann and I aren't exactly the best of buddies."

I said nothing.

She lifted her tissue to her face. "Things hadn't been good between Ed and me for a while. Not his fault. Not my fault. No one's fault. It's just the way things are. But we loved each other once, and I can't forget that. And no, despite what you might have heard, he did not spend our marriage pining for Julie-Ann. He broke up with her because she was a whining, possessive, jealous, controlling woman and he was glad to be rid of her, and he scarcely gave her another thought in all the years since."

I didn't know what to say, so I said nothing. When she talked about Ed, Trisha's voice had been soft, sad. It turned on a dime when she mentioned Julie-Ann. Whether or not Ed had thought about Julie-Ann over the years, Trisha clearly had. And not fondly.

I needed to get to work, but Trisha, I thought, needed to be with someone, so I stayed with her. We sat together for a while, watching the activity on the water. Charter fishing boats bobbed in the bay and a whale-watching boat went past, headed for the creatures' feeding grounds in the open ocean at the top of the peninsula.

"How long had Ed been drinking that tea?" I asked.

"He had a heart attack a year ago. His doctor ordered him to lose fifty pounds, reduce his beer consumption, exercise more, and cut out red meat and caffeine. The only part of that advice Ed accepted was eliminating caffeine. The police confiscated what I had left of it. The so-called tea isn't anything special. I bought it at a health food store back home in bulk and packaged enough for this trip. The police seem to believe someone tampered with it."

"So they say."

"I can't stop thinking about who would do such a thing."
The tissue in her hands was now nothing but shreds. "The
only . . ."

"Yes?" I prompted.

"Nothing. Poor Ed."

I stood up. "If you need someone to talk to, I'll be in the
tearoom all day. And there's always Rose and Sandra." I
called to Éclair and we walked away, leaving Trisha staring out to sea.

Chapter 13

I'd been afraid that our brush with notoriety would have a negative effect on business, but Tea by the Sea was fully booked all day. We even had people without reservations arriving in hopes of being seated. We don't take advance reservations for the patio tables, in case of unexpected rain, but today was another lovely warm summer's day, so we were able to seat most of our arrivals. While they waited, the overflow customers were told they were welcome to tour the gardens or walk down to the bluffs to enjoy the views over the bay.

The time I'd spent in the kitchen yesterday had been worthwhile, and I was stocked with enough baking to get a start on the day. I'd told Marybeth and Cheryl not to answer any questions about the death of Ed French. Better to pretend they didn't know anything about it.

I was folding dough for currant scones when Rose and Bernie came in.

"Where were you this morning?" I asked my grandmother. "You should have dealt with the police, not left me to do it."

"I decided discretion was the better part of valor," she replied.

"Meaning?"

"Meaning," Bernie said, "she was still in bed and didn't want to make an appearance without preparing herself for her public."

This morning, Rose was fully made-up, with dark red lipstick, slashes of blush across her cheeks, thick black eyeliner and purple eye shadow, her short steel-gray hair sprayed into spikes. She wore a pair of voluminous black pants printed with huge yellow sunflowers, topped by a red and yellow T-shirt featuring a hummingbird sipping from a purple flower. Her feet, clad in orange socks, were stuffed into a pair of sturdy Birkenstocks.

"If you walked up from the house," I said, "you should have brought your cane."

"I don't need it. Bernie's with me."

"I told her that," Bernie said, "but she said not to fuss. She tells me she's not that old yet."

"Maybe not," I said, "but her bones are."

"Please don't talk about me as though I'm not here," Rose said. "I'm pleased to see you're putting currants in the scones. A proper scone is made with currants. Not that ridiculous stuff they add these days. Imagine, chocolate chips in a scone." She shuddered. "Never mind drenched in icing, of all things."

"I like chocolate chip scones," Bernie muttered under her breath.

"Morning, Rose. Hi, Bernie." Marybeth came into the kitchen. "One order of full afternoon tea for four, and one light tea for two. Sorry, can I get by?"

Bernie pressed herself against the butcher block.

"Thanks." Marybeth squeezed past and took down the tea canisters.

"What tea have our guests selected?" Rose asked.

"You're kinda in the way here, Rose." Cheryl came in with a tray full of used cups and teapots.

"Pay me no mind," Rose said.

"Hard to do that as I'm trying to get to the dishwasher." Cheryl lifted the tray high and passed it over Rose's head to Marybeth. Fortunately, Rose is barely five feet tall. "Don't mind us. We only work here."

Marybeth scooped tea leaves into infusion balls, placed them in teapots, added water from the air pots, and set the timers. One hot-water dispenser is kept at 210 degrees and one at 180 degrees and we time the immersion carefully. Different teas require different steeping times and temperatures.

"For this table," Marybeth said in answer to Rose's question, "Creamy Earl Grey, a Darjeeling, an oolong, and a Lapsang souchong."

"A nice variety," Rose said.

I cut circles out of the dough with my cutter and laid them on the prewarmed baking sheet. "We're busy here, Rose. Did you want to talk to me about something?"

"I was on the phone again this morning with friends in Iowa. I learned something of interest." She glanced at Cheryl, who was carefully arranging food on the three-tiered trays.

"Don't mind me," Cheryl said. "I never repeat anything I hear in this place."

"Except to me, Mom," Marybeth said as she left the room with her teapots. "Don't forget to fill me in."

"I see you added a touch of curry powder to your egg sandwiches, love," Rose said. "I'm glad you took my advice."

"Your advice? You said it was sacrilege, an affront to tradition."

"Tradition is all well and good, but we mustn't be afraid

to try the new and modern." Rose leaned around Cheryl and helped herself to a sandwich. I thought Cheryl showed great restraint by not slapping her hand away.

I myself never worry about showing restraint. "Stop that! Those are for our customers."

"You can make more." Rose chewed. "Maybe a touch too much curry powder."

Bernie laughed. I glared at her. She composed her face into serious lines.

"I need another sandwich to replace the one snatched by ravenous wolves," Cheryl said. "Can I get to the fridge, please, Bernie."

"Oh. Sorry." Bernie sucked in her stomach and moved aside a couple of inches, giving Cheryl enough room to slide one arm into the fridge so she could grope around for what she needed.

"Morning, all," Simon said from the back door. "Looks crowded in here. What did you want to talk to me about, Rose?"

"Would you like a biscuit?" Rose said. "I see some nice shortbread on the cooling rack. Lady Frockmorton was particularly fond of her shortbread and she ensured Cook taught me how to make it properly. I, of course, taught Lily. I attempted to teach Petunia, but she had a remarkable way of never hearing a word I said. On any subject."

I threw my cutter down and my hands up. "Oh, for heaven's sake. Let's get it over with so I can get back to work. Outside, everyone. No, not you, Cheryl!"

Rose, Bernie, and Simon obediently filed outside, followed by me. We gathered in the shade of the ancient oak standing guard over the kitchen door. From here, I could see the traffic passing on the highway. I closed my eyes and lifted my face to the hot sun and tried to take deep, calming breaths.

"Now that I have your attention," Bernie said, "tell her what you told me, Rose."

"I was on the phone to a friend in Grand Lake this morning." Rose turned to Simon. "That's in Iowa, where I lived for fifty years. You needn't bother putting it on your list of places to visit while you're in America."

"Isn't it nice there?" he asked.

"It's very nice. It was a marvelous place to live and to create a happy life and raise a family. I couldn't get away fast enough as soon as I no longer had those responsibilities. Hundreds of miles from the nearest coast is no place for an Englishwoman."

"All of which is a discussion for another time, if anyone wants to hear it," I said. "What did you learn?"

"Shame and scandal, love. Perhaps not much shame, but still plenty of scandal and fodder for gossip. It would appear that Julie-Ann and Lewis are, as the young people say, heading for splitsville."

"I doubt very much anyone has said splitsville since the days of sock hops and poodle skirts," Bernie said.

"What's a sock hop?" Simon asked.

"You mean they're getting divorced?" I said.

"Lewis moved out of their home a month ago and is in the process of obtaining a legal separation. Julie-Ann remains in the house with the children, but it's up for sale."

"Why did they come on this trip together, then?"

"For the children maybe?" Bernie said.

"Tyler and Amanda aren't babies. They can travel with one parent or neither."

"Bringing the whole family to the Cape was Brian's idea," I said. "Not Heather's. She only invited her parents. Maybe Brian and Darlene don't know Julie-Ann and Lewis are . . . uh . . . splitsville."

"Hard not to know," Rose pointed out, "in a town the size of Grand Lake."

"Maybe they're wanting to give their marriage another try," Bernie said.

"If they are," I said, "it's not working. I could chill my butter and cream in the air between the two of them. It's pretty noticeable, or it is to me, anyway, that they are not getting on."

"Are they sharing a room at the B and B?" Bernie asked.

"Yes," Rose said. "One with a double bed. Tyler and Amanda are in another room."

"I agree that it's hardly our business, but in light of what happened in my tearoom, someone in Heather's family made it our business," I said. "So you might want to ask the housekeeping staff if there are signs of one of them sleeping in an armchair. They might have only come on this trip together because Heather's paying for it, so why not?"

"Room 103 has a chaise longue," Rose said. "That could double as a single bed."

"Sorry," Simon said, "but I don't understand what these people's marital arrangements have to do with that man's death. Which is, I assume, why we're talking about it."

"Julie-Ann and Ed were a couple at one time," I said. "Which was years ago. They broke up, and Ed married Trisha, and Julie-Ann married Lewis. Insinuations have been made that some of the parties regretted that."

"You think Lewis bumped Ed off all these years later because Julie-Ann had left him to go back to his rival?" Simon asked.

"Oh. I didn't even consider that." I looked at Rose and Bernie. "Should we? Consider that Lewis might be the killer?"

"It's as good a possibility as anything else we have," Bernie said. "Julie-Ann openly accused Trisha of killing Ed because she knew he wanted to be with her. Did Lewis think she wanted to be with him?"

"Tough parsing out your pronouns," Simon said, "but I get the drift. Julie-Ann and Lewis are divorcing, and Julie-Ann might have wanted to hook back up with the late, not overly lamented, Ed, her ex-boyfriend. But Ed's wife, Trisha, has reason to object to that, as might Julie-Ann's soon-to-be ex-husband, Lewis, especially if Lewis doesn't want to be an ex. Is that it?"

"Close enough," Bernie said. "Although having met Ed, I have a heck of a hard time imagining him to have been such a Lothario he inspired the sort of jealously that would lead to murder."

"No accounting for taste," Rose said.

"Did you notice anything between them?" I asked. "Secret glances between Ed and Julie-Ann? Or Trisha and Lewis looking particularly angry?"

"No," Bernie said. "I only met them all that one time at the tea. I was sitting next to Ed, and he regaled me with the difficulties of running a computer services company in a small town in the Midwest these days. The rest of the conversation at the table wasn't any more interesting—sorry, Rose—so I spent most of my time working out the latest plot snag I've gotten myself into. Which reminds me, you were going to help me with that."

"I've had other things on my mind," I said. "Speaking of which, I need to get back to work. Has anyone told Detective Williams what Rose learned?"

"Not yet," Rose said. "I'm reluctant to, for two reasons. First, he's likely to pat me on the head and tell me not to listen to the idle gossip of a bunch of old ladies. Second, he's equally likely to run out and arrest some innocent person based on the idle gossip of a bunch of old ladies. Come to think of it, I have another reason. He's equally likely to accuse me of deliberately muddying the waters so as to distract attention from my guilt."

"Why would he think you did it?" Simon said.

"For no better reason than he's a fool, and he knows I know he's a fool."

"Tell Amy Redmond, then," I said. "She's no fool."

"I fear Detective Redmond has once again been sidelined. Williams can't allow her competence to overshadow him."

"Step carefully, Rose," I said. "You don't want to make an enemy of him."

"Even *more* of an enemy," Bernie said, "than you already have."

"I can be trusted to show some restraint," my grandmother said through her dark red lips as the fabric of her enormous black-and-yellow pants fluttered around her legs in the wind.

Bernie coughed, and I said, "Right. Restraint is your middle name."

I turned to go back inside, and then I remembered Simon. "Sorry, why did you come to the tearoom in the first place? Did you want something?"

"Rose called me. Rose?"

"Tell me more about foxglove," my grandmother said. "I know it's quite commonly grown and it is distinctive. I believe I saw some at friends' homes in Grand Lake. Is it difficult to grow?"

"They can be fussy," Simon said. "They don't like the soil too dry or too wet—but, otherwise, anyone can grow them successfully. I asked about it in the gardening chat room. Quite a few of the local gardeners said they had it. One person warned me that foxglove shouldn't be used in homes with children or pets who eat plants."

"I wonder what sort of children wander out into the garden to munch on the foliage," Bernie said. "Don't they get fed inside?"

Simon smiled. "More a matter, I think, of not planting it

near a vegetable bed or letting babies crawl around in it. Other than that, I didn't learn anything new. No one confessed to picking it and feeding it to their enemies."

"What about longevity?" I said. "Do you have any idea how long the active ingredient remains active—therefore dangerous—after the leaves have been picked?"

"No, I don't. I'll try and find out."

"Is that relevant?" Bernie asked.

"It might be," I said, "if we accept that our killer snuck into Linda's garden in the dead of night on Sunday and picked foxglove."

"Who? What?" Simon said.

I quickly filled him in.

"Seems a stretch," he said. "This woman didn't actually say her foxglove had been vandalized?"

"Not at the time, but the police were going to go back and talk to her again."

"Phone Detective Redmond," Rose ordered me, "and ask her."

"Why me?"

"Because you seem to have developed a rapport with her."

"I have not."

"Yes, you have."

"I have—"

"Never mind that now," Bernie said. "What are you thinking, Lily?"

I took a deep breath and gathered my thoughts. "Rose, you know where Linda's house is. Would you say her foxglove plants are visible from the road?"

Rose scrunched up her face in thought. "I can't say for sure. A hedge runs around the property, and I've never paid enough attention to try and see through it. I'll check into that."

"Let's say the killer did go scrounging for foxglove on

Sunday," I said, "and did somehow find out where to get some. Which means that as of Sunday night, they planned to kill Ed. But does it mean they made the decision to do so on Sunday?"

"Not before," Bernie clarified.

"Right. Why didn't they bring the foxglove with them? Because they hadn't yet decided to kill him?"

"Maybe they didn't want to take it on the plane," Bernie said. "That's assuming they flew here, which most of the group did. If they got searched at security, the guard might remember it."

"Remember a few apparently harmless dried leaves among the possessions of the thousands of people they search in a day?" Rose said. "Unlikely."

"It could also mean," Bernie said, "that the killer didn't know Ed was coming."

"Which brings us full circle," Rose said. "Other than Heather, who invited him, and Trisha, who came with him, none of them knew he was going to be here."

Chapter 14

Tea by the Sea had been full all day with happy, satisfied customers. Once I managed to get rid of Bernie, Rose, and Simon, I'd been able to get the day's needed baking done. I made one more batch of scones after closing, while Cheryl and Marybeth cleaned up the restaurant and laid the tables for tomorrow. Then at six o'clock, I locked up and walked down the long driveway to the house.

After a busy day, when we've been pretty much cleaned out, I usually stay after closing to start on the next day's food, but I decided I had enough from my baking binge of yesterday that I could leave early. I wanted to find out what, if anything, Bernie and Rose had learned since our meeting under the oak tree.

The McHenrys and Trisha were supposed to be leaving in the morning, but they were still under police advisement (orders?) not to leave town. I wondered what Rose was going to do about accommodating them, as well as receiving a fresh batch of weekend B & B guests.

I found Rose and Sandra rocking themselves on the front veranda, their nightly refreshment—G&T for Rose and a glass of wine for Sandra—at hand. Heather's car was in the parking lot, but the one remaining rental was not. The vehicle Ed and Trisha had rented on Monday had been picked up by the rental company after his death.

"Good evening," I said.

"You're finished early, love," Rose said. "How was your day?"

"Good. We were full to bursting all day. Our brush with notoriety didn't do our reputation any long-lasting harm. I stopped by to check in with you. Any developments?"

"Bernie and I scouted out Linda's place."

I glanced at Sandra, who put her glass on the table next to her. "I'll check on Trisha. See if she needs a hand. I know you and Lily are trying to help, Rose, but I can assure you no one in my family killed Ed or anyone else. The police are making something out of nothing, and you're allowing your imagination to run away with you. And taking Lily along with it, I see. Excuse me." She gripped her cane and tapped her way into the house.

"Problem?" I asked.

"Sandra has always been a stubborn woman. Not everyone considers that to be a refreshing trait. She refuses to accept that Ed was murdered. She insists he had a bad heart, and if something in his health store tea killed him, then that tea needs to be taken off the shelves or warning labels slapped onto it."

"Understandable." I dropped into the now-vacated chair. "Murder's a hard thing to accept. Even more, I suppose, when the suspects are your own family. What's happening with Trisha? Is she leaving? Are they all leaving tomorrow? Do I have to move into Bernie's?"

"Trisha's leaving Victoria-on-Sea, but not North Augusta. Tensions here are reaching the breaking point. She and Julie-Ann almost came to blows when they met on the stairs earlier. I used the local hoteliers' online grapevine and found her a room."

"Lucky for Trisha. I thought most everything would be fully booked for the weekend."

"It is. Can't find a room for love nor money. Except at the Blue Water Bay Resort."

"That's got to cost a pretty penny."

"A room for the last weekend in June at last-minute notice? Five hundred a night. Two night minimum."

"Wow."

"Wow, indeed. Heather agreed to pay for it."

"That was nice of her, I guess. What about the rest of them? What are they going to do?"

"Heather's paying for that, too. The Blue Water Bay Resort had a large group cancelation at the last minute—a wedding party in which the groom decided two days before the wedding weekend began that he doesn't want to get married, after all, and has instead fled to Hawaii to take up the life of a surf bum. The Blue Water Bay Resort is now in the fortunate position of holding on to the prepaid room charges from the first group and renting out the suddenly available rooms at their regular exorbitant rates."

"If the purpose of Trisha moving is to get away from the McHenrys, it's not going to help if they all arrive at the same hotel right after her."

"Oh, no, they're not moving. Heather's paying the difference for the guests who were supposed to be staying here to go to the Blue Water Bay Resort. I've been on the phone all afternoon explaining. Not many guests complained, not when I pointed out where they were moving to."

"Heather's paying for all this?"

"I explained the situation to Heather and Sandra. I had to, love. I told Sandra you'd give her your bed, and Heather could have the couch, but I couldn't help the others. I mentioned that Trisha was moving, where and why they have rooms free, and Heather came up with this idea.

She told us the best thing about having money is how easy it makes solving problems."

"Must be nice," I said, thinking of how much Cheryl, Marybeth, and I missed the two days' income lost when the tearoom was closed.

"Regarding the other matter," Rose said. "Linda's perennial patch where foxglove holds pride of place along the border is visible from the road, but only if one is taking notice of one's surroundings. The view passes in a flash when the hedge opens at the driveway. One wouldn't normally pass Linda's house driving between here and town, but people get lost or want to explore their surroundings."

Heather came out onto the veranda, carrying a bottle of wine and two glasses. "Hi. I thought Gran was here."

For the place, and the time of day, Heather was overdressed in a deep-cut silk blouse that was all ruffles and layers and a double row of gold buttons, and extra-full black pants, with a black belt and large gold buckle. Her earrings were huge gold hoops, and a necklace of thick gold chains nestled in her cleavage.

"She went inside for a moment," Rose said. "That's her glass there. Please join us."

I jumped up to pull a third chair into the circle. Heather put the glasses on the table and twisted the cap on the bottle. "Lily?" she said to me.

"Sure. Thanks."

Heather poured and handed me a glass. Then she helped herself and settled back in her chair. "This is such a beautiful place. You can be sure I'll be back, Rose. I'm thinking I might like to buy a vacation home near here. I've been browsing the listings on the Internet and have seen some promising properties."

"How did you do that?" I asked. "Did you get your phone back?"

The diamonds flashed as she dismissed that trifle with a wave of her left hand. "I bought another. The police can keep the old one, for all I care. I was planning on upgrading when I got home, anyway. As for buying a house, with all that's going on right now, it might not be the best time to start looking seriously, but I'll be back. Where do you live, Lily?"

"About fifty feet that way." I pointed. "I have the cottage next to the bluffs."

She clapped her hands. "How absolutely delightful."

I looked up at the sound of a car bouncing down the driveway to see Bernie's Honda Civic. She parked, got out of the car, and trotted toward us. "Hi, all."

"What brings you here?" Rose asked.

"Once I finished the . . . business I was doing for you, I tried to get back into my book, but I still haven't gotten over that tricky plot point and I want to talk it over with Lily. I figured she'd be making scones or tarts for hours yet and could provide a sounding board."

"You don't need a sounding board, Bernie," I said. "You need to sit down and write the darn thing. Start typing and it'll work itself out."

"But it's not working itself out. That's the problem." She dragged a chair over and dropped into it. "Okay, here's what's happening. Rose—my Rose—and Tessa are looking into the death of a girl who worked in a sweatshop, and—"

"Would you like a glass of wine?" Heather said.

"Thanks, that would be great."

"Lily?" Heather said. "Do you have any more glasses?"

I pushed myself to my feet. "I'll get one."

When I returned from my errand, glass in hand, Bernie was explaining that she wasn't entirely sure whether or not to go for a hard, gritty, realistic tone in her description of the life of the poor women who worked in sweatshops or keep it vague so as not to darken the mood of the book.

"Shouldn't you have decided this long ago?" Rose said. "As in before you wrote the first word? The mood of the entire book has to be consistent."

"I'm struggling with that," Bernie said.

I handed my friend the glass, and Heather poured wine into it. "Bernie's a great writer," I said to Heather. "Absolutely top notch. When she knows what she wants to write and actually writes it, that is. She's had some short stories published and they're really good." I wasn't just saying that because I was her friend. They were good—more than good—and the reviews had been enthusiastic. But Bernie had been working on this novel for two years now and was nowhere near getting it finished. She was scarcely past getting it started.

"I have a close friend who's an editor at one of the big publishing houses in New York City," Heather said. "When you're ready, I'll show him your work, if you like."

Bernie let out a completely un-Bernie-like squeal. "You would? That would be great."

I grinned at Heather. That promise might be the kick in the pants Bernie needed to get herself on track. She'd changed her book more times than I change the scone menu at the tearoom and she was constantly getting distracted. I feared she was so frightened of finishing it, and finding out no one wanted it, that she was subconsciously seeking ways to avoid that ever happening.

A suitcase thumped onto the veranda, accompanied by Sandra and Trisha. Trisha had made some attempt to tame her wiry mop of hair, and was dressed in jeans and thick sandals. Today's flower-patterned T-shirt declared it had been bought at BUTCHART GARDENS, VICTORIA, BRITISH COLUMBIA. "I'm ready to go. I took what I want to keep of

Ed's and left his suitcase in the hall. You said you'd take care of it, Rose?"

"I'll see it gets to the charity shop." Rose gave the woman a smile. "Your husband's things will be much appreciated."

"Thank you. Does anyone have a phone they can call me a cab with?"

"I'll do it." I jumped up to let Sandra have her chair back.

"Have a glass of wine while you wait," Heather said. "This bottle's almost empty, but I have another in my room. Run up and get it, would you, Lily?" She tossed me her key and I grabbed it out of the air. I wasn't a maid here, but I decided not to point that out.

"Where are the others?" Trisha asked. "Not coming to see me off?"

"Julie-Ann took the kids to the beach," Sandra said. "Brian and Lewis went fishing again."

I placed the call to the taxi company as I ran up the stairs and let myself into Heather's room. Twenty to thirty minutes, they told me.

Heather had been given the second-best room in Victoria-on-Sea; Sandra had the best. Heather's was in a corner with a sea view in two directions and a small balcony. All the guest rooms are decorated as though they're in a stately home nestled in the English countryside and Queen Victoria might be expected to pop in at any moment. Heather's room is papered and painted in shades of soft green and light gray. The four-poster double bed is covered in a thick garden-patterned duvet, with a ruffled green bed skirt, and mounds of matching pillows. An oval mirror with beveled edges hangs over the white vintage dressing table and stool, and a matching nightstand stands beside the bed. Next to the windows, two sage-green damask-covered wingback chairs are gathered around a small table. A six-light chandelier hangs from the center of the ceiling, and the gilt-framed paintings on the walls are of pale-faced, dark-haired women in formal gowns and long white gloves.

Ornate is the word that best describes this room.

The housekeeper had been in, and the room was tidy and the bed made. I don't do any work in the B & B other than make the breakfasts; I rarely, if ever, have reason to come into the guest rooms so I didn't know where things were kept.

A pile of loose papers with the letterhead of a law firm had been tossed on the dressing table, and my eyes passed over them as I looked around to see where the fridge might be hidden. A handwritten note was scribbled in the margins: *Ensure it's final?*

A credenza, with a set of double doors, sat against the wall next to the bathroom. I opened it and found a tiny fridge containing a couple of bottles of white wine nestled inside. I grabbed a bottle, left Heather's room, and locked the door behind me. I stopped in the kitchen for another glass, and when I went outside, I found the others engulfed in gales of laughter. Even Trisha had a smile on her face.

"A car's turning in," I said. "Might be your cab, Trisha."

"That was quick. I won't have time for that glass of wine, after all. Thank you for your hospitality, Rose. I'm sorry I can't stay longer, but this is for the best. And thank you for arranging my new accommodation, Heather. You have no reason to be kind to me, but you were."

Heather stood up and wrapped the other woman in her arms for a long hug. When they separated, she said, "Ed was my husband's beloved brother. I'm sorry they were so bitterly estranged in their last years."

"That's not a taxi," I said as the car came to a screeching halt in front of the veranda steps. "It's the police. And there's another one following it."

Officer LeBlanc leapt out of the cruiser and Detective Williams emerged from the passenger seat.

"I don't like the look on his face," Rose muttered under her breath.

"Something's up," Bernie said. "And it's not good news."

LeBlanc hung back while Williams climbed the steps. The second cruiser parked beside the first. Two more cops got out. Neither of them was Amy Redmond.

"Good evening, Detective," Rose said in her best hostess voice. "May I offer you a glass of wine?"

He ignored her. He ignored all of us, except for Trisha. He stood on the veranda, almost bristling with aggression. Trisha slowly got to her feet. All the blood had drained from her face. "Detective?"

"Patricia French," he said, "I am arresting you for the murder of Edward French."

Chapter 15

I stood in the doorway and watched while the police searched what had been Trisha and Ed's room. Whereas Heather's room had been ornate and lush and feminine, this one was smaller, with a more masculine feel in shades of brown and deep red.

While we'd all shouted questions, to which we received no answers, Williams had told Trisha to turn around, slapped her in handcuffs, and bundled her into the back of the patrol car. He and the driver got in and they drove away in a spray of gravel and sand. Trisha hadn't said a single word; she'd blinked at Williams as though not understanding what was happening.

They were gone so quickly, no one had a chance to tell the detective that the suitcase on the veranda belonged to her.

"If you can tell me what you're looking for," I said. "I might be able to help."

"Unlikely." The female officer checked the closet, empty of everything except a row of hangers and two white robes. "There's not much here."

"Nothing in the bathroom, either," said the other officer.

"Which would be correct," I said, "as I could have told you, if anyone had taken the trouble to ask, because the guest checked out. I called her a cab."

The woman turned and stared at me. The man emerged from the bathroom. "She did?"

"Yes. She did."

"Why didn't you say so?"

I decided, as Rose would put it, that discretion was the better part of valor, so I didn't say, "Because you didn't ask." Instead, I said, "Detective Williams asked me to show you to Mrs. French's room. Which I have done."

The woman dropped to her knees and lifted the dark red bed skirt to peek under the bed, while the man studied the top of the dresser. "What's this?"

A ten-dollar bill was tucked under a plastic bag containing brown and green vegetation.

"The tip for the housekeeper, I assume."

"Do people tip cleaning women?"

"Some do."

He opened the bag and sniffed it. "And this?"

"I don't know for sure, but it's most likely the tea the late Mr. French drank." I was surprised to see it. I'd assumed the police would have taken Ed's entire supply, but they must have only analyzed the amount Trisha had with her at the hospital. "When people don't want to take things home with them, they sometimes leave them here, in case the staff can use it. Mrs. French didn't drink the special tea her husband did, so she had no reason to take it with her."

The two cops had put on thin latex gloves. He picked the bag up. "We'll take this with us."

The woman got to her feet with a grunt. "Nothing under there. Not so much as a dust bunny."

"We have good housekeepers," I said.

I led the way downstairs. We found Rose sitting at the reception desk in front of the large empty spot the computer had previously occupied. Bernie was leaning against a wall and straightened up when she saw us. She threw me a questioning look. I shook my head.

Someone had brought Trisha's suitcase inside and put it with the other.

"Are those the woman's suitcases?" the cop asked.

"Yes," I said.

"The red one belongs to Mrs. French," Rose said, "and the brown one contains her late husband's things. I was going to drop it off at the charity shop."

"We'll take them with us." He made no move to pick the cases up, but instead glanced around the hallway.

"Detective Williams told you to search Mrs. French's room," Rose said. "That was all. Thank you so much for your time."

"Let's go, Rick," the female cop said. "We're done here." She grabbed the handle of the red suitcase and dragged it away. Rick LeBlanc shrugged and took the other.

I let out a long breath when the door slammed shut behind them. Rose's shoulders slumped and she rested her elbows on the desk with a groan.

"Where are Sandra and Heather?" I asked.

"Heather's calling her lawyer," Bernie said. "She's going to ask him to recommend someone in North Augusta to help Trisha. Sandra went with her. Do you think she did it?"

"I've no idea," I said. "The police must have some reason for arresting her."

"Try and find out what that reason is, love," Rose said.

"How am I supposed to do that?"

"Ask."

"Williams isn't going to accept a call from me."

"Ask Detective Redmond."

"Who is equally unlikely to share police information with me."

"It doesn't hurt to ask," Rose said.

"I can try to find out what I can about the Frenches' financial situation," Bernie said. "Maybe he had a big insurance policy or a lot of debts to the mob. Or something."

I stared at her. "I hate to think that sort of personal information is sitting around waiting for people like you to find it. I hope you don't know all my secrets."

"You mean you have secrets other than the ones you told me? Never mind, don't answer that. Is your financial information stored on a computer somewhere? If it is, it's available to anyone who knows how and where to look. But don't worry, I won't be looking. I doubt I can find anything about Ed and Trisha French, either. I have no contacts in Iowa. But I can give it a try."

"Debts to underworld figures might be something worth following up on," Rose said. "We're assuming Ed's killer was part of the group he joined here. But it might have been an outsider acting for reasons we don't know."

"May I remind you," I said, "that the killer had to have been in the tearoom at the same time as Ed."

"Perhaps someone was following him and saw their chance. A hired killer."

"Or perhaps a Russian agent. Come on, Rose, the guy was a computer salesman from Grand Lake, Iowa."

"Someone thought it worth going to the trouble of killing him. That's not a task one takes on lightly," Rose said.

"She's got you there," Bernie said, and I had to admit my grandmother was, as usual, right.

Heather and Sandra came down the stairs. Sandra

gripped the banister, and Heather had a firm hold on her grandmother's other arm. "I called my lawyer in New York," Heather said. "He'll see someone gets to the North Augusta police station tonight."

"Trisha," Sandra said, "I can't believe it."

"Nothing's been proven, Gran," Heather said.

"If there's anything we can do . . . ," Rose said.

"The police wouldn't have arrested her if they didn't think she did it," Sandra said. "Still, better her than someone in my family."

"You don't mean that," Heather said.

"Of course, I do. Julie-Ann said Trisha was jealous, knowing Ed would rather be with Julie-Ann than her. Looks like she was right. You never should have invited them on this trip, Heather. You're too kind for your own good sometimes."

"That, obviously, was a mistake," Heather said. "I can't deny that, but I was trying to do the right thing. It was time to reconcile with Ed, like you said. It's what Norman would have wanted."

"Sandra needs to sit down," Rose said. "Let's go outside. I believe we left a bottle of wine untouched. Just this once, I'll have a glass of wine myself."

I took my grandmother's arm and helped her to stand.

"Did you know Trisha well?" Bernie asked Heather, once we were settled into our chairs on the veranda, glasses in hand. "Before you moved away, I mean."

"Not well, no," Heather said. "I knew her, of course. She and Ed were married when Norman and I started dating. I never . . ." Her voice drifted off.

"You never?" Bernie prompted.

"Nothing. I always found Trisha cold and distant, but that's just the way she was. She was certainly possessive of Ed. Jealous when she had no reason to be. Maybe he *was* going to leave her for Julie-Ann."

"Believe it or not," Sandra said, "Ed French was a handsome man in his youth and considered to be quite the catch."

"You knew him before Heather married his brother?" Bernie asked.

"Oh, yes. The McHenry and French families have always been close. As in closely intertwined, not close as in good friends." She smiled at Heather. "Not until Heather and Norman fell in love."

Heather reached over and took her grandmother's hand. "And I'll never forget that the only one who supported me was you, Gran. My dad was particularly nasty about Norman, and he turned Mom and Lewis against our marriage. Dad had been in business with Ed at one time and it had not ended well. I don't know the details."

I exchanged glances with Rose and Bernie.

"But," Heather said, "that's all water under the bridge. Dad and Mom are having a great time on this holiday. It's doing them good, wouldn't you agree, Gran?"

"I would," Sandra said. "Except for the murder part."

"Uh, yeah." Bernie left her wine untouched and got to her feet. "Except for that. And when that kid almost killed himself on Simon's bike."

"That boy's spoiled rotten," Sandra said. "It's driving Brian to an early grave."

"Don't interfere, Gran," Heather said. "Dad shouldn't, either. Tyler's not his son."

"Hard not to," Sandra said. "Any grandmother worth her salt wants to do everything she can to help her grandchildren and great-grandchildren. Isn't that right, Rose?"

"It is," Rose said.

"I'm on my way," Bernie said. "Good night."

"Good night," they chorused.

"See you tomorrow," I said.

"Uh, Lily, can I have a word?"

"About what?"

Bernie's red curls flew as she jerked her head.

"Oh, a word," I said. "Right. I have to let Éclair out, anyway. Catch you all later." I took my barely touched wineglass with me.

"I hope we'll be able to go home, now that they've found the guilty party," Sandra said.

"What do you want to talk to me about?" I asked as Bernie and I crossed the lawn.

"You need to phone Redmond and ask what they have on Trisha."

"Why?"

"If she did it, fine. If the cops have a good case against her, fine. But if she didn't, then someone else did, right?"

"Why is it up to us to determine that?"

"Because Williams is a lazy cop. You know that. I know that. Redmond knows that. Even Williams knows that. He might have grabbed at the smallest clue pointing to Trisha, and he's hoping the whole thing can be dumped on her and off his workload. This way, he can get back to arresting teenagers for underage drinking and go home for his supper at a reasonable hour."

We rounded the big house and my little cottage came in sight. I knew I was wasting my breath, but I spoke, anyway. "Bernie, I have two jobs. I have a business to run and this is the busiest time of the year. You quit your job and cashed in all your savings so you could take the chance of a lifetime and write your book. Isn't that enough?"

"Would you let an innocent woman go to jail so you can spend more time making scones?"

"That's not what I meant."

"I know it's not," she said with a sigh. "You're right. You are busy. I'll ask Rose to make the call."

"Manipulative much? Okay, I give in. Let's see if Redmond will talk to us."

We went into the cottage to be greeted by an enthusiastic dog. Bernie greeted her equally enthusiastically. Greetings over, I put Éclair into the enclosed yard, and while she went about her business, I phoned Detective Redmond.

I almost didn't expect her to answer, but she did.

"Hi," I said, trying to sound cheerful and friendly. "It's Lily Roberts here. From Victoria-on-Sea?"

"I know who you are, Lily. What can I do for you?" Her voice was distant and tinny. She was on a speakerphone. I heard the soft hum of an engine and guessed she was in her car.

"Are you aware Trisha French has been arrested?"

"I am."

"Good. I mean, good that you are aware. Not good that she's been arrested. Are you . . . uh . . . okay with that?"

"If I was not okay, as you put it, I wouldn't tell you. Not in so many words."

Maybe I was reading undercurrents that weren't there, but I took that to mean Redmond was not okay with it.

"Are you still on the case?"

"It's a busy time in North Augusta," she said. "A massive influx of visitors, but no additional police resources to cope with it."

I took that to mean she was no longer on the case.

"What's she saying?" Bernie whispered.

I turned my back to her. Bernie walked around me.

"Can you give me some idea of why Trisha was arrested? Something must have happened. Williams must have learned something new. I was with her when he got here, but he didn't say anything. Just cuffed her, stuffed her in the car, and drove away."

"He doesn't have to explain his reasoning to you, Lily."

"I know that. I'm just . . . trying to understand."

"Invite her to come over for a drink," Bernie whispered.

"Is Bernadette Murphy there?" Redmond asked.

"Yes, I am!" Bernie yelled.

"What about Rose Campbell?"

"She's at the house with Sandra and Heather." I decided to tell a little white lie. "Sandra was upset at the arrest of her family friend."

"For heaven's sake," Bernie said, "give me that. She knows why we're calling, don't beat around the bush." She snatched the phone out of my hand. "Detective Redmond, Bernie here. If it's not breaking police confidences, can you tell me why Trisha French was arrested?"

I leaned in so I could hear the reply.

"It'll be in the paper tomorrow," Redmond said. "And no doubt on social media before that. What will not be in the paper is that I tried to stop it, but Detective Williams made a statement to the press from the steps of the police station moments ago."

"How did the press know he'd have something to say?"

"They'd been sent an anonymous tip." Redmond cleared her throat.

Edna had told me Chuck Williams was fonder of media attention than he should be. The chief of the North Augusta Police Department was notoriously camera-shy and more than happy to let Williams grab the spotlight.

"For my pains," Redmond said, "I've been sent to North Truro to liaise with them about handling crowds expected for the forthcoming music festival weekend. I'm on my way there now."

"Music festival," I said. "That could be important. Hard-rock fans can get out of control."

"Chamber music festival," Redmond said.

Bernie scrunched up her nose.

"In answer to your question as to why Trisha French was arrested. Her iPad was used to search for information about gardens in North Augusta and environs."

"That's it? Maybe she likes plants," I said. "She is, was, on vacation."

"Or maybe she was looking for something in particular. I'm not saying the evidence isn't valuable. I thought, I still think, the arrest was premature, that's all. Any reasonably competent lawyer will have her out tonight."

"Heather French has someone heading for the station as we speak," Bernie said.

Redmond didn't reply.

"Is that all you have?" Bernie asked.

Redmond said nothing for a long time. I assumed her car window was down, as I could hear traffic zipping past. I looked at Bernie. Bernie looked at me. She shrugged.

Eventually Redmond said, "You tipped me off about the intruder in Linda Sheenan's yard. I went there the following day and had a look around. It's been several days since the supposed incident, and the woman and her gardeners have been tramping all over everything, so no chance of finding any evidence. She gave me a nice tour, though. It's a lovely garden. Plenty of foxglove. I asked if they might have been interfered with, and she said she'd thought the bed around them had been trampled on. I realize that's an extremely leading question, but I simply couldn't get the information otherwise. She was more concerned that the intruder might have intended to climb up her drainpipe into her bedroom window and murder her in her bed."

"Is that possible?" Bernie asked.

"For Spider-Man, perhaps. No one with lesser abilities. To make her feel better, I advised her to cut back some of the ivy growing on the side of the house, although I tested it myself and it came away with a strong tug."

"And this ties into Trisha how?" Bernie asked.

"Mrs. Sheenan keeps a blog about gardening and gardens. Trisha accessed it from her iPad. It contains lots of pictures. Some of which include the foxglove. On the other hand, the blog doesn't have her address, or even name the town. It just says the garden's located on the Outer Cape. Mrs. Sheenan's house is part of the forthcoming garden tour put on by the local gardening club, and her name's mentioned on their page. Again, no address, but information about the tour says it's limited to homes within North Augusta. Mrs. Sheenan has a landline at her house and the address has an entry on 411-dot-com."

"Okay," Bernie said.

"All freely available information for anyone to access. No hacking skills required, Ms. Murphy."

"I hope you're not implying—"

"I never imply. If I ever intend to accuse you of engaging in illicit computer activity, I'll do it. Trisha French's iPad accessed Mrs. Sheenan's blog, and it also checked the North Augusta garden club page."

"What about 411-dot-com?"

"No evidence of that. There are, of course, other ways of finding addresses and other computers."

"Did the iPad show any attempt to hide these searches?" I asked. "Surely, if she'd been planning to steal foxglove to murder her husband, she would have tried to cover her tracks?"

"Criminals are not always as clever as TV programs make them out to be. Otherwise, we'd never catch half of them."

"There's a cheerful thought," Bernie said.

"If the person who killed Jack Ford had been smart enough to shut up and lay low," I said, "they wouldn't have been caught." I was referring to the late, unlamented real-estate developer who'd met his end at the bottom of the bluffs not long after getting into an altercation with Rose.

"It's only because you put yourself in danger over that," Redmond said, "that I'm talking to you two about this at all. And that is not, by the way, an invitation to you to do so again."

"I have no intention of ever again running through the night pursued by a deranged killer armed with one of my kitchen knives." I shuddered at the memory.

"Glad to hear it," Redmond said. "I've got to go. I'm about to arrive at my destination."

"Enjoy your meeting," Bernie said.

Redmond harrumphed and the line went dead.

"That was interesting." I took back my phone.

"Wasn't it? Not only the information she gave us, but the fact that she obviously trusts us more than she does her so-called partner, Detective Chuck Williams."

"Would you trust Detective Williams? I wouldn't trust him to deliver a breakfast order, but I'm surprised she talked so freely to us."

"She needs someone to kick ideas around with," Bernie said. "Williams is so full of his own importance, and at the same time so terrified people will recognize that he's an idiot, he can't just let go and allow his mind to wander. It's unlikely he can accept that she might have some good ideas."

"I can buy that. So, what do we do now? If Trisha is innocent, and we don't know she is, we should try to help her."

"Agreed. Let's see if she gets released tonight. If so, we can go around to her hotel first thing tomorrow."

"I have to work tomorrow."

"You're your own boss, Lily. You can take as much time off as you like."

"I'm my own boss, Bernie, which means I work harder than my employees. In addition to running the tearoom, someone has to make the breakfasts for the B and B guests." I grinned at my best friend.

"I don't care for that look," she said.

"The sooner we get the breakfasts over with, the sooner we can leave, and the sooner I can get to the tearoom. I'll see you in the kitchen at six-thirty. Don't be late."

Chapter 16

"Éclair needs a walk and so do I. We'll go with you to your car." I grabbed the leash off the hook by the side door and went outside. Recognizing the signs of a walk, Éclair danced around Bernie's and my feet. I opened the gate and the dog raced across the grass toward the edge of the bluff.

I called her to follow us and she turned around and charged ahead.

"Are you planning to get some work done on the book tonight?" I asked Bernie as we watched Éclair stop to sniff under every bush and at every blade of grass between my cottage and the big house.

"If I don't, I'll never admit it to you. You're like my mother asking if I have homework tonight."

"You once told me you rely on me to keep your nose to the grindstone. If that's not the case, tell me."

She said nothing. Something rustled in the undergrowth and Éclair took off after it. She's the terror of the neighborhood squirrels. Little do they know that if she ever cornered one, she wouldn't know what to do with it. Ask it to play probably.

The squirrel ran up a tree and Éclair trotted back to us.

"I'd like to write tonight," Bernie said, "but I need to try and find out what I can about Trisha and Ed and their marriage. She might well have done it. Redmond said the case wasn't strong, but she didn't say there wasn't one. Trisha, of all people, would have been able to interfere with Ed's tea."

"That's true. We've been assuming someone slipped the foxglove into his teapot when we were all outside, but it might have been added to the mixture earlier."

"You're forgetting that the police tested the unused tea, and found nothing in it."

"They tested the unused tea Trisha gave them. She could have separated one portion, added the foxglove, and given it to the tearoom staff to steep. Still, I can't see it, Bernie. Surely, Trisha would have had far better opportunities to rid herself of him, if she wanted to, than doing it in a way that puts her smack-dab in the center of a limited circle of suspects."

"Remember what Redmond said about criminals not being very smart? Maybe she didn't think that far ahead."

"Maybe. I don't want to get myself in the position of knowing how criminals think." Time to change the subject. "If you ever want me to read your writing, I'd be happy to."

She shook her head and I didn't push it. I'd made the offer before, and Bernie always declined, saying she didn't like to show unfinished writing to anyone. "Too open. Too raw. Not until all the kinks have been worked out and the punctuation put in the right places," she'd said.

We rounded the house and I could see Heather, Sandra, and Rose on the veranda. They'd been joined by another group of guests, two middle-aged couples. Several wine bottles and cans of beer were on the table, along with a basket of bread and crackers and a platter of cheese.

"Don't say anything to the others about what Redmond told us," Bernie said. "We can tell Rose later."

"Why?"

"If Trisha didn't do it, someone in Sandra's family did."

At that moment, a car pulled up, parked, and the McHenry family spilled out. Julie-Ann, Amanda, and Darlene glowed pink from a day spent on the beach. Julie-Ann carried a beach bag and a stack of towels, and Darlene unloaded plastic supermarket bags and handed them to Brian, while Lewis took a case of beer out of the trunk. Éclair ran over to greet them, her ears up and her tail wagging.

"There you are, you little darling!" Amanda cried as she bent down to give Éclair a pat.

Laughing and smiling, the family climbed the veranda steps, with us in tow.

"Hey," Lewis said, "looks like the party's started without us."

"Did the police come by?" Amanda straightened up. "They said they'd bring our phones back when they were finished with them."

"Is that all you can think about?" Brian said. "You haven't stopped moaning all day about that blasted phone. You could at least say hello to your great-grandmother."

Amanda pouted, but she said, "Hey, GeeGee. You missed a fun day at the beach."

"What's happened?" Darlene said. "Sandra, is everything okay?" Finally someone had noticed that none of us were smiling.

"No," Sandra said, "it's not. The police were here earlier, not to return phones, but to arrest Trisha."

Darlene sucked in a breath. Brian shook his head.

"Cool," Tyler said. "Too bad I missed it."

"Ha!" Julie-Ann shouted. "I knew it." She turned to her

husband. "I told you so. I told you she'd done it. What do you have to say now?"

Lewis shrugged.

The four people who'd joined Rose's circle shifted uncomfortably in their chairs.

"Don't be so quick to gloat, Julie-Ann," Darlene said. "It doesn't become you. The whole situation's nothing but sad."

"I'm not gloating," Julie-Ann said. "I'm saying I knew it all along, that's all."

"We'll leave you people alone now." The eldest of the women who'd joined Rose and Sandra got to her feet. "You obviously have things to discuss. Thank you for the restaurant suggestion, Rose. I'll let you know what we think of it." She and her friends scurried inside, taking their glasses and bottles with them. Éclair sniffed at the low table containing the food.

"An arrest is not a conviction," Heather said.

"Might as well be," Julie-Ann muttered. "I'm going to change out of this bathing suit and wash the salt off, and then come down for a glass of wine. We bought cheese and pate and bread and crackers, but I see you have some already. Amanda and Tyler, come with me."

"If the police have arrested someone," Amanda said, "then they don't need my phone anymore, right?"

"Good night, Rose, everyone," Bernie said. "I'm off home."

"Good night," they chorused.

Bernie took a step toward her car and then stopped. She slapped her forehead and turned around. "Lily, I totally forgot. I have an appointment to take my car into the shop first thing tomorrow."

"Do you have something planned?" Rose said.

"I was going to . . . uh . . . give Lily a hand with the breakfasts."

"Why on earth would you do that?"

I shot a look at my grandmother.

"Oh," she said. "I forgot. You like to do that sometimes."

"I can drop the car off tonight and bike over in the morning," Bernie said. "It's not far, but I can't drive us on our . . . errand. If we have an errand, that is."

"You can take my car," Rose said. "I have no plans for tomorrow. Lily?"

"Fine with me."

"Thanks," Bernie said. "Call me later, Lily. When you know what's happening about our errand."

"Will do," I said.

"What errand is that?" Sandra asked.

"Nothing," I said. "Just . . . uh . . . business to do with Bernie's book."

"Don't forget," Heather said, "I told her I'd introduce her to my publishing friend, and I meant it."

"Believe me, Bernie isn't going to forget."

"Your friend's writing a book?" Darlene said. "Isn't that nice? I'm going up for a shower. Brian, do you want to go first?"

"You go ahead," he said.

"I wonder if the police will let us go home now?" Lewis said. "I'm going to give that cop a call and ask."

Before taking myself off to bed, I called Detective Redmond, hoping for an update on Trisha's situation. I got voice mail and left a message. She did not return my call, so when I got up the next morning, I didn't know if there was any point in Bernie and me going to the Blue Water Bay Resort to try to speak to Trisha.

Still, helping in the B & B kitchen wasn't something I'd ever discourage Bernie from doing.

I let Éclair out and then showered and dressed for the

day. The forecast was for more perfect weather, so I tied my hair into a high, tight ponytail and pulled on a pair of shorts and a T-shirt. The dining areas of the tearoom were air-conditioned, but the kitchen wasn't, and it could get hot in there when both ovens were on and the small space crammed with people.

I locked the cottage behind me, called to Éclair, and we walked the short distance to the back door of the B & B. As always, I took a moment to stop and admire the peaceful morning view. I put my hands on the wooden railing that protects people on our property from the sharp drop-off of the bluff. The tide was out, and down below a few people stepped carefully on the wet rocks, studying the tidal pools or searching for shells. Gulls circled overhead and a storm petrel dove for her breakfast. Boats loaded with fishermen headed to the open sea or rocked at anchor in the warm shallow waters of the bay, and an aircraft flew high above, heading east toward Europe.

I took a deep breath and let the fresh, salty sea air fill my lungs. My one small, brief moment in a busy day to truly experience heaven on earth.

"Nice morning," Simon said at my side. Éclair rushed to greet him.

I turned to him with a smile. "It is. Getting an early start?" I nodded at the pruning shears in his hand.

He bent over and gave the dog a hearty pat. Greetings over, she went off to follow her nose to something that lay beyond the range of my feeble human senses.

"I like to see to the plants out here first thing in the morning," Simon said, "when it's peaceful and I can watch the bay come to life. I can cut the grass and trim the hedges anytime."

We stood together, close but not touching, staring out over the bay. We didn't speak, and I felt no need to fill the quiet with mindless conversation.

"Contemplation over," I said at last. "The workday begins. Come on in. I'll put the coffee on."

"Won't say no to that."

We descended the three stone steps to the kitchen door and I unlocked it. Éclair ran ahead of us and sniffed at all the corners. I took coffee beans out of the fridge and ground them, while Simon poured fresh water into the pot.

"Trisha was arrested yesterday for the murder of her husband," I said as I switched the coffeemaker on.

"I caught the news on Twitter last night. Do you think she did it?"

"I don't know. I really don't know."

"The police will get to the bottom of it."

"If not, Bernie will." I turned to him with a smile. "She can be determined that way." I took down mixing bowls and got ingredients for strawberry muffins out of the cupboards and fridge. "Coffee's ready. Help yourself."

Simon took a plump juicy strawberry out of the basket and popped it in his mouth. "Are these local?"

"From a farm not more than a few miles from here."

"You can taste it. Like eating pure sunshine. Can I pour you a cup?"

"Thanks."

"I like Trisha." Simon served us coffee. "Anyone who's interested in gardens can't be all bad, as me dad always says. She spent a long time looking around ours."

I was about to reply when Éclair lifted her head and let out a single bark, and Bernie clattered down the stairs and came into the kitchen. She wore sleek black bike shorts and a matching shirt and carried her helmet. She shifted the helmet to her left hand and saluted me with her right. "Reporting for duty, ma'am!"

"You're working here today?" Simon asked.

"Hard to believe, I know. But I am. Lily and I have an errand to run as soon as breakfast is over."

"Is that what you're wearing?" I said. "You can't wait tables in Rose's dining room in bike shorts."

Bernie looked at Simon and gave an exaggerated sigh. "I didn't know I was expected to wait on tables. I thought I was helping you cook."

"Can you cook?" Simon asked.

"No, but how difficult can it be? Lily does it all the time."

"Most amusing. I need you to do whatever I need you to do."

She dropped her helmet on the table and poured herself a cup of coffee. "Last time I helped in here, you mocked my attire."

"That's because you were dressed like a Victorian housemaid."

"I was getting into the mood of one of my characters. I told you that. Enough cheerful banter. What do you want me to do first?" She took a frilly pink-and-green apron down from the hook by the door and tied it around her waist. It looked, I thought, ridiculous with her high-tech athletic clothes, but I didn't say anything.

I tossed the dry ingredients together for today's muffins. "First, get the muffin tins out of that cupboard there. Then you can pour coffee into the white carafe and take it and the jugs of milk and juice out to the dining room." Breakfast service was supposed to begin at seven, but people often came early to get a start on coffee and juice.

"As I seem to be in the way," Simon said, "I'll be off." He held up his cup. "I'll return this when I'm finished."

"Anytime," I said.

"You're having morning coffee with the delectable Simon," Bernie said once the door had closed behind him. "Anything of interest happen yesterday after I left that you want to tell me about?"

"Not that it would be any business of yours if it did, but

no. He usually comes in here to grab a coffee before start-ing work."

Edna was next to arrive. "I see Bernie wearing one of my aprons. Does that mean I've been fired and I can go home? Please say yes."

"No such luck," I said. "Bernie and I have something to do before I go to the tearoom, so I want to get out of here as soon as I can. You can start on the fruit, please."

Edna took cantaloupe and a honeydew melon out of the fridge and the remains of the basket of strawberries off the counter and sat at the table to slice them. "Shall I assume you'd like the news on the French arrest?" she asked casu-ally.

I asked Bernie to start chopping mushrooms and toma-toes, while I mixed the batter and poured it into the tins. "You assume correctly."

"A lawyer arrived last night, posthaste, and sprang her. I know him. He's a local guy, does a few low-level criminal cases, but as far as I know, he's never had anything like a murder. Still, she's out of jail, but under orders not to leave the grounds of her hotel pending her appearance before a judge."

"That's what we expected would happen," Bernie said.

"Is she still staying here?" Edna asked.

"No. Things were getting rather tense between Trisha and some members of the McHenry family, so she moved. That's not for publication."

"Don't worry," Edna said. "I don't gossip. Much. Infor-mation between Frank and me goes one way only."

Voices came from the dining room and Edna stood up. I asked Bernie to finish the fruit salad. "As you're not dressed to appear in proper company, you can help me in here. Be ready to serve up the plates when Edna places the orders."

*   *   *

The last of the breakfasts was cooked and served by quarter to nine, and I was able to leave Edna to tidy up. Rose hadn't put in an appearance, and I was pleased about that. I didn't want her tagging along on our errand, and I didn't want to have to lie to her about where we were going. Fortunately, I know where she keeps the keys to the car—on a hook by the kitchen door next to the aprons. I grabbed the keys as I passed.

"I need to take Éclair home first, and then we can go. What will we do if Trisha doesn't want to talk to us?"

"We'll leave," Bernie said. "What else can we do? We're not going to bring out the rubber hoses and switch on the powerful lights."

I half turned to watch Éclair greet a B & B guest out for a breath of air after breakfast. Bernie glanced at my cottage and let out a snort of laughter and said, "One step ahead of us, as always."

Rose was sitting on my front porch, resplendent in her usual purple and yellow. It was too late for us to turn and run. She'd spotted us and was waving as she got to her feet.

"Ready to go?" she asked cheerfully as we walked up.

"Go where?" I said.

"Wherever you two plan on going in my car. To visit Trisha, I suspect." She hefted her cane. "Let's be off then."

"Three people might be intimidating," I said. "We don't want to frighten her. Why don't you stay behind, and we'll tell you what we learn. If anything."

"I agree three's overdoing it," Rose said.

I smiled at Bernie.

"So you will remain in the car, while Bernadette and I speak to Trisha," Rose said.

Bernie smothered a laugh.

Rose set off across the lawn toward the garage at a brisk pace. Éclair started to follow, but I called her back and shoved her into the house. I then had to run to catch up to Bernie and my grandmother. I went in the side door of the garage and slapped the automatic door opener.

"Want me to drive?" Bernie said.

"Why not?" I tossed her the keys.

Rose got into the front passenger seat, leaving the back for me. As Bernie was reversing out of the garage, Rose turned to me. "How much time have you spent with Trisha, love?"

"Me? Almost none."

"Why would you expect her to confide in you? Or in Bernie?"

"Because we'll ask nicely?"

"I assumed that was your plan. Although I assume it's Bernadette's plan, not yours. In this instance, she also hasn't thought it through."

"I always think things through." Bernie turned the wheel to point the car down the driveway to the highway. "We'll show up, helpful and friendly, and ask what she knows. Isn't that good enough?"

Rose shook her head. "No, it is not good enough. Fortunately for you, I did go to the trouble to get to know her a bit. I could tell she wasn't at all comfortable here at Victoria-on-Sea, not with the McHenry family around. Her husband didn't seem to mind that they didn't want him tagging along on their holiday. If anything, I got the feeling he relished their discomfort. Trisha, however, didn't like it. Then, when Ed died, she was not only grieving, but was even more isolated. Heather and Sandra did their best to be nice to her, but they couldn't climb over the decades of animosity between the French and McHenry families. Trisha will talk more comfortably to me than to two virtual strangers she has no reason to trust."

Although I hated to admit it, that made sense.

"Do you think she did it?" Bernie asked. "Murdered her husband?"

"No, I do not. She mourned Ed quietly and in her own way. They no longer loved each other, and their marriage was more a matter of neither of them wanting to go to the bother of moving out of the house, at least not while their children are still in school. But Trisha hadn't forgotten that she and Ed had once meant the world to each other."

Silence fell over the car. "That's sad," Bernie said at last.

"That's life," Rose said, "for some. Eric had been the center of my world from the day I knocked him off his feet outside the butcher's shop on Holgate High Street until the day he died."

I reached across the seat and rested my hand on my grandmother's shoulder. She lifted her hand and patted mine.

Traffic was light on the highway running along the coast. Once we'd passed the turnoff to North Augusta itself, the road got rougher and less used. Before long, Bernie slowed and turned into the long, steep private drive leading to the Blue Water Bay Resort, one of the nicest, and most expensive, places on this section of the coast. Golf course, swimming pools, a small patch of sandy beach at the bottom of a steep set of stairs, hiking trails, conference facilities, restaurants and bars, its own dock and small harbor. The main building was perched high on top of the cliffs, with the golf course on the other side of the highway. The view of the hotel and property spread before the open waters of the bay was one of the best in North Augusta.

The car picked up speed, and Bernie took the first curve on two wheels. I clutched at the seat belt crossing my chest. "We're not in that much of a hurry, Bernie."

We sped on. The next curve came toward us way too fast. The car took it, but barely managed to cling to the road.

"Bernie!" I called. "Slow down."

"Can't."

"What do you mean you can't?"

Her right leg was pumping hard on the brake pedal, but nothing was happening. The car was going even faster now. A silver Lexus approached, heading in the opposite direction, filling the narrow roadway. At the last minute, the driver yanked the wheel hard to his right and the car passed us with barely an inch to spare. He leaned heavily on his horn.

"Brakes," Bernie said. "Gone."

Chapter 17

The freckles scattered across Bernie's cheeks and nose stood out against skin turned frighteningly pale. She twisted the steering wheel hard and barely made the next bend.

Rose gripped the dashboard in front of her.

"Hold on," Bernie yelled.

The car went even faster.

I leaned forward and thrust my arm over the top of the seat in front of me. I pushed hard on the top of Rose's head. "Duck! Get your head between your legs."

A sharp curve in the road loomed in front of us, nothing but sky and sea straight ahead. A feeble-looking wire fence with a yellow warning sign offered no protection to two tons of speeding metal and three terrified women. Far below, the sea crashed against the rocks.

I wanted to close my eyes. But I didn't dare. "Do something, Bernie!"

The edge of the cliff lay directly in front of us, coming up fast. The road turned sharply to the right. A tourist bus was lumbering up the hill toward us.

"Hold on!" Bernie wrenched the wheel to the left. We crashed off the road, bounced over the rocks, plowed through scraggly bushes, and finally, at last, the drifting sand gripped the wheels of the car, and we came to a shuddering halt. The front bumper was inches from a gnarled old tree.

"Goodness." Rose slowly uncurled her body. "That was exciting."

We sat in the car, stunned.

People came running from all directions. The tourist bus screeched to a stop and the driver and passengers piled out. Golf carts sped toward us. A security guard ran up the road shouting into his radio.

Car doors were wrenched open. Faces peered at us.

"Are you out of your mind?" the bus driver yelled at Bernie. "You could have been killed. You could have killed us all."

I staggered out of the car on legs that could barely support me. "My grandmother," I gasped.

"You're okay, ma'am," a woman said to Rose. "Here, take my arm."

"Don't mind if I do," Rose said. "I feel slightly unsteady."

The bus driver stuck his face in Bernie's. He sniffed.

"No," she said, "I have not been drinking. My brakes failed."

"Old car like that," a bus passenger said, "not surprised. Some people don't keep their checkups regular enough."

"I've called the police," the security guard said. "Should I cancel them? Do you need an ambulance for the old lady?"

"Heavens, no!" Rose said. "I'm not dead yet. I'll be perfectly fine in a moment."

A woman cheered. "That's the British spirit. Stiff upper lip. Like you showed in the Blitz."

Rose huffed.

"I want to talk to the cops." Some color was returning

to Bernie's face. Her hands shook. She caught my eye and gave me a pained grin before she dropped onto a rock.

"We'll wait here," I said. "In the meantime, can someone please take my grandmother to the hotel? She needs to sit down and have a glass of water."

"I'm not leaving," Rose said.

"Oh yes, you are. Just this once, I insist you do what I tell you. You've had a shock."

"So have you," Rose pointed out. "So has Bernadette."

"Yeah, but I wasn't in the front seat. I didn't really see what was going on until it was all over." I lied. The image of the edge of the cliff with nothing but air and sea beyond was burned into my brain. "Bernie's the Warrior Princess. She can recover from anything."

"Please, ma'am. The young lady's right. Allow me to assist you." The man who spoke was middle-aged and gray-haired, dressed in lurid orange-and-brown checked pants and a white golf shirt with orange trim. He bowed and swept his arm out to indicate one of the golf carts. "My chariot awaits."

Never one to resist gentlemanly charm, Rose gave in and allowed him to take her arm. I leaned into the car and found her cane, then ran after them and threw it into the back of the golf cart. "We'll be up to get you soon as we can. If you feel at all unwell, call for an ambulance."

The man smiled at me. "I'll take care of your grandmother as though she were my own mother."

Sirens blared as a cruiser pulled into the resort drive and sped toward us.

"Can we be going now?" a woman asked the bus driver. "Excitement's over."

"I need to make a statement to the police." The driver was puffed up with his own importance. "That woman shouldn't be allowed behind the wheel ever again."

Bernie sat on the rocks and said nothing.

"Brakes failed," I said.

"I saw what happened," the security guard said. "I'll talk to the cops. Off you go, Fred."

Fred gave Bernie one last glare before abruptly turning and marching back to his bus. His passengers followed like a line of goslings hurrying after their mother.

"Have a nice day," Bernie called after them. She almost visibly gave herself a shake and then pushed herself to her feet with a grunt as the police car screeched to a halt. The driver was the female cop who'd searched Trisha's room yesterday.

"What are *you* doing here?" she said to me.

I jerked my head at her and we walked away from the crowd. The security guard watched us, but he didn't try to follow. Bernie joined us, and we stood in a patch of scruffy bushes that were barely clinging to life in the rocks and sand. The only sizable tree in the area was the old oak that had almost abruptly halted our progress.

"You need to call Detective Redmond," I said. "Get her down here. I believe this is related to the French murder."

One eyebrow rose. "How so? Dispatch said a car was driving dangerously on this road."

"It was driving dangerously," Bernie said, "because I didn't have any brakes."

The cop glanced back toward the car.

"I'm Lily Roberts and this is Bernadette Murphy," I said. "You are . . ."

"Jocelyn Bland."

"Officer Bland," I said, "my grandmother's car's old, but I can assure you she takes excellent care of it. It was in the shop for regular maintenance less than a month ago. If the brakes had been anywhere close to total failure, they would have noticed."

Officer Bland glanced over her shoulder at the car. A

man was leaning in the open driver's door. "Step away from the vehicle please, sir!" she shouted.

He straightened up and lifted his hands in the air.

"You." She pointed to the security guard. "Keep people away."

He stood slightly straighter and gave her a thumbs-up. "Excitement's over, folks. Off you go." Slowly, and in some cases reluctantly, people began to disperse.

Officer Bland spoke into the radio at her shoulder. "I have Lily Roberts from Victoria-on-Sea here. We need a detective."

"You needn't make it sound like I've been arrested for something," I protested.

"Ask for Redmond," Bernie said, "not Williams."

"We don't take custom orders." Officer Bland spoke into her radio again. "The detective might want to have this car towed to the police garage."

The reply was totally incomprehensible babble lost in a burst of static.

"We'll wait by the car," Bland said to us.

Bernie and I took seats close together, hip to hip, shoulder to shoulder, on the ground in the shade of the single tree, while Bland studied the tire marks that indicated the path of our car. The initial shock was passing, and I was feeling surprisingly calm.

"Good driving," I said.

"Thanks," Bernie said.

"Good thing Rose wasn't behind the wheel."

"She would have managed."

"I wouldn't have thought a woman who'd spent her entire life in Manhattan could drive like that."

"Funny what we can do when we need to." Bernie's hand felt for mine. I squeezed hers in return. "Do you really think someone fiddled with the brakes?" she said.

"Had to have. It's true what I told Officer Bland. Rose takes the car to the garage regularly. When we get home, I'll have a look at the bill from the last time it was in to make sure they didn't advise her to have the brakes fixed, but if they had, she wouldn't have ignored it."

"That's what I figured."

A golf cart pulled up and a woman got out. Dressed in a gray skirt suit with stockings and pumps, she was obviously not on her way to the links for a round. She introduced herself as the day manager. She asked how we were, told us the hotel was at our disposal, and assured us the road was properly signposted and maintained. Her primary concern seemed to be that Bernie not sue. An ambulance had not come screaming down the road, so I assumed Rose was fine. The manager told us my grandmother had been given a cup of tea and a piece of toast, which was all she'd asked for.

A cruiser pulled up and both Redmond and Williams got out. Williams glanced at us, shook his head, and they went to speak to Officer Bland.

That didn't take long and they soon approached us. Bernie and I let go of our intertwined hands and got to our feet.

"Good morning, Detectives." The wind whipped Bernie's red curls around her head. "What brings the two of you out this fine day?"

Redmond narrowed her eyes and studied Bernie's face.

"Delayed shock," I said. "Never mind her. Or me. We had the fright of our lives."

"Looks like you almost went over that cliff," Williams said. "You had a lucky escape."

Next to me, I felt Bernie's body shudder. My own blood ran cold, and despite the hot sun beating down on us, I shivered and rubbed my arms.

"We were in a meeting with the chief, discussing where to go next with the French investigation," Redmond said, "when the call came in. We both decided to respond."

I could tell by the look on Williams's face—sucking lemons came to mind—the joint response hadn't been his idea.

"Someone cut the brakes on the car," Bernie said. "It has to be related to the French murder."

"I suggest we go inside and find someplace to talk," Redmond said.

"Good idea," Williams said. "Take care of arranging that, will you, Detective?"

She threw him a look, but turned and walked toward the hotel manager, who'd gone to talk to the security guard.

"You need to take this car to a garage," Bernie repeated. "The brakes have been cut."

"You know this because of your extensive experience with automotive mechanics, do you?" Williams said.

"Don't be a fool," Bernie snapped. "I know this because I was driving the car and I can tell when the brakes stop working."

"You waited until you were at the edge of the cliff before pulling off the road. You couldn't have done that earlier? Less of a show, maybe?"

"How dare you!"

"Now see here—"

"No, you see here." Bernie stretched herself to her full height, which was considerably more than Detective Williams's. Her chest expanded, her shoulders straightened, her eyes blazed green fire, and her red hair streamed behind her. The Warrior Princess was on the attack.

I didn't think attacking Williams was such a good idea. I put my hand on Bernie's arm and said, "Let's discuss this calmly."

"I'm done with being calm! I could have been killed. I almost was killed, not to mention you and Rose, and this idiot's patting me on the head. I'd like to see you do better, Detective. At first, I didn't understand what was happening. I tried to regain control of the car, still thinking I could slow down. When I did realize the situation, a car and then a bus were coming toward me. In case you didn't notice . . ." Bernie stopped talking in midbreath and burst into tears. I wrapped my arms around her.

Redmond ran over to us. "The hotel manager will show us to a private room. We can take her cart. Let's go. Detective Williams, you need to stay here and secure the scene until the tow truck arrives to take this car to the state police garage."

"I—" he started to say.

"I've called them, and they're on their way."

Before Williams could say anything more, Redmond hustled Bernie and me into the back of the golf cart. She took the passenger seat.

The manager jumped behind the wheel. "Hold on, everyone."

I've never ridden in a golf cart before. It's not a comfortable ride. I put my arm around Bernie's shoulders as we bounced down the road toward the main building. "You okay?"

She wiped at her eyes with the back of her hand. "I can't imagine what came over me. Never show weakness in the face of your enemies."

Redmond twisted in her seat to look at us. "Detective Williams isn't your enemy."

"At that moment," Bernie replied, "he was. I'm not trying to make excuses for bad driving, you know."

"That," Redmond said, "I believe. Ms. O'Leary here tells me Rose was with you and is now resting in the hotel.

Do you think she has anything to add to what you two can tell me?"

"No," I said. "We were in the car screaming in unison."

"I'll let her rest then."

We pulled up to a side door of the hotel and clambered out of the cart. The manager swiped her pass to let us in and showed us to a small room with several chairs around a table that was probably used for staff meetings and breaks.

Bernie and I dropped gratefully into the closest chairs. The manager left, shutting the door behind her. She returned a moment later with a carafe of ice water and two glasses.

I smiled my thanks at her.

"So," Redmond said, "what happened?"

"I don't know," I said.

"Brakes didn't work." Bernie poured herself a glass of water and drank deeply. Her hands had stopped shaking.

I surreptitiously studied my own and was pleased to see they were still. I was feeling surprisingly calm.

"You were driving, Bernie," Redmond said. "Why don't you go first. Take your time. Tell me what you remember."

There wasn't much to tell: Bernie turned down the private road to the hotel; when she applied her foot to the brakes, nothing happened.

"If," Redmond said, "it's discovered the brakes were deliberately tampered with and didn't fail of their own accord, do you have any idea when that might have happened?"

"As far as I know," I said. "the last time we had the car out was Wednesday evening when we went into town for ice cream. I drove and I didn't notice anything at all wrong. Rose takes good care of that car. I know I keep repeating that, but I want to be sure you understand."

Redmond nodded. "What garage does she take it to?"

"North Augusta Motors. When she was sick one day over the winter, I took it in for her. I don't have a car of my own, so we share hers. I didn't use it yesterday, and Rose didn't say anything to me about going out. She doesn't always, so you should check with her."

"You have a garage at your place."

"Yes, we do. Rose's car's kept in there. Always. The sea air, as you no doubt know, isn't good for cars. The garage door's kept closed at all times because of visitors wandering the property, but it isn't locked. We have two sets of keys to the car. One's kept on a hook in the kitchen and one in Rose's suite."

"If someone fiddled with the brakes," Bernie said, "they had the time and the privacy to do it."

"As for that someone," Redmond said, "who knew you were taking the car out today?"

Bernie and I exchanged a look. "It might not have mattered to whoever it was," I said. "If the apparent accident happened today or any other day."

"They all knew," Bernie said.

"All of who?" Redmond asked.

Bernie turned to me. "You remember, Lily. Last night, I was about to get in my car to go home when I remembered that I had to take my own car in today, and I said I'd bike over this morning and we could take Rose's car to come here."

"That's right." I drew up a mental picture of the scene. "The McHenry family had returned from their day's outing, but they hadn't gone to their rooms yet. Rose and Sandra were having drinks on the porch with some other guests. Rose asked us where we were planning on going, but we didn't tell her."

"No doubt," Redmond said, "you exchanged secretive looks."

"Do we do that?" I asked.

She rolled her eyes.

"Every one of the McHenry/French bunch heard us," Bernie pointed out. "With one obvious, and highly significant, exception."

"Trisha," I said, "who'd been carted off to the clink."

"Although," Redmond pointed out in return, "Trisha was at the B and B until yesterday evening and thus could have tampered with the car at any time."

"Why would she do that?" I asked. "Why would any of them?"

"Because we're getting close," Bernie said. "We're onto them. Or they *think* we're onto them, because in reality, we don't have a clue."

"If we'd been killed." I suppressed a shudder. "It would have been a fluke. Most of the roads around here are fairly level. It's only dangerous near the bluffs. More likely, we would have plowed into a patch of sand or bumped into another car at a stoplight in town."

"A warning, then," Bernie said.

"A warning," I agreed.

Redmond stood up. "Don't get ahead of yourselves. You're making a lot of assumptions. First, that the brakes were deliberately tampered with. And secondly, that someone wanted to stop you from investigating the French murder." She cleared her throat. "Someone, that is, other than the police, who've told you not to get involved."

"Just trying to be helpful." Bernie gave her a big grin.

"And how's that working out?"

"Maybe not so well," I admitted.

The door flew open, and Detective Williams marched in. "Are you ladies finished with your little tea party? Good. The car's been taken to the state police garage. I told them I want the results ASAP. If you don't have grounds to arrest Ms. Murphy for dangerous driving, Detective, let's go. The chief wants an update."

Bernie leapt to her feet. "Great! We're off. We'll wait for your report, Detectives. I can be contacted at any time."

We ran out of the meeting room.

"I suppose," Bernie said, "as long as we're here, we might as well do what we came to do."

"You mean talk to Trisha? I'd totally forgotten about that."

"Rose is probably right that Trisha's more likely to talk openly to her than to us. Let's try and find her. I just hope she isn't too traumatized by our recent brush with death."

Chapter 18

We found my grandmother happily ensconced in a game of bridge in a big sunny room overlooking the sparkling waters of Cape Cod Bay.

"My arrival was timely," she said when Bernie and I arrived. "These ladies were in need of a fourth hand. Two spades."

"Sorry," I said, "but we have to go."

"Three hearts," the woman to her left said.

"Once I've finished this hand," Rose said.

Her cane was hooked over the back of her chair. I lifted it off and handed it to her. "Remember why we came here? To visit someone. We'll ask reception to call her room."

"But I have a good hand," the three-heart woman said.

"No table talk," Rose's partner snapped.

"I've already attended to that," Rose said.

"To what?" I asked.

"You two were busy, so I spoke to Trisha. I suppose you want to know what she had to say. If I must. Sorry, ladies, duty calls." Rose laid her cards on the table and spread them out faceup. Scarcely a face card among them, and not many spades, either.

"But you don't have anything," her partner said.

"I was bluffing." Rose got to her feet. "It would have worked." She indicated the woman to her left. "She doesn't have enough for nine tricks, but she enjoys bidding. Thank you for the game, ladies."

"Does she think we're playing poker?" Rose's partner said as we walked away.

"Where's the car?" Rose asked.

"The police have impounded it. We're pretty sure the brakes were cut," I said.

"That's what I suspected," Rose said. "As we are now without transportation, ask the young lady at the desk to call us a cab."

Bernie took care of that, while Rose and I went outside to wait. An iron bench was under the portico by the front door, and Rose settled herself onto it.

We watched hotel guests come and go, many of them lugging golf bags. No one paid us any attention. The crowd at the final bend in the long lane had dispersed.

"The cab'll be here in about fifteen minutes," Bernie said. "You shouldn't have spoken to Trisha without us."

"I saw no need to waste time," Rose said. "It was just as well I did. She was about to go for a walk. If we had delayed, we would have missed her."

"She's been asked to stay on the hotel grounds," I said. "We would have found her."

"The point of working as a team, love, is that we can cover more ground than working individually."

"We're a team? I wouldn't call us that."

"Never mind. It's done," Bernie said. "What did she have to say for herself?"

"She assured me she didn't kill Ed," Rose said.

"That's to be expected," I said. "Anything else?"

"Her lawyer ordered her not to speak to anyone in the

McHenry family, not even Heather, who's paying his bill. I told her I might be Sandra's friend, but I wasn't a member of the family and she can trust me. She freely admits she searched for information about gardens in and around North Augusta. She's a keen gardener and enjoys visiting them when she travels."

"That might be true," I said. "I saw her walking in our garden not long after they arrived, and she seemed to be taking her time admiring the plants. Simon told me the same."

"Last night," Rose said, "she was wearing a T-shirt from Butchart Gardens in British Columbia, which would indicate she does like to visit gardens when on vacation."

"She might have gotten it as a gift."

"When she arrived, the T-shirt she had on was from the Desert Botanical Garden," Bernie said. "The evidence isn't conclusive, but it all helps toward building a pattern."

"She never did have a chance to visit the places she was interested in," Rose said, "because of Ed's unexpected death. She claims she wasn't searching for any plants in particular, just wanting to see what was available to tour. Her lawyer has assured her that simply looking at publicly available tourist information is hardly grounds for charges. He's going to try to have the police's case thrown out."

"Williams acted prematurely," I said. "Redmond thinks so, too."

"Tell us something we don't know," Bernie muttered. "Man's way over his head in a murder case that wasn't witnessed by half-a-dozen people in a bar in a shady part of town."

"I didn't know there were any shady parts of North Augusta," Rose said. "Are there?"

"That's the totality of the police case?" I said. "Trisha's Internet searches?"

"As far as she knows."

"What about Julie-Ann's accusations?" I asked. "Did you ask Trisha about that?"

"A bad word or two might have escaped Trisha's lips when I mentioned Julie-Ann," Rose said. "They haven't spoken in years, but the animosity doesn't seem to have diminished because of that. Mostly, according to Trisha, on Julie-Ann's part because of Julie-Ann's jealousy over Trisha marrying Ed."

Bernie snorted. "For heaven's sake. The man wasn't exactly male model material."

"Perhaps he had a kind heart," Rose said. "Trisha's aware, as is almost everyone else in Grand Lake, that Julie-Ann and Lewis have separated. She thinks Julie-Ann's interest in Ed was rekindled because of his financial prospects."

"What financial prospects? Was he about to come into money? I didn't know that," I said.

"You know these businessmen, love. They're always about to discover the next big thing. The fact that Ed's brother did create the next big thing might have made Ed think he could do so, too."

At that moment, a taxi arrived and we got to our feet.

"Do you want us to drop you off?" I asked Bernie.

"I need to get my bike. Besides, I want to see their faces when we arrive unscathed. Maybe the guilty party will expose themselves."

"That would be convenient," I said.

"Victoria-on-Sea," Rose said to the driver.

He headed up the hill and turned slowly at the first bend. A scrap of yellow police tape fluttered in the wind. Our car was gone, but deep gouges in the sand marked where it had gone off the road.

"I keep tellin' 'em they need to fix that bend," the driver

growled. "Someone's gonna go right over that cliff one day, and *bam!*" He pounded the steering wheel with his hand. Bernie, sitting in the seat next to him, yelped and hit her head on the roof. I swallowed heavily and put my hand on Bernie's shoulder. She laid hers on top of it. Rose took my other hand in hers.

"You ladies visiting Cape Cod for the first time?" the cabbie asked. "I hope you enjoy your time here. I can recommend things to see if you'd like. You should try the restaurant down at the pier in North Augusta. Best seafood this part of the Cape. And that's sayin' somethin'." He chattered on, not noticing or caring that none of us replied with anything but grunts.

It was almost noon and I needed to get to work. As we waited for the police to arrive, I'd called Cheryl and told her I was delayed. She and Marybeth could open the tearoom, make sandwiches, and serve the first lot of customers with what scones and pastries we had in the fridge and freezer. But they couldn't work both the kitchen and dining rooms, so I had to get in there.

The cab turned into our driveway and drove past Tea by the Sea. Cars filled the parking lot and most of the tables on the patio were taken, but I didn't ask the driver to stop and let me out.

Like Bernie, I was hoping to be able to make some deductions based on the reactions of the McHenry guests when we arrived home safe and sound. Although carless.

That idea came to naught. Their cars were gone and none of them were in.

We walked through the front door as the housekeeper clattered down the stairs, the vacuum cleaner bouncing along behind her.

"Are any of the guests in their rooms?" Rose asked.

"Nope. All gone out. Not a day for people on vacation to be sitting indoors, now is it?" She dragged the vacuum down the hall.

"What now?" Bernie asked.

"I'm going to work," I said.

"All we can do is wait for the police to tell us what they find," Rose said.

"We know the brakes were cut," Bernie said. "I don't need Detective Williams telling me as though he arrived at that deduction all by himself."

"No," Rose said. "But they may find something else. Fingerprints, perhaps? Maybe something distinctive about the tool used."

"Do you think it would be worth asking them to finger-print the garage?" Bernie said. "We're assuming the car was interfered with there."

"Might be," I said. "If they decide to take the matter further. No one was hurt, and there's no evidence pointing to what happened with our car having anything to do with the death of Ed French."

"Once again," Bernie said, "all we can do is wait. I hate doing that. Rose, don't say anything about what happened. Not even to Sandra. We'll pretend nothing did and see if one of them slips and gives something away."

"Like spies," Rose said.

"Precisely. I need to get home, anyway. While we were in the taxi, I had a great idea for a scene in my book and I want to get the idea worked out and down on paper. Get this! Rose—my Rose—and Tessa are in a runaway carriage heading for the edge of the cliff. Someone has put burs under the horse's saddle and it bolts. Do you think they should save themselves—maybe Tessa spent lots of time with the horses back on the estate in Ire-land—or should the handsome young farmworker come to their aid?"

"Neither," Rose said. "Carriage horses don't wear saddles. Thus burs cannot be placed under them."

"You know what I mean," Bernie said.

"He should if this is intended to be a romance. Is it?" I asked.

"I'm not sure yet."

"Maybe that's something you need to figure out," I said.

Bernie got her bike and we walked up the driveway together. "My problem," she said, "is that I want to do it all. And I end up doing nothing. I have so many marvelous ideas for this book, all tumbling around in my head. But when I sit down to write the scenes, nothing comes."

"All right, then. Monday evening, I want to see a detailed plot outline. Tuesday night, character sketches of the main characters."

"What?"

"You told me you don't want me reading your rough work. That's fair enough. I don't give people unbaked dough to taste so they can tell me what they think of it."

"Nothing better than raw cookie dough."

"Not my point, Bernie. You can show me what you're thinking of doing. Get it down on paper. Let me see it. Then set yourself to follow the plan. No more wild ideas and rushing off in a totally different direction. You have to make up your mind. Time's passing. Your savings won't last forever."

She turned and grinned at me. "Lily Roberts, you are the best friend ever!"

"I wouldn't go that far."

"I'm on it! That's a great idea. Bye." She leapt on her bike and peddled away in a cloud of writerly enthusiasm and sand.

Whether or not Bernie would follow my plan, I didn't know. I'd done what little I could.

I went into the tearoom through the back door. Mary-beth was at the counter peeling hard-boiled eggs to combine with curry paste, mayonnaise, and a touch of Dijon mustard and salt and pepper for tea sandwiches. "Everything okay?" she asked.

"Fine. Sorry to be late. The place looks full."

"It is. And reservations for the rest of the day will keep it full. We had two tables for Royal Tea already, and we're running out of those orange scones. We'll need plenty more sandwiches."

"You and your mom are lifesavers, or at least tearoom savers. You know that, I hope. With all that's been happening, I've left more work to you than I should, and I'm sorry."

Marybeth smiled at me. "Not your fault the police shut the place down, Lily. You've been trying to help your grandmother and her friend, and so you should. I know you've been worried about us—Mom knows, too—and we appreciate it. We're good here."

"In that case," I said, "I'll start with the scones and then do sandwiches. Finish what you're doing there and then go and help Cheryl."

I got out my mixing bowls and dry ingredients and set to work. As I mixed and sliced, rolled and cut, I thought back over what had happened earlier, trying to reach some sort of conclusion.

Nothing came. I was stymied. We'd learned nothing of significance from Trisha and had no idea who would have sabotaged Rose's car, in what I could only assume was an attempt to kill us.

I opened the oven to pop in the first batch of orange scones. I froze as a thought hit me.

To kill us? Or to kill Rose?

It was Rose's car. We'd talked last night, in front of the

McHenry group, about going out in Rose's car. But plans change all the time.

I shoved the baking trays in the oven and set the rooster timer. I washed up the bowls and measuring cups and spoons and then I did a quick inventory of the fridge and freezer. We had enough scones and pastries to last a while but, as Marybeth had said, the supply of sandwiches was getting low.

"One order of traditional tea for four and one children's tea for two," Cheryl said. "Have a nice morning?"

"Very nice, thank you."

"We have a bus tour of twelve coming in at four. Thirteen, including the driver."

"We'll be ready." The difficulty in running a restaurant serving afternoon tea is that unlike more traditional meals served in courses and individually, for us the food has to all be served at the same time for everyone, all at once. At least, with a large group booking, I know in advance what we'd be serving.

I took a cooked chicken out of the fridge and slapped it on a chopping board. The chicken had been poached yesterday in Darjeeling tea and I'd mix it with mayonnaise, lemon juice, celery, grapes, and diced red onion to make sandwiches using whole wheat bread. Today's other sandwiches were curried egg, smoked salmon on pumpernickel, and open-faced roast beef and arugula. For the children, we'd serve ham and cheese sandwiches sliced into fingers and peanut butter and jam pinwheels (after checking for allergies). For pastries, our little guests would be offered mini cinnamon buns, vanilla cupcakes, and chocolate-dipped strawberries.

The children's food was plainer, but served on the same quality china and linens as the adults got. If they didn't want tea, their choice of iced tea or juice came in crystal flutes. Afternoon tea, I believe, is to be served properly or not at all.

As I went through my daily routine, baking, making sandwiches, taking orders from Marybeth and Cheryl, I resumed my earlier train of thought and kept turning the events of this morning over and over in my mind.

What had been the intention of whoever sabotaged our car?

Assuming they had an intention and weren't simply out to cause trouble—which, I had to remind myself, was a possibility. Someone had killed Ed French. If Trisha didn't do it, and it hadn't been a random attack or mob-contracted hit (which wasn't even worth considering), then whoever did kill Ed was currently staying at Victoria-on-Sea.

Whoever sabotaged Rose's car had no way of knowing that when we needed the car's brakes the most, we'd be driving down one of the few truly dangerous roads in North Augusta. More likely for us to have been in a fender bender on Main Street or to strike an innocent pedestrian in the crosswalk than to be plunging over the edge of the cliff to our doom.

Maybe it didn't matter what the end result was: The disruption was intended to be the end in itself. Rose was hale and hearty and as fit as a woman of her age could be. But she was a woman of her age, and even a minor car accident could put her in the hospital.

With Rose in the hospital, all my focus would be on her.

If we'd been involved in an accident with another car or a pedestrian, and it was clearly our fault, then we'd be tied up in legal complications.

Even a small accident—if it ended with one of us injured or facing legal problems—would have taken over our concentration.

That hadn't happened.

And, I thought as I rolled out chilled pastry to make tart shells, I was now focused more than ever on the case.

I knew, or thought I knew, why Rose's car had been sabotaged. To stop Rose and Bernie and me from asking questions about the death of Ed French.

The big question, of course, was who did it.

Who could tamper with brakes on a car? Not everyone. I wouldn't have the faintest idea how to go about something like that. Not many women I knew would.

Brian or Lewis? Brian and Lewis owned a car dealership. Did that mean they had some familiarity with basic mechanics?

Possibly.

Had Brian or Lewis taught Tyler?

Possibly.

The phone-obsessed Amanda? Unlikely, but I wouldn't take anything off the table.

Darlene and Julie-Ann? Highly unlikely, but, again, not impossible.

Heather? With her designer clothes, fresh manicure, and flashy diamond rings? Even more unlikely.

Sandra? Almost certainly not. Women of her generation simply didn't learn how to maintain cars.

How difficult was it to cut a brake line, anyway? It happens all the time in books and movies. Maybe that's the sort of thing you can learn with a quick glance at the Internet. I made a mental note to check into it after work. I filled the shells with pastry cream and set them aside to be decorated later. Then I washed my hands and pulled my phone out of my pocket.

"One order of Royal Tea for two." Cheryl dumped a load of used dishes onto the counter next to the sink.

I lifted a finger to tell her I'd be right there. She took a bottle of sparkling wine out of the fridge and two flutes off the shelf.

Amy Redmond answered her phone. "Lily, what can I do for you this time?"

"I have a . . . uh . . . suggestion."

"You mean instructions about how I might work my case?"

"I . . . uh . . ."

She chuckled. "Go ahead. You're like a dog worrying a bone, and that's not necessarily a bad thing when it comes to my line of work. What's up?"

"I don't know anything about cars, other than how to drive them and how to tell when they need gas, but I'm wondering how hard it is to sabotage the brakes. Is that something you have to have the equivalent of an advanced degree in or can you look up how to do it on the Internet to find step-by-step instructions with pictures and everything?"

"Why are you asking that, Lily?"

"I thought maybe you could have a look at the search history on those phones and tablets you confiscated and . . . uh . . . check if anyone did. Search, I mean."

"That's a good idea, Lily," she said. "We didn't specify something as specific as that, but if our techies had found such a search, they would have included it in their report. *Probably* they would have included it. I'll check. Thanks for the tip."

"You're welcome. Has the garage found anything yet?"

"They're scheduled to start on your car later this afternoon. I'll let you know what, if anything, they find."

"Thanks." I hung up. I was pondering what Redmond had said when a loud crash came from the dining room, a woman screamed, and someone cried, "Oh, no!"

I ran out of the kitchen.

I found Marybeth lying in the center of the main room, flat on her back, surrounded by broken china, sandwiches, and pastries. A pistachio macaron rolled across the floor toward me. A woman stood over Marybeth, wringing her hands together and saying, "I'm so sorry. I'm so sorry. I didn't see you there."

Marybeth grunted.

I ran to her and dropped to my knees. Cheryl came in from the garden at a run.

Marybeth blinked at me.

"Are you okay?" I asked. "Lie still."

"I'm . . . okay."

"Don't get up."

"No, I'm fine." She struggled to sit.

"I'm so sorry. I'm so sorry," the customer wailed. "It was all my fault. I didn't look where I was going."

Cheryl took one of Marybeth's arms, I took the other, and we carefully helped Marybeth get to her feet. She wobbled and gave us both a sickly grin. "Really, I'm okay." She took one step and gasped in pain. Between us, Cheryl and I half carried her into the kitchen. As I passed the counter, I grabbed a chair it and dragged it after me. I shoved it beneath Marybeth, and her mother helped her lower herself onto it. Beads of sweat were popping up on Marybeth's forehead.

"Do you think something's broken, honey?" Cheryl asked.

"Is she okay?" The woman had followed us. "I can take her to the hospital."

"No. Really," Marybeth said. "I just need a minute."

"You stay with her," I said to Cheryl. "I need to clean up out there before we have another accident." I turned to the customer. "Why don't you come with me and give me a hand?"

"I'm so sorry. I pushed my chair back the moment she was passing and . . . I'm sorry."

I grabbed the broom and dustpan out of the corner and shoved them into the woman's hands. While she swept up shards of my beautiful china and squashed pieces of my precious baking and scooped the fugitive macaron out from under a table, I assured the customers the waitress was fine and she only needed to rest for a few minutes. I'd have their tea and food out shortly. So sorry for the delay.

Back to the kitchen.

"I don't think anything's broken." Cheryl was crouched in front of Marybeth, probing her ankle lightly.

I let out a sigh of relief. That was excellent news, but Marybeth didn't look too good. She was pale and dripping with sweat.

"You need to go home," I told her. "We can manage here."

"But—"

"But nothing. I can't have you fainting in the middle of the dining room."

"I came with Mom in her car."

"You shouldn't be driving, anyway. I'll call you a cab. Did you hit your head?"

"No. I don't think so."

"Good."

"I'll pay for the cab," the apologetic customer said. "It's the least I can do. I feel so bad."

"Thanks. You've been very kind. Go and finish your tea. We're fine here."

She hurried away and was soon back, waving two twenty-dollar bills. "Will this be enough for the taxi?"

"Yes, thanks," I said.

She shoved the money at Marybeth and then left, still apologizing. Marybeth said, "I can't just up and leave. We're full for the rest of the day. A big group's coming in at four."

"We'll manage," I said, wondering how I could possibly manage with only one waitress. Then I had an idea.

I sent Simon a text: **Other duties, as assigned. Drop everything and come to TBTS kitchen.**

The reply came almost instantly: **On my way.**

I called the cab and it arrived at the same time as Simon. Cheryl told Marybeth to call her if she started feeling worse and helped her daughter into the taxi.

"Scones," I said after I'd told Simon what had happened. "I need scones in the oven and then cupcakes, and the strawberry tarts have to be assembled. I'll make sandwiches, do dishes, and help Cheryl wait tables, particularly when big groups arrive." I looked down at my jeans and well-worn sneakers. "Nothing I can do but put an apron on and hope no one notices."

He spent a long time at the kitchen sink, scrubbing good Cape Cod earth off his hands. He grabbed a tea towel, dried his hands, and then turned to me with a wicked grin. "I'm on it."

I smiled back. "You're a lifesaver."

He tugged at an imaginary forelock. "I serve at m'lady's pleasure."

"Ooh," Cheryl said, "I love a man with an English accent."

Simon laughed and began measuring flour.

For the next several hours, Simon baked scones, shortbread, tarts, and cupcakes. We had enough macarons at hand to last through the day. I prepared sandwiches and did the dishes, and helped Cheryl make tea and serve the guests.

At one point, when all the tables had been served and she could take a brief break, Cheryl called Marybeth and then reported back to me. "She's watching afternoon TV, eating an entire bag of salt and vinegar chips all by herself, and enjoying the rare quiet while the kids are at their day camps and Dave's at work. She tells me she's thinking of taking up the life of a lady of leisure. I told her I'd pick her up at quarter to ten tomorrow as usual."

"Glad to hear she's okay," I said. "She probably didn't need to go home, but better safe than sorry."

"I'd like to take up the life of a lady of leisure," Simon said.

"To do that, you'll have to snag a rich husband like Heather did," I said. "Although, to be fair, he wasn't rich when she married him. I don't know if she has a job. She never said. I haven't spent much time with Rose's friends." A memory flashed through my mind. "Although Heather did mention—"

"Showtime." Cheryl's head popped into the kitchen. "The bus tour's here."

"Once they're seated, take their tea orders. I'll start arranging the food." I checked that the hot-water dispensers were full and took teapots and three-tiered trays off the shelf. The rooster timer my sister gave me, which I use only for timing scones, crowed and Simon slipped on oven mitts and lifted a fragrant tray out of the oven.

I glanced at the scones. Sheer perfection made out of nothing more complicated than flour and butter and a splash of milk.

I'd been about to say something, something about Heather. The thought was gone now. I arranged the sandwiches on the bottom tier of the trays.

Chapter 19

"I can't thank you enough for this," I said to Simon. "Cheryl and I never would have been able to do all that on our own."

"Sure you would," he said.

The last of the guests had finally finished lingering over their tea, and I'd locked the door with a contented sigh. A good day, and disaster averted. I told Cheryl she could leave early, as she was anxious about Marybeth, and Simon and I would clean up and prepare the tearoom for the next morning. He was making a final batch of tart shells as I loaded dishes into the dishwasher.

"Do you know much about cars?" I took a leftover egg sandwich off a tray and popped it into my mouth. It was the only one left—clearly, everyone at that table had been too polite to take the last one.

"I know as much about cars as the average bloke," he said. "Why?"

"I take that to mean you know way more than I do. Can you do basic maintenance on your car yourself, if you had to?"

"I've never owned a car," he said, "as I prefer motor-bikes. I love bikes, so I learned how to look after them. The principle's the same, so I can help Mum sort out small things on her car. Why are you asking?"

"Just wondering."

"If you're having a problem, I can have a look at Rose's car, but don't expect me to do much. I'd never attempt a major repair. Cars these days have too many computer components, and you can ruin a warranty by doing the wrong thing."

"Rose's car is long past worrying about a warranty, but that's not it. I'm helping Bernie with her book. We're wondering how easy it is to cut the brakes on a car—so they stop working, I mean."

Simon put down my marble rolling pin and studied my face. "I thought Bernie's book was historical. Horses and carriages and sailing ships historical."

"She keeps changing it."

"That's quite the change. Lily, did something happen to your car?"

I never was a very good liar. "Yeah. Brakes failed on Rose's car this morning. We're pretty sure it was deliberate."

His eyes opened wide. "What do you mean *deliberate*? Where's the car now?"

"The police have it."

"That's good. Obviously, you're unhurt, and Rose also, I'll assume." He picked up the marble pin and finished rolling out pastry. "I'll get these in the oven and then have a look at the garage."

"What will the garage be able to tell you?"

"Maybe nothing, but it won't hurt to look. A brake line isn't cut, per se, as in severed. Otherwise, the car would crash on its way out of the parking space. If the line providing the fluid to the brakes has a leak, once all the fluid's leaked out, the brakes'll stop working. A small hole isn't easy to do, not if you don't want the driver to realize immediately that something's wrong, but it is doable. Let's check the floor of the garage and see if any fluid leaked out overnight."

"How easy would it be to do that? For someone who isn't a qualified car mechanic, I mean."

"Probably not all that difficult, not for someone with a basic knowledge of the workings of a motor vehicle. I'm sure you can find specific instructions on the Internet. There's videos on how to do just about anything these days."

"Brian and Lewis McHenry own a car dealership. Do salespeople work on the cars?"

Simon laughed. "I doubt that means anything. A lot of them can barely tell one end from the other without a map."

My phone rang. Amy Redmond.

"This might be an update," I said to Simon as I answered.

"I thought you'd want to know what the mechanics found on your car," she said.

"I do." I waggled my eyebrows at Simon.

He popped the tart shells into the oven and came to join me. I held the phone so he could hear and we tilted our heads together.

"Definite signs of interference with the brake fluid," she told us. "The line was punctured within the last week, they assured me, probably less than that."

"Is it possible this was an accident?" I asked. "Or as a result of regular wear and tear on the old car?"

"No," Redmond said. "The puncture's distinctive and clean. As for everything else, as you assured me, your grandmother keeps her vehicle in good condition. Our mechanics were impressed enough to say so."

"Detective, Simon McCracken here, listening in. Can you tell anything about who might have done this?"

"Sorry, no. No fingerprints. The line's clean. As in wiped down. No business cards dropped into the engine or scraps of clothing conveniently caught on a protruding nail."

"Thanks for letting me know," I said. "What's happening with the French investigation? The case against Trisha's very flimsy. Do you have any other suspects? Are the McHenrys going to be allowed to leave?"

"Heather French has a mighty powerful city lawyer who's been on the phone yelling at our chief. She's saying we can't expect Heather to stay here indefinitely. Not now that someone has been arrested. The chief gave in and Heather will be allowed to leave North Augusta tomorrow. We couldn't let her, the one with the big-bucks lawyer, go and continue to keep the others here. So they all, except for Trisha French, will be allowed to leave if they want. Other than that, you'll know at a suitable time, Lily." She hung up.

"I was hoping," I said with a discontented sigh, "that as she was sharing information, she'd keep doing so."

Simon grinned at me.

I finished setting the tables for tomorrow while Simon washed up the baking dishes and utensils and waited for the last batch of tart shells to bake. When they were out of the oven and packed away, and the kitchen was once again clean and tidy, I swept the floor, took off my apron, and left the tearoom.

Simon and I walked up the long driveway to the big house together. Redmond had confirmed that the brakes on Rose's car had been interfered with, but Simon wanted to check out the garage, anyway. "I really appreciate your help," I said.

"Anytime." He cleared his throat. "Have you ever ridden on a motorbike?"

"Heavens, no. Not a lot of call for bikes in Manhattan. They look dangerous."

His face fell and I added quickly, "Although you obviously don't think so."

"Nothing like being on a bike. The feel of the open road. The speed. The freedom." His eyes glowed with the sheer joy of the memory. "I haven't had a chance to do much exploring since I've been here . . ."

"Because we're overworking you?"

He chuckled. "Slave drivers that you and Rose are. I'm thinking of taking a day off next week and driving up the coast to Provincetown. See the sights, go to the beach, maybe have lunch in town."

"Sounds nice," I said.

"Would you"—he hesitated, then continued—"like to come with me?"

"You mean on your bike?"

"Yeah." He was no longer looking at me.

I hesitated. I was single; Simon was single. We were the around the same age. I liked Simon, and I got the feeling he liked me. But as I'd told Bernie, I wasn't looking for a relationship. This summer needed to be all about getting Tea by the Sea up and running. Even if I was looking for a relationship, Simon was going back to England in the fall.

Then again, maybe I was reading too much into his simple question. Maybe all he wanted was some companionship. He'd come to the Cape specifically to take the job here, so he didn't know anyone other than us. Maybe he didn't like eating in restaurants alone. Maybe he liked introducing people to his motorcycle. Maybe he wanted other people to love it as much as he did.

A thought burst out of my subconscious. I sucked in a breath.

"What?" Simon asked.

"You said you love motorcycles, so you learned how they work."

"What of it?"

"I bet you talked to your parents about your bike. Did you?"

"I tried at first, but that didn't last long. Mum's terrified that I'm going to come to a bad end on it, and Dad told me it would be better just to pretend I gave the bike up, even though I drive it to their house for Sunday lunch most weeks. Why do you ask?"

"People who are passionate about something—a sport, a hobby—usually encourage the people close to them to love it, too. To play the sport, to enjoy the hobby. So they can do those things together."

"Yeah, I guess. I went out for a long time with a girl who loved bikes. I didn't like her all that much, but I loved her enthusiasm for bikes. She had a better one than mine, and she let me ride it sometimes. What of it?"

"Heather's late husband, Norman, was an antique-car enthusiast. From what little I know about antique cars, they require a great deal of highly specialized maintenance because regular garages can't handle them. You can't buy the parts the cars need; they have to be individually made."

I slowed to a stop. I looked toward the grand old mansion. It was still full daylight, but the sun was sinking over the bay ready for its nightly dip. The trees threw long shadows across the lawn, and birds darted between the bushes and buzzed around the flowers. A butterfly flew past my face, and the soft pounding of the surf against the shore sounded in my ears. At the house, the lights above the veranda hadn't yet come on. I could see Rose in her rocking chair, but she was alone. Heather's car and Brian's rental were in the car park.

"You think Heather knows cars?" Simon asked. "That's possible. Doesn't mean she fixed your brakes, though."

"No. It doesn't." Snatches of overheard conversations and fragmented thoughts flashed through my mind. "At the time of Norman French's death, Ed was suing his brother for a share of what he'd earned from the sale of his company on the grounds that he was equally involved in the development of . . . whatever the company made. Norman died and the lawsuit died with him. Now, four years later, Ed came on this vacation at the invitation of Heather."

"That means nothing, Lily. Families fight and they get over it."

"Yes, they do. But Ed was expecting to come into some money soon." What had Trisha said to Rose about Julie-Ann? She only wanted to get back with Ed, all these years later, because he was about to see an improvement in his financial situation. Surely, before breaking up two marriages, Julie-Ann would have expected a *substantial* improvement in Ed's finances.

"Maybe he and Heather came to an agreement, and she was going to cut him in?" Simon speculated.

"That's what I'm thinking. But now, I'm also thinking, what if, for some reason, Ed thought there was going to be an agreement, maybe an out-of-court settlement, but Heather had no intention of honoring it? Had she invited Ed and Trisha on this trip under the pretext of talking it over? If so, he died before that could happen."

"Convenient," Simon said.

"Very," I said.

"You have absolutely not one iota of proof that that's what happened, Lily. I have to tell you, I don't think you have much of a case, anyway, even if it did happen that way. Plenty of people can fix a brake line—I can, and I hope you're not considering me for it—and plenty of people reconcile with estranged relatives. Some even come to legal and financial arrangements without going to court. My sister's father-in-law didn't speak to his brother for years after their parents died, because he thought the will wasn't fair. They got over it. Without anyone killing anyone."

"But in this case, Simon, someone has been killed. Ed French. Why would Heather invite Ed and Trisha to come here, knowing the amount of bad blood between Ed and Brian and Lewis? Someone said that since Heather doesn't live in Iowa anymore, she might not have realized everyone hadn't moved on. That's possible, but I don't think Heather's naïve. She wasn't surprised when Ed and Trisha arrived to not a very enthusiastic welcome. If anything, she was amused at the others' reactions when the Frenches checked in."

"If everything you're saying's true, Lily, Heather's not going to confess to killing Ed. Even if you ask her nicely."

"So I won't ask. I'll tell. She's going to be on her way home tomorrow, probably the second she gets word she's free to go. Then she'll be surrounded by a phalanx of New York lawyers, well out of the reach of not only me, but Detective Redmond also. I have an idea. Let's go back to the tearoom."

Chapter 20

Tea by the Sea was dark and quiet when we let ourselves in through the front door. We passed through the vestibule into the main room. The clean white tablecloths glowed in the golden evening light streaming through the windows, and the glass bowls full of flowers sparkled. The dining room smelled of tea and the end-of-day baking.

My place. I loved it so. But tonight, I hadn't come back to admire it.

"You don't have to stay if you don't want to," I said to Simon. "I can handle this."

"Of that," he said, "I have no doubt. But just in case . . ."

"Thanks. Now be quiet and let me talk."

I took a deep breath and placed a phone call.

"What is it now, Lily?" Detective Redmond allowed a hint of impatience to creep into her voice. Maybe *creep* isn't the right word. More like *stampede.*

A car turned off the highway and drove slowly up the long lane to the big house.

I got straight to the point. "I believe Heather French killed Ed because he had a claim to his late brother's fortune. I intend to accuse her of that. I thought you might like to join us."

"Are you out of your mind? If you have proof of what you're saying, come down and tell us about it and let me . . . I mean us . . . handle it."

"I don't have proof, Detective. Not yet. But I intend to get it. I'm at Tea by the Sea now. Can you be here in ten minutes?"

"Lily, this is a mistake."

"Ten minutes. I know what I'm doing. You can trust me. Park on the road behind the tearoom. You can't see that spot from the house. Come in the back way. I'll unlock the door for you." I hung up.

Simon eyed me warily. "It sounds as though Detective Redmond isn't overly chuffed with this idea. I'm on her side."

"Trust me," I said again. "Tea?"

"Why ever not?" he replied.

"I'll be right back." I went into the kitchen, unlocked the back door, and then filled a small kettle. One thing my grandmother had taught me: There's nothing like a cup of tea in a crisis. I scooped leaves of English breakfast, strong and dark, out of a tin, pressed them into a tea ball, and set the timer. While the tea steeped for precisely three minutes, I took three of Simon's strawberry tarts out of the fridge. Might as well reward the man for his patience with his own baking. I didn't think the bribe would go very far toward mollifying Redmond, but it might lighten her mood a fraction.

I heard the front door open and footsteps cross the floor. I was annoyed at Redmond for disregarding my instructions—orders?—and potentially ruining my plan by coming in the front way, where she could be seen. Then I recognized the tap of Rose's cane and hurried out.

"What are you two doing here?" Not only Rose, but Bernie had arrived.

"I'm here for an end-of-the-day meeting," Bernie said. "We wanted to ask if you heard anything from Detective Redmond about the car." She glanced at Simon. "Sorry if we're interrupting something."

"You are, but it's not what you think. The more the merrier."

Rose pulled out a chair. Simon leapt forward to assist her.

"Don't sit down!" I said.

"Why not?" my grandmother asked.

"Because you'll ruin everything. This is a highly delicate, closely timed operation."

"What is?" Bernie said.

"You have to leave. Now."

"I'm not leaving until I know what's going on," Rose said.

"Yes, you are," I said.

"No, I'm not."

"Yes, you are."

"This isn't getting us anywhere," Simon said. "Like it or not, you're stuck with us, Lily. Where do you want us?"

"In the kitchen. All of you. But first, Rose, have you seen Heather today?"

"She and Sandra went for a walk along the bluffs earlier," Rose said. "They're back now, and as far as I know, they've gone to their rooms before going out for dinner. The police called earlier to say they could have their phones and iPads back, and Lewis went to the station to get them. He also picked up our computer, but I haven't checked it yet. I hope they haven't interfered with anything."

"Never mind that. Did Heather seem . . . surprised to see you?"

"You think it was Heather who fixed the brakes?" Bernie asked.

"Yes, I do. And that means she killed Ed French. Rose?"

"She didn't appear surprised to see me," Rose said, "which might be, if what you suspect is true, because she would have heard me before seeing me. I spent most of the day in the office working on the accounts. Around six, I called Sandra and asked if she was ready to meet for our drink. Sandra and I had just settled ourselves on the veranda for a nice chat when Heather came out of the house. Heather asked Sandra if she felt like a walk and they left. I would have liked to have gone with them, but I was not invited. Just as well, as Bernie arrived a few moments ago and we decided to talk to you and find out if you have news of any developments."

"Off you go," I said, "I've made tea and laid out some tarts in the kitchen."

"All this excitement is over a tea party?" Bernie said.

"Redmond will be here any minute, and I don't think I can keep her for long. She didn't sound as though she was in the mood to linger over tea. I have to make my phone call now. Simon?"

"Okay. Come on, ladies, I'll explain when we're in the kitchen. You have to keep your voices down."

"Why would I want to do that?" Rose asked.

"By *voices down*," I said, "he means *shut up*. And I mean it, too. Not a peep."

They left, Rose complaining that there weren't any chairs in the kitchen, and Bernie still demanding to be told what was going on. Simon grabbed a chair as he passed and dragged it after him.

I took a deep breath and placed my call. If Heather took the bait, fine. If not, then I'd look like a fool. That would be fine also.

"Hello?"

I didn't bother with pleasantries. "I know all about it, Heather."

"Who's this and what do you think you know?"

"It's Lily Roberts. You must have been surprised to see Rose home this afternoon, hale and hearty, and totally un-upset by her recent brush with death."

"You're talking nonsense, Lily."

"You know I'm not, Heather. You cut a hole in the brake line in Rose's car. You did it last night when the car was in the garage after you heard Bernie and me planning to take the car out this morning. You guessed, correctly, that we wanted to have a talk with Trisha, because I know Trisha didn't kill Ed, and I'm wondering who did."

"As long as you're on the line, Lily, I want to thank you for making my grandmother and my family so welcome. We'll be checking out tomorrow. Sorry for any inconvenience over the bookings. You can move Trisha back here if you have the room, but I'll no longer be paying her bills."

I heard the back door opening, the squeak of the hinges, the creak of the loose floorboard, and whispered voices in the kitchen. Detective Redmond had arrived. I clutched the phone closer to my ear. "My dad was a car mechanic." I lied. "He was a big believer in girls learning nontraditional occupations, so he taught me a lot. Much to his disappointment, I became a pastry chef, but that's neither here nor there at the moment. As soon as our car came to a shuddering halt mere inches from the edge of a cliff, I crawled under the car and had a look around before the police arrived. I found several threads of wool caught on a . . ." My nonexistent knowledge of the undercarriage of a car failed me. I cleared my throat to give myself a moment to think. ". . . protruding nail. Nice bit of cloth. Good-quality wool. Oatmeal with a thin blue thread."

I held my breath. The breeze off the bay had been cool

last night. Anyone venturing out of their room under the cover of darkness would have been likely to throw on a sweater, particularly if they were wearing their pajamas. It was summer in Cape Cod. Not many people would bring more than one sweater and maybe a light jacket on a short vacation break.

Heather, who seemed to have an outfit for every occasion, had worn that sweater twice. I was counting on her having brought only the one.

"What do you want, Lily?" Her voice turned cold. Hard.

"You could have killed my grandmother, never mind me. That's bad enough, but that you did it can mean only one thing. You murdered Ed French, and you know Rose, Bernie, and I have been asking questions about that. I haven't told Detective Redmond, who, by the way, is a close friend of mine, about the fabric I found. I will, if I have to, take it to Detective Williams. I'll also show him the picture I took the other evening of Rose when we were having ice cream on the pier." I hadn't taken such a picture, but Heather didn't need to know that. "You're in the background, by the way, wearing that sweater, so if you throw it into the sea tonight, I still have proof it's yours. I'll make up some excuse about tidying the car after the near-accident and not realizing the cloth was important until later. Silly me. Williams isn't that bright. He'll believe me. The police will then wonder why you'd do such a thing. And they'll come to the same conclusion I have. Eventually. A hundred thousand should do it."

"You want me to give you a hundred thousand dollars?"

"Yup. I'm in the dining room of the tearoom. No one else is here. You can come over now. You give me the money, you can watch me burn the cloth."

"I don't have a hundred thousand dollars in cash lying around my room."

"Don't be a fool, Heather. I don't want cash. I wouldn't know what to do with a suitcase full of cash. A check will do. An online electronic transfer will do even better. You make the transfer in front of me, and I'll hand over the fabric and you can watch me delete the photograph."

"You might have made copies."

"Yes, but without the cloth, the picture proves nothing. I'm here alone working late, as I usually do at the end of the day. Be here in five minutes or I call the cops. Come in by the main door." I hung up. I breathed.

She'd come or not. If I was wrong, if she had nothing to hide, she wouldn't show.

If I was right . . .

Before putting my phone away, I switched on the recorder. "She's on her way," I called out. "Everyone stay quiet!"

"What about this cloth?" Redmond called to me. "Do you have it?"

"I lied. I don't have any such thing. You told me you found no fingerprints. You have no proof Heather did it. I'm trying to get the proof for you."

"You're nuts," Bernie said.

"Shush. If you won't leave, at least be quiet." I walked across the tearoom and stood at the window. A slight figure ran down the steps of the B & B and walked down the driveway at a rapid pace.

Heather was on her way.

I took a seat at the big table in the center of the main room, from where I could see the door. Only when I'd sat down did I realize this was the table at which the fatal tea had been served. I tried to suppress a shudder. I needed to look strong. Strong and ruthless.

A woman in control.

My mother was a singer and an actress. She'd achieved some success on Broadway and in Hollywood and still got a fair amount of work for a woman of her age. She wanted me to follow in her footsteps, but I'd had no interest and absolutely no talent. Even as a child, I'd felt a total fool trying to pretend to be something I wasn't.

Right now, I felt a fool trying to pretend to be strong and ruthless. I wiped my hands on my jeans and attempted to control my breathing.

The front door opened, footsteps sounded in the vestibule, and Heather walked into the tearoom, her face set into hard, angry lines. She was dressed in tight white ankle-length jeans, fashionably shredded at the knees, a black-and-white striped T-shirt, and white sandals with two-inch heels. She held her phone in her hand. "I'm here. Let's get this nonsense over with."

I held out my hand. Then, remembering that people were listening and I was trying to record this, I said, "Give me the money."

"I'll give you ten thousand dollars and no more. And that's only to get you out of my hair. I might have fiddled with your grandmother's car, but it was just a joke, because I could and I'm bored. My husband taught me a lot about cars, but I sold his collection when he died and I don't get much of a chance to tinker with them anymore. I figured you'd crash before you so much as left your driveway. Like Tyler did."

"Did you put Tyler up to stealing Simon's bike?"

"Hardly. What do I care what the silly boy gets up to?" She pressed her thumb to her phone to open it. "Give me your email address and I'll transfer ten thou. Then I want the cloth and I'll be on my way. Tonight. If that cop thinks I'm going to stay here a moment longer, she can contact my lawyers."

"What about the rest of your group?"

"What about them? Gran can come with me, but Mom

and Dad and the rest are on their own. I've spent enough money on them. Ungrateful bunch."

"Is that why you killed Ed? Because he wasn't grateful."

"I didn't kill Ed. Or anyone else." She snapped her fingers at me. "Hand it over."

I needed her to say the words. To confess. With the sort of lawyers she could afford, if she was charged with tampering with Rose's car, she'd get nothing more than a slap on the wrist. Unlikely, even that. No one had been hurt. No damage done.

"I want a hundred thousand. Ten isn't enough."

"You're lucky I'm offering you ten. Take it, or I'll go down to five. Keep arguing and I'm walking."

"You killed Ed because he wanted half of what his brother had gotten for the company and the software."

"Ed might have wanted half, but he wasn't going to get it. Despite what he said, he could never prove he contributed anywhere near as much as Norman to the original idea or the development of the program. And that, Lily, is because he didn't. Now, can we please get this over with? You've just wasted five thousand dollars of my time. All you're getting is five."

I rattled off an incorrect email address, and she punched buttons on her phone. I didn't know if I'd be compromised if her money did show up in my account. "Trisha said Ed was about to come into money."

"As you're finding out, in your own annoying way, I prefer to pay people off rather than put up with their constant pleading. Dealing with greed gets so tedious. I offered Ed ten million dollars to put it all past him and leave me alone. He accepted. End of story.

"I've set up the electronic transfer for you. Give me the cloth and I'll press the final key. Put it on the table, Lily, and then we'll be done."

I floundered around, trying to find something, anything, to keep her talking and eventually admit all. My phone was heavy in my pocket. I desperately wanted to take it out and check it was recording. Redmond needed to hear a confession of murder, not just of playing a prank on an old woman's car. "Why did you invite Ed on this weekend, anyway? If you wanted him to leave you alone?"

"It wasn't my idea, but it wasn't a bad one. I knew it would make Dad and Lewis mad if Ed showed up. The thing with Julie-Ann and Trisha was a lovely extra bonus. Keeps things interesting."

"Not your idea? Then whose?"

A figure stepped into the room. Heather turned around.

"It's time to put an end to this tedious discussion, dear," said a frighteningly calm voice.

"I'm handling it," Heather said.

"Not very well. She's a babbling fool, but she knows too much. It's time for me to take matters into my own hands. Once again. Please get out of the way."

Heather looked at me, and then she ducked her head so her hair fell over her face and took two steps to her left.

Sandra lifted the gun in her right hand.

Chapter 21

I yelped. Then, remembering the kitchen full of listeners, I said, "Sandra. It was you all along. Put down that gun!"

"Please leave us, dear," Sandra said to Heather. Her arm, I couldn't help but notice, was as steady as her voice. She stood tall and straight, her cane nowhere in sight. She'd played me—and my grandmother—for a fool. And it had worked. I'd seen Sandra jump to her feet when Tyler had crashed Simon's bike, and then walking on the bluffs, comfortable and steady, when she hadn't known she was being observed, but I hadn't thought anything of it. The cane, the feeble old lady needing a strong hand on the stairs: all for show.

"Please, Gran . . ." Heather's voice was nowhere as calm as her grandmother's. "You don't need to do this. We can leave now. Go back to New York. I'll give her the money she wants and she won't mention it again." Heather turned to face me. Her eyes were wide as she pleaded with me to agree.

"We're back to a hundred thousand," I said, "and I won't mention a word of this to anyone."

"Too late," Sandra said. "I thought you were a mindless bimbo, happy to play with your scones and pretty teacups, while Rose and the redhead pretended to be detectives. But I should have realized any granddaughter of Rose Campbell had to be as sharp as a tack. My mistake. I won't be making another."

In the kitchen, one of the old floorboards settled as it was stepped on. Heather threw a look toward the back. "What was that?"

Sandra didn't react and her gun hand didn't quiver. She might be spryer than she pretended to be, but she was still an eighty-year-old woman who refused to admit she was hard of hearing. She hadn't heard the noise.

"Mice." I raised my voice. If Redmond was on the move, I needed to give her some cover and some time. "We have lots of mice in here. Don't tell the health inspectors." The hinges on the old back door squeaked.

"The health department is the least of your worries." Sandra's eyes were once again fixed on my face. Something very dark moved in the depths, and I swallowed. "Heather," she said, "go and check it out. Then leave by the back way. Rose isn't on the veranda, and the redhead's car's here. They must have gone to Rose's room, no doubt to keep poking into my family's private affairs. Tell Rose I'm not feeling well and we're leaving tonight. I'll deal with this nuisance."

"Gran, I don't . . ." Heather's voice trailed off.

"I said, I'll deal with this. You need to trust me. Once again."

Heather threw me a look that might have meant she was sorry. But not sorry enough. She ducked her head and slunk across the dining room, staying close to the walls, taking care to keep herself out of my reach.

She went into the kitchen and I heard a soft grunt. Sandra did not.

I judged the distance between me and Sandra and realized I had no chance of overpowering the woman. A table—perfectly arranged for afternoon tea—stood between us, and by the time I covered the distance, she'd have fired. I hoped my phone was still recording. If she killed me, Redmond would have the evidence she needed. "You murdered Ed French because he wanted money from Heather. Heather would have paid him off, she could afford it. But you decided to deal with him in a more direct way."

"He wanted ten million. For now. Once he had that, he'd want another ten million, and then another. Get that idiot wife of his involved, and then who knows what they'd be insisting on? They'd make Heather's life a nightmare."

"You're wrong about that, Sandra. If Ed thought he was entitled to ten million dollars from his brother's estate, and Heather agreed, that would have been the end of it." When I'd been in Heather's room the other night fetching a bottle of wine from her fridge, I'd seen legal papers on the desk. I hadn't stopped to read them, but I had seen a note scribbled in the margins saying, *Ensure it's final?* "Not everyone's as dishonest and distrusting as you appear to be."

"I'm not wasting time justifying myself to you. Your death will break Rose's heart, and I'm sorry about that. She was a good friend to me. Can't be helped. I'll console her at your funeral."

A shrieking figure wrapped in purple and yellow flew out of the vestibule. A pink stick flashed through the air and came down hard on Sandra's outstretched right arm. Brittle old bones snapped and Sandra screamed. The gun clattered to the floor.

Chapter 22

I staggered backward and fell. Fortunately, a chair was behind me and I dropped into it.

Amy Redmond and Bernie ran into the room. Redmond's gun was drawn, and Bernie clutched my marble rolling pin in both her hands, wielding it like a baseball bat.

Sandra cowered on the floor, moaning, holding her left arm over her head to protect herself from the wrath of the woman standing over her. Rose yelled rude English words, brandished her cane, and kicked the gun across the floor. It came to rest under a table.

Bernie dropped the rolling pin, grabbed Rose around the waist with both arms, and dragged her away. Redmond kept her gun and her attention on Sandra as she spoke to Rose. "I believe I told you to take a seat in the garden, Mrs. Campbell, and to leave the matter to me."

"Did you, love?" Rose said. "I must have missed that. I don't hear as well as I used to, you know."

Redmond hid a grin and spoke into her radio, asking for backup and an ambulance.

"I wouldn't have let her do it! I was going to get help," Heather protested as she was frog-marched into the dining room by Simon. He had one hand on her shoulder and was holding one of her arms up behind her.

I heard sirens approaching and turning into the driveway.

"You had them on standby," I said to Redmond.

"Of course. If I didn't think there was *something* to your plan, I wouldn't have come out. We've been talking to our colleagues in Grand Lake, Iowa, and learned some interesting things about Mrs. Sandra McHenry and what happened to anyone who crossed her path."

"Not Heather?"

Redmond glanced at Heather, who'd stopped struggling and was crying quietly in Simon's grip. The detective shook her head.

"Help me up, please," Sandra moaned. Her voice had changed; no longer confident and authoritative, it had turned old, timeworn, timid, quavering with pain and fear. Helpless. "I'm an old lady. You can't leave me lying here. She broke my arm. I'm going to sue."

"Help is on its way," Redmond said. "In the meantime, Sandra McHenry, I am arresting you . . ."

"Come on, Rose," Bernie said when Redmond had finished the warning. "Let's get out of the way. We'll be in the garden if you need us, Detective. Is that okay?"

"Yes. Lily, you can join them. Mr. McCracken, I suspect Ms. French isn't going to try to run. Are you, Heather?"

Heather said nothing.

"But," Redmond said, "just in case, I'd like you to stand with her for a few moments longer until my colleagues can take over."

Bernie, Rose, and I walked out of the tearoom as paramedics and cops rushed past us.

We took seats in the garden and watched the activity. It was getting dark now; the white flowers in the garden glowed in the dusk, and lights were coming on in the guest rooms of the B & B. The wind had picked up, and the teacups hanging from the big old oak tree tinkled merrily. Simon soon joined us.

"Sandra," Bernie said. "I never would have believed it."

I touched my grandmother's hand. "Are you okay, Rose?"

"No," she said. "I am not. My faith in humanity, never mind my own judgment of character, of which I've always been so proud, has been shattered."

"Don't blame yourself," I said. "Judging by that snippet of information Redmond dropped, Sandra has fooled a lot of people."

"Eric never liked her, but he never said why. Eric never said a bad word about anyone." Rose shook her head. She looked every one of her years, and my heart turned over.

The parking area of the tearoom was crowded with emergency vehicles, lights flashing and sirens wailing. Lewis and Julie-Ann McHenry burst through the gate, accompanied by Amanda and Tyler. Brian and Darlene hurried down the driveway behind them. Other B & B guests gathered on the veranda. Matt Goodwill tore across his property heading in our direction.

"What's happening?" Lewis gasped for air. "Have they caught the person who killed Ed?"

"It's not Trisha, then?" Julie-Ann said, with what I thought an unseemly trace of disappointment.

Brian and Darlene arrived, and Matt came next.

"Is my mother here?" Brian said. "She's not in her room. Is she okay? What's happening? Where's Heather?"

"Your mother," Rose said, "has had a . . . minor accident. The medics are tending to her."

He ran to the tearoom, but the uniformed officer posted there blocked his path and wouldn't allow him in despite his protests. Darlene and Lewis joined him. They all shouted at the cop, who stood firm, her legs firmly planted and her hands resting on her belt, and said not a word.

"You guys okay?" Matt took a seat next to Bernie. He studied her face.

She gave him a weak smile. "We're all good."

"What's happening?"

"We caught Ed's killer. I'll tell you later."

Detective Redmond came out of the restaurant and spoke to Brian and Darlene. "Your mother has a broken arm and she'll be taken to the hospital and tended to there."

"A broken arm?" Brian said. "What happened? Did she fall? What does that have to do with you? Why are all these cops here? Why can't I see her?"

Redmond held up a hand to stop the barrage of questions. "First, I have to inform you that Mrs. Sandra McHenry is under arrest for murder and two counts of attempted murder."

Brian laughed. Then he realized no one else was laughing. "What?"

"My goodness," Julie-Ann said.

"That's the most ridiculous thing I've ever heard," Lewis said.

Amanda and Tyler simply looked stunned. Amanda recovered first and pulled out her phone.

"Heather!" Darlene put her hands to her chest. "Where's my daughter?"

"She's also under arrest," Redmond said. "Accessory after the fact and attempted murder."

Darlene's legs gave way and she would have fallen, had not Lewis been standing next to her. He half carried his mother to a garden chair and lowered her gently.

"You can accompany Mrs. McHenry to the hospital," Redmond told Brian. "But no one else."

At that moment, Heather was marched out of the tearoom. Her hands were cuffed behind her back, her head was down, her hair fell over her face, and an officer gripped her arm. Darlene screamed. Heather didn't look at her mother, or anyone else, as she was taken to a patrol car and stuffed into the back.

A car screeched to a halt in a spray of gravel and sand, and Detective Williams leapt out. The tail of his shirt was half out, and the front of the shirt buckled because the buttons had been pushed through the wrong holes. He had on one slip-on black shoe and one brown shoe with untied laces. "What's going on here?" he yelled.

"Heather!" Darlene screamed as her daughter was driven away.

A stretcher was wheeled out of the tearoom. Sandra's right arm was wrapped in a splint and her left wrist handcuffed to the gurney. "Brian!" she yelled. "This is a mistake. It's Rose. Rose did it. She tried to frame me, and she put her idiot granddaughter up to trying to bribe Heather. Get me a lawyer. And not that incompetent moron from Grand Lake, either."

My grandmother put her head in her hands. I draped my arm over her frail shoulders and felt her tiny body heave.

"Bummer," Tyler said.

"Oh, my gosh!" Amanda said into the phone, her words tripping all over themselves in the rush to get out. "They are, like, doing a takedown of my great-grandmother. She's totally going to be on the warpath over this."

"Lewis," Brian said, "follow Heather to the police station and get a lawyer down there as fast as you can. I'll go with your grandmother."

"Where are the car keys?" Lewis said.

"In our room."

We all watched while Sandra, still protesting, still accusing Rose, was loaded into the ambulance. Brian jumped in after her, and Redmond joined him. The ambulance drove away, not bothering with lights and sirens.

"I'm going with you," Darlene said to Lewis after the ambulance had turned onto the highway and disappeared. "I need to lie down. This is all too much. Julie-Ann?"

"You go ahead," Julie-Ann said. "Amanda and Tyler, go with Dad and Grandma."

"But I want to watch," Tyler said. "This is exciting. Do you think GeeGee really did kill Ed?"

"Don't be ridiculous," Darlene said.

"The cops think so," he pointed out.

"Go," Julie-Ann repeated. "And tell your sister to get off the phone."

"Like that ever happens," Tyler said.

I looked over Rose's shoulder at Julie-Ann. Sandra's granddaughter-in-law didn't look shocked. "You have anything to say?"

She shrugged. "I can't say I'm entirely surprised. I always figured Sandra was too fond of getting everything her own way."

"Will you be quiet," Lewis snapped. "That's a terrible thing to say about my grandmother."

Julie-Ann turned on him. Spittle flew as she yelled, "She wanted me to go back to you. 'For the sake of the children,' she said. I told her that wasn't going to happen, and if you were so concerned about the welfare of our children, you might have tried being a responsible husband and father. But Sandra couldn't have that. If I didn't see things her way, your precious grandmother implied that I wouldn't be able to find work anymore."

"We'll talk about this later," Lewis said before he turned and walked away.

"We certainly will!" Julie-Ann called after him.

When Lewis had gone, holding his mother's arm and

being trailed, reluctantly, by his children, Julie-Ann turned to us. "I'm a bookkeeper, and I have my own company. I specialize in small family businesses and local nonprofits. Sandra's on the board of a lot of charities, and if she isn't on the board, she's friends with those who are. She knows a lot of people in our town, and everyone of any importance. A couple of carefully placed rumors and she would have ensured my reputation was ruined. I agreed to come on this stupid vacation to get her to back off, let her think I was considering going back to Lewis, while I shored up my defenses. By the way, any feelings Ed and I had toward each other in the past were long behind us, and the meetings we'd had over the past few months were strictly about business. He was no friend of Sandra's, either, but he thought she was mellowing in her old age and wanted to try to get on. More fool him."

"Why didn't you tell the police this?" I asked. "After Ed died."

"Tell them what? That a sweet old lady who didn't want me to divorce her grandson asked me to make one more attempt at saving my marriage by coming on an all-expenses-paid vacation, so she must be a murderer? I knew she and Ed didn't get on, but if Sandra killed everyone she considered her enemy, the population of Grand Lake would be depleted considerably. Even after Ed died, I didn't see any reason for Sandra to have killed him. Why'd she do it, anyway?"

I glanced at the police officer guarding the door. Williams had gone inside. I remembered that Julie-Ann had been quite happy to accuse Trisha of killing Ed. There was more than one poison-tongued person in their family. "I don't know. We'll have to wait to find out."

"I'm assuming our family farewell dinner isn't going to happen. I can only hope Heather made the new flight bookings before she was hauled off to the pokey." Julie-Ann walked away.

"Happy families," Bernie said. "Not. Rose, why don't I walk you to the house? You also need to lie down."

"What I need is a gin and tonic, and heavy on the gin. I'll have to take your arm, young man," she said to Matt, "as my cane has been confiscated as police evidence. I do hope I get it back. I like that one."

Matt stood up and graciously extended his arm. Rose slipped hers through it. "Are you coming, love?" she said to me.

"Not yet. Once again, I feel compelled to sit here and watch the police rifle through my place. Good thing nothing happened in the kitchen. Maybe this time, they'll stay out of my baking."

"I wouldn't count on that," Simon said as Detective Williams came out of the tearoom, munching on a strawberry tart.

Chapter 23

The others returned to the house, but I stayed in the tea-room garden with Simon sitting quietly at my side until the police had finished what they had to do and left. The few curious guests had drifted back to their rooms long ago. Redmond phoned me, saying she'd be around in the morning to take Rose and my statements. Something else had been bothering me, and I told her about it. She said she'd see what she could do.

Simon and I walked to the house together. Darkness had fallen, but a full moon hung in the sky, lighting our way. He took my hand in his and I left it there, glad of its warm strength. We found Bernie and Matt in rocking chairs on the veranda, the chairs pulled close together, a bottle of red wine on the table in front of them. "Where's Rose?" I asked.

"She went to her room," Bernie said. "I suggested she sit with us and have a drink, but she wants to be alone."

"I'll go check on her."

"Perhaps better not to. I offered to sit with her, but she said no. She's pretty shook up. More, I think, at her misjudging Sandra so badly than at what happened."

"Sounds like a lot of people misjudged Sandra," Matt said.

Bernie had her phone open on her lap. She typed a line and pressed a button and closed it.

"What are you doing?" I asked.

"Matt's helping me with the plot points of the book I'm stuck on." Bernie gave him a big grin. "Isn't that nice of him?"

He looked up and gave me a wink.

Bernie slipped the phone into her pocket. "When did you first realize—"

"Not now," I said. "I'm beat and I'm also shook up and I need to process this."

"Can I pour you a drink?" Matt asked. "Simon?"

"No, thanks," I said.

"I'll walk you home." Simon came with me to my door. I let Éclair out, and while she snuffled under bushes in search of squirrels, we stood on the porch, watching the movement of the sea and listening to the sound of waves lapping at the shore and the whispers of the wind in the trees.

I took a deep breath and felt the clean, salty air fill my lungs. "Thank you. I'm okay now. You should probably come to the kitchen first thing tomorrow. Redmond will want to talk to you, too."

"Good night, Lily," he said.

"Good night."

He kissed me on my cheek. He smelled of good Cape Cod earth.

He turned and walked away, and I called to Éclair.

"Poisonous families." Rose shook her head. "No good comes of grievances allowed to fester. Perhaps I'll give your mother a call, love. It's been a while since we had a nice chat."

I touched her shoulder. "Why don't you do that? Maybe invite her down for a few days. She can have my room. I'll sleep on the couch."

We were gathered in the kitchen of Victoria-on-Sea the morning after the drama in the tearoom. To my surprise, Rose had arrived before me. She was unable to sleep, she'd said.

"Sandra killed Ed," Bernie said. "I still have trouble believing it. That old lady."

"We old ladies can be more competent than you young people realize," Rose said. She'd dressed in her usual colors and had applied her makeup with her normal heavy hand. She looked, I thought, perfectly chipper. Nothing like that English stiff upper lip.

"Fear not, Rose," Bernie replied. "I'm well aware that you can do anything you put your mind to."

About the last thing I felt like doing this morning was making breakfasts. But if there's one job that has to be done regardless of what mood one is in, it's feeding people. The McHenry family I'd gladly see starve, but we did have other guests. "You didn't leave a note telling me how many people we have for breakfast, Rose," I said.

"I scarcely know, love. The house is full, but if the McHenry family show their faces, I'll be surprised. Other than Julie-Ann and the children, that is. Do what you think best."

I took down the mixing bowls.

Redmond had texted me at six to say she'd be around to take our statements at nine o'clock. I thought it considerate of her to wait until I finished with the breakfasts.

She must have texted the others, too, as minutes after I'd unlocked the kitchen door, first Simon and then Bernie came in. Matt wasn't far behind.

Even Edna arrived at work early. "Frank got a call as

we were finishing up dinner. He was out the door while still hopping on one foot putting on his socks. More excitement at Tea by the Sea."

"Never a dull moment," I said. "Unfortunately. Since you're all here, you might as well work. Simon, make the muffins. I have apple cinnamon planned for today. Matt, fruit salad. Bananas are on the table and you'll find everything else in the fridge. Bernie, start on the tomatoes and mushrooms. Rose—"

"Why don't I make the tea?" Rose said.

"Excellent idea," Edna said. "Okay, fill me in. Sandra McHenry and Heather French have been arrested. That's a shocker."

"Sandra killed Ed French," I said.

"Allegedly," Matt said from the depths of the fridge.

"Not according to me. Sandra killed Ed because Ed wanted money from Heather, and Heather planned to give it to him."

"That makes no sense," Edna said. "Why didn't Heather just say no to Ed and tell Sandra to mind her own business?"

"Heather didn't say no," I said, "because she and Ed had come to an agreement. She had a lawyer draw up a contact to settle the dispute. From what I saw last night, Heather's totally dominated by Sandra, and Sandra didn't trust Ed not to keep demanding more money."

"Sandra," Rose said, "considered everything that went on in her family to be her business. I failed to realize to what extremes she could go."

"She fooled us all," I said. "Me, most of all, with the feeble-old-lady bit. I should have realized, knowing you, Rose, what elderly women are capable of."

Rose sniffed. "I hope you're not suggesting that if anyone else around here is murdered, I'm a good suspect."

"There will be no more murders around here," I said. "And that's that. When Ed and Trisha arrived, Heather told her father she'd invited them. But later, she told me it was Sandra's idea, although Sandra said at one point she wished Heather hadn't invited Ed. I thought nothing of it, but I should have. Sandra had orchestrated the whole thing. She knew they'd be here, therefore malice afore-thought was involved."

"What about the foxglove?" Simon asked.

"More feeble-old-lady distraction. Who would have thought Sandra would creep out of the house in the night and nip around to Linda Sheenan's place to steal plants? Yet, that's what she did. I suspect she slipped Heather's car keys out of her bag. Heather might have known she took them, or she might not. She pretended not to notice a lot of things when it came to her grandmother. Sandra had invited Ed and Trisha here with the intention of killing Ed and would have been on the lookout for something she could use that wouldn't cast suspicion onto her. Linda's foxglove garden is visible from the road, and the McHenrys were out and about quite a bit. If she hadn't seen the foxglove, I've no doubt she was resourceful enough to come up with another idea. She would have wanted to kill him well away from Grand Lake, where people who know the history of the McHenry and French families might have asked questions."

"And getting the foxglove into his tea?" Bernie said. "She couldn't have known Tyler would steal Simon's bike and cause a distraction."

"No, but she probably had the foxglove on her, waiting for the right time to use it. She probably planned to slip the stuff into the bag Trisha kept in her purse when the opportunity presented itself."

"Throwing suspicion onto Trisha? Why would she do that?"

"Sandra didn't have anything against Trisha, but she wouldn't have much cared if Trisha went to prison for the crime."

Bernie shuddered. "Did anyone else just feel a cold breeze blow through here?"

"Rose is making tea," Edna said. "Must be hell freezing over."

"You can't get good help in the Colonies these days." Rose poured boiling water into a sturdy brown teapot.

"I'm starting to get an idea for my next book," Matt said.

"Everything I'm telling you is nothing but guesses and conjecture on my part," I said. "You'll have to talk to Detective Redmond for details you can use in a book."

"And wait for it all to wend its way through the courts. I've waited longer for material before. Maybe this won't work as a book on its own, but part of something larger. I wonder if there's much of a history of elderly people being murderers. Do you know, Rose?"

Rose carried the teapot to the table and sat down. Simon stirred batter, and Matt and Bernie continued chopping. Edna seemed to be enjoying having help and had made no move to start carrying things into the dining room. Éclair ran from one person to the other, tail wagging, tongue drooling, ears up, happy to have company this morning. Robbie perched on a shelf, not happy to have company this morning. I placed sausages in the hot frying pans.

"Everyone, so they say, is capable of murder if the conditions are right," Rose said. "What's stopping people of a certain age isn't motivation, but physical ability. Then again, some of us have learned to get over it, as the young people say."

"And that," I said, "is why no one even thought to suspect Sandra. When everyone else was in the garden fussing over Tyler and Simon's motorcycle—"

"Me, most of all," Simon muttered.

"Rose and Sandra went inside. You told me the ladies' room was occupied, so you used the men's while Sandra stood guard."

"The ladies' room was occupied while everyone was supposedly outside?" Bernie said. "Why didn't I know that? You didn't think to ask who might have been in there? That person might have been the killer, hiding until the coast was clear."

"Oh," I said. "You're right. I never thought . . ."

"Some detective you are, Lily Roberts."

"Except that Lily did solve it." Simon poured batter into the muffin tins.

"Except for that," Bernie admitted.

"While Rose was otherwise occupied, and no one was watching her, all Sandra had to do was nip across the room and dump foxglove into Ed's teapot. Put the lid back on the pot and be once again standing at the men's-room door, all innocent and smiling, when Rose emerged. A matter of seconds."

"For someone who could move quickly," Matt said.

"When she wanted to," I said.

"Did Heather know what Sandra was planning?" Matt asked. "Or what she'd done after the fact?"

"I don't know. Judging by the bit of conversation the two of them had when . . . when Sandra was about to kill me, she didn't have a lot of respect for Heather."

"Heather fixed the brakes. Not Sandra," Simon pointed out.

"Sandra might be spryer than she put on, but she is eighty years old. She's not capable of crawling around on the floor of the garage or doing detailed work in the near dark. It's highly unlikely she knows anything about cars, anyway. But Heather does."

"Sandra probably told Heather it was a prank. Or a way of putting a fright into Lily and me to stop us asking questions. Remember," Bernie said to Rose, "no one knew you'd be coming with us that morning."

"If that's supposed to console me about the actions of my friend"—Rose sipped her tea—"it does not."

"Hello!" a voice called from the dining room. "Anyone here?"

Edna picked up her tray. "And it's off to work we go."

I returned my attention to the stove and flipped the sausages.

"I'm thinking of bringing Rose's grandmother into my book," Bernie said to Matt. "She can be the brains behind the detective agency, thinking it all through back at the office while the two younger women follow her instructions. What do you think?"

Most of what I surmised, Amy Redmond told me, was right. Probably right, anyway.

Allegedly.

We met in the drawing room over coffee and apple and cinnamon muffins. I gave her my statement, going over what I'd guessed (incorrectly) and what I'd tried to accomplish (and would have failed at, if not for Rose and her cane). Before calling in the others, Redmond filled me in on what was happening down at the police station.

Sandra remained tight-lipped, demanding she be treated in a way that respected the dignity of her years. Heather, on the other hand, was talking. Crying mostly, but talking despite her lawyer's advice. Unfortunately, Heather didn't have a lot to say. Sandra had been furious when Heather told her she wanted to come to an agreement with Ed and pay him some of what he claimed he deserved—just to get him to go away.

"It seems, from what I can gather, that Sandra has Heather firmly under her thumb. Much of the estrangement between Heather and her parents and her brother comes from Sandra's meddling. Basically, she likes pitting one party against another and leaning back to enjoy the fallout. It appears to be her modus operandi on the boards she's been on in Grand Lake. Not many people in that town think well of her, but most of them have been afraid to say so. She has a long reach and she doesn't forget an injury."

"I'm surprised she took my grandmother in. Rose is pretty sharp."

Redmond gave me a soft smile. "I suspect Rose simply didn't have anything Sandra wanted. Except friendship. I'd guess Rose isn't a woman who listens to gossip."

"No, she doesn't. She prefers to make her own judgments about people. Finding out what Sandra is really like . . . Well, that's hard on her."

"Other than Julie-Ann, who did have occasional business transactions with Ed French, the McHenrys haven't had anything to do with Ed or Trisha for years. Which seems to be the way everyone wanted it. But Sandra kept tabs on Ed and Trisha, the way she kept tabs on everyone. I called the health food store in Grand Lake this morning."

"Why would you do that?"

"It's a small store in a small town. The clerk is friends with Darlene McHenry. She confirmed that she told Darlene about the special tea Trisha was buying for Ed. Just local gossip, she thought nothing of it. Trisha told the clerk Ed was trying to be more conscious of looking after his health."

"And Darlene told Sandra."

"Yup. Sandra might have been planning to get rid of him for some time, but the opportunity never presented itself. Ed seems to have been fairly patient about waiting to get his share of his brother's money. There is, by the way, nothing we can find that indicates he threatened Heather in any way. He sent her a few emails over the last six months, asking if they could get over old grievances and talk, and to remember they'd both loved Norman. Three weeks ago, Heather replied that she was talking to her financial advisor and she'd have something for him soon. Sandra must have realized time was running out, but she wouldn't have wanted to do anything to Ed in Grand Lake, where everyone knows everyone else's business and the police hear the local gossip. What better than a nice family vacation at a neutral B and B on Cape Cod?"

"I remembered something when I was making the breakfasts this morning. Believe it or not, I think Sandra made one last attempt at warning Ed off."

"When?"

"I heard people arguing late one night when I was walking Éclair. I didn't see the people or recognize the voices or hear much of what was said, but a man told the other person to stay out of it whatever it was, and then called the other person an interfering busybody. It's not proof positive, but busybody is usually an insult aimed at women, and older women at that."

"Irrelevant," Redmond said, "if she killed him. And I believe, thanks to you, we have enough proof to get a conviction."

"And Heather?"

"Heather fixed the brakes on your grandmother's car at her grandmother's suggestion. She continues to insist it was a lark, because she was bored and misses fiddling around with cars, and, besides, she thought you wouldn't get any farther than the end of the driveway. Which doesn't matter in court, because you would have been killed if you'd gone over that bluff, and that counts as attempted murder in my book. You might be interested to know that the idea of sending Trisha and your rebooked guests to the Blue Water Bay Resort was Sandra's, not Heather's. Heather wanted to move to what she calls a proper hotel, with a pool and room service, but Sandra insisted they remain here. Not because it's so nice, I hate to tell you, but to keep an eye on you and Rose. I intend to argue before a judge that because Sandra ordered Heather to disable your car, Heather must have known Sandra had killed Ed. Accessory after the fact."

From the hall came the sound of suitcases clattering down the stairs and people yelling at each other. The McHenry family was checking out. As predicted, only Amanda, Tyler, and Julie-Ann had dared to show their faces in the breakfast room.

I let out a long sigh. "So that's that. Can I go back to work now?"

"You can," Redmond said.

I stood up. "Where's Detective Williams this morning? I'd have thought he'd be eager to hear the whole story, if only to relate to the press conference later."

"Chuck's on his way to New York City. Send Bernadette in next, please."

Chapter 24

A week after the near-fatal showdown in the tearoom, I was taking the last batch of scones out of the oven. Marybeth and Cheryl had gone home, ready to collapse at the end of a busy day. Summer on Cape Cod was in full swing. Every room in the B & B was booked for the next three weeks, and the reservations book at Tea by the Sea overflowed.

A light knock sounded on the back door, and Simon came in. "Smells nice in here."

"You say that every time."

"Because it smells nice in here every time."

I pulled off my hairnet and shook out my hair. "You look very presentable this evening. Going someplace special?" Simon had changed out of his overalls into jeans and a clean blue shirt, scrubbed the dirt off his hands and rinsed it out of his hair.

"I am," he said. "And so are you."

"I am? Where am I going?"

"Wash up and I'll take you."

"This sounds very mysterious.: I washed my hands and

splashed cold water on my face, while Simon put the fresh scones in containers.

I checked the ovens were off, switched off the lights, and locked the door behind us.

"I might have guessed we're going for a motorcycle ride," I said, "but I don't see your bike and you're not wearing your leathers."

He took my hand and we walked up the driveway. Instead of going straight, toward Victoria-on-Sea, we crossed onto Matt Goodwill's property.

"That's Bernie's car next to Matt's," I said. "And one I don't recognize. What's going on?"

"Matt's having a party. A select number of guests, and one very special guest."

"What's the occasion?"

"You'll see."

From a distance, Matt's house looks like any other grand old Cape Cod mansion, although one surrounded by tough weeds and wild grasses. Only when you approach can you see the potholes in the driveway, the rot in the porch pillars, the crumbling gingerbread trim, the holes in the roof, and the loose floorboards of the porch. I hadn't been inside, but I couldn't imagine it was much nicer there.

We didn't go inside. Simon led me around the side of the house. Plywood was nailed over ground-floor windows, and weeds struggled for purchase in the cracks in the walls.

"Matt does have his work cut out for him," I said.

"He does."

We rounded the house. The view from the back was the same as from behind Victoria-on-Sea: Cape Cod Bay spread out in all its glory.

What had once been a fishpond overlooking the bay was now a puddle of slimy green rainwater. The French doors at the center of the house opened onto an enormous patio, now more cracks than concrete, but the patio had been swept and the glass table on it was sparkling clean, as were the six wicker chairs covered with bright blue and yellow cushions. The table was laid with platters of food, cocktail plates and napkins, and crystal flutes. A bottle of prosecco rested in a silver bucket, and a glass pitcher contained slices of lemon and lime in ice water.

Éclair rushed across the lawn toward us, ears flying, barking greetings. I bent over to give her a pat.

Matt, Bernie, Rose, and Amy Redmond sat at the table. Matt stood up when he saw Simon and me. "Good. You got her. I was afraid we'd have to send out a kidnapping expedition."

"What on earth is going on?" I asked. "Bernie?"

She grinned at me. Bernie was wearing her tea dress, complete with pearls and gloves. Rose also wore a dress, blue with swirls of yellow, and Matt had on, of all things, a suit and tie. Redmond had her usual dark slacks and leather jacket, but the jacket was thrown over the back of her chair and she'd rolled up the sleeves of her white shirt.

"Please," Matt said. "Have a seat."

I sat. Simon took the chair next to me, and Éclair curled up between us. Bernie passed around plates and napkins. A giant silver bowl overflowed with potato chips, a matching dish contained dip. Slices of store-bought flatbreads were on marble platters, next to glass bowls of olives and nuts.

"I wanted to have a proper tea party," Matt said. "But Tea by the Sea doesn't cater. And as I don't bake . . ."

"This all looks great," I said. "But I still don't get the occasion."

Matt lifted the jug, poured water into the glasses, and passed them around. I glanced at Simon. Surely, the flutes were for the wine, not water? I sniffed at mine. Just ordinary water.

"Originally," Matt said, "this was going to be a . . . ahem . . . private party." He glanced at Bernie. "But she wanted to invite you, Simon, and Rose."

"Inspector Redmond paid a call on me earlier," Rose said. "With news. As I knew you'd all be interested, I suggested she join us this evening."

"But first," Matt said, "a toast." He drank his water until the glass was empty. Bernie did the same. Rose, Simon, and Amy Redmond sipped at theirs and looked confused. Matt crossed the patio to the back door. He flicked a switch on the wall and the lights overhead came on.

Simon laughed. "I get it. Congratulations, mate! I'll drink to that." And he did so.

"To what are we drinking?" Redmond asked.

"The fresh, clean water you are enjoying came straight from the tap in the kitchen. And the light you are now basking in is real electricity—provided by the good people of the electricity company."

Rose clapped.

"No more lugging in cases of water. No more trying to hammer nails by flashlight or using a hand-operated drill. Empty your glasses, everyone, and we'll have a toast with the real stuff to my progress on this house." He lifted the bottle out of the cooler with a flourish. We all cheered.

When we had refilled glasses in hand, Rose said, "Your turn, Inspector Redmond."

"Detective," Amy Redmond muttered.

"She knows that perfectly well," I said.

Redmond looked around the table, waiting until she had everyone's attention. That didn't take long. Even Éclair sat up. "Sandra McHenry has been charged with the murder of Norman French."

"Wow," Bernie said, "I didn't see that one coming. You don't look all that surprised, Lily."

"I can't say I am. If Sandra was prepared to kill Ed French because he wanted a small amount—comparatively—of money from Heather now, how far would Sandra have gone to stop him from getting a full half of the sixty-five million he thought he was entitled to?"

"Lily mentioned that to me," Redmond said, "And I . . . that is, Detective Williams and I thought it worth following up."

"Norman French had to die," I said, "as Sandra saw it, because he was going to share his good fortune with his brother. You told me, Rose, Sandra was in New York when Norman died. I started wondering if that was a coincidence."

"You were right about the killer, Lily," Redmond said. "But wrong about the motive. If Sandra wanted to ensure Ed didn't get a share, she would have tried to kill Ed."

"As she did here," Matt said.

"Precisely. No, Norman had to die, as far as Sandra was concerned, because Norman was going to divorce Heather."

"Really?"

"Really. Heather swears she didn't know Sandra killed Norman, but I don't believe her. Heather grew up close to her grandmother, and she would have known Sandra was ruthless in getting her own way, if perhaps not sure of the ends to which she was prepared to go. Heather must have had her suspicions, but she insists she and Norman would have worked out their difficulties despite the fact that Norman was in the process of moving out of the marital home and moving in with a twenty-year-old receptionist he met at his new offices."

"The swine," I said.

"The NYPD was never entirely satisfied that Norman's death had been an accident. The cabbie who hit him said

Norman stumbled onto the roadway with enough speed to indicate he'd been pushed. But it was a crowded intersection at midday, and accidents happen. When they found out about the separation, the detectives looked into Heather, but she had a good alibi. She was at the spa, and the spa attendants remembered her. Norman's new girlfriend was at work. They checked into some of his business partners, but nothing threw up a red flag. His brother, with whom he'd had a falling-out over the sale of the company, was at his office in Iowa."

"No one thought to ask where Sandra had been?" Bernie asked.

Redmond lifted her glass to Rose. "The widow's grandmother? Of course not."

"I went to that funeral," Rose said. "Sandra wept copiously, as I recall. She also kept a firm hand on Heather's arm the entire time. I thought she was supporting her in her overwhelming grief."

"She was warning Heather," I said, "not to say a word. And Heather never did. What a burden to live with."

"Don't feel sorry for Heather," Bernie said. "She was happy to carry on enjoying Norman's money, never mind what it had cost. I don't see that she devoted the rest of her life to charitable works out of a sense of guilt. Hey! I've just realized something. I didn't like Heather the moment I first laid eyes on her, but you, Lily, told me to cut her some slack. The poor widowed thing. Ha!"

There'd be no living with Bernie now. I helped myself to a giant handful of potato chips.

"While I was ripping up floorboards and hanging drywall," Matt said, "I started some preliminary outlining on the idea I had for a new book. I'm seriously wondering if there are many other cases of the extreme elderly as killers. When, and if, the French/McHenry case is public record, I might include that, but right now, I'm doing some preliminary research. Anything you want to share with me, Detective?"

Redmond lifted her glass. "Good wine, this."

" 'Extreme elderly,' indeed," Rose sniffed. "I'll have you know, young man, that Sandra's younger than I am. I don't have one foot in the grave yet."

"I'll drink to that," I said.

Recipes

Chocolate Chip Cookies

You don't normally find chocolate chip cookies as part of the afternoon tea sweets selection, but Lily makes these for the children's tea. This recipe makes a very soft and chewy cookie.

Makes approx. 12 large cookies. The recipe can easily be doubled if you need more.

Ingredients
8 Tbsp salted butter
½ cup white sugar
¼ cup packed light brown sugar
1 tsp vanilla
1 egg
1½ cups all-purpose flour
½ tsp baking soda
¼ tsp salt
¾ cup chocolate chips

Instructions
1. Preheat oven to 350 F. Microwave butter until just barely melted. Should be almost entirely liquid.
2. Using stand mixer or electric beater, beat butter with white and brown sugars until creamy. Add vanilla and the egg; beat on low until incorporated, 10–15

seconds (if you beat the egg too long, the cookies will be stiff).

3. Add the flour, baking soda, and salt. Mix until crumbles form. Use your hands to press the crumbles together into a dough. It should form one large ball that is easy to handle (right at the stage between "wet" dough and "dry" dough). Add the chocolate chips and incorporate with your hands.

4. Roll the dough into 12 large balls (or 9 for HUGE cookies) and place on a cookie sheet. Bake for 9–11 minutes until the cookies look puffy and dry and just barely golden. (DON'T OVERBAKE: This is essential for keeping the cookies soft. Take them out even if they look like they're not done yet. They'll be pale and puffy.

5. Let them cool on the pan for a good 30 minutes or so. They will sink down and turn into dense, buttery, soft cookies. They will stay soft for several days if kept in an airtight container.

Shortbread Cookies

Nothing goes better with a cup of tea than a slice of buttery shortbread, and they're quick and easy to make, so Lily makes a lot of these at Tea by the Sea.

This makes about 60 cookies, depending on the size. The recipe can be halved if you don't want so many.

Ingredients
1½ pounds unsalted butter, room temperature
2¼ cups icing sugar
1½ cups cornstarch
¼ tsp salt
4½ cups all-purpose flour

Instructions
1. Preheat oven to 275 F. Prepare cookie sheets (Lily uses silicone liners).

2. Cream butter and sugar in electric mixer.

3. Combine cornstarch, salt, and flour together in medium bowl.

4. Knead flour mixture into butter mixture.

5. Roll out dough ¼ inch thick and cut with cookie cutters or by hand.

6. Place on cookie sheets and bake for 35–45 minutes until cookies are pale gold on the bottom.

Curried Egg Salad Sandwiches

Makes 4 full-sized sandwiches.

Ingredients
8 hard-boiled eggs
1/3 cup light mayonnaise
1 tsp Dijon mustard
1/2 tsp mild curry paste
1/4 tsp pepper
1 pinch salt
8 slices white sandwich bread, crusts removed

Instructions
In bowl, finely chop eggs. Mix in mayonnaise, mustard, curry paste, pepper, and salt.

Spread on lightly buttered bread, top with another slice of bread, and cut into triangle shapes.

Read on for a special preview of the next
Tea by the Sea mystery . . .

MURDER SPILLS THE TEA

Lily Roberts pores over the clues in a piping-hot new case when a confrontational celebrity chef is murdered at her Cape Cod tearoom during the filming of a popular baking show in the latest Tea by the Sea mystery from national bestselling author Vicki Delany . . .

The country's hottest TV cooking show is coming to Cape Cod. And against her better judgment, Lily Roberts is entering *America Bakes!* with her charming tearoom, Tea by the Sea! Filming is already proving disruptive, closing the tearoom during Lily's busiest season. But tensions really bubble over when infamous bad-boy chef and celebrity judge Tommy Greene loses his temper with Lily's staff, resulting in an on-camera blowout with Cheryl Wainwright. Just as Lily thinks the competition can't get more bitter, Tommy is found dead in Tea by the Sea's kitchen . . . murdered with Cheryl's rolling pin.

Suspicion immediately falls on Cheryl, but the temperamental star has racked up plenty of culinary clashes in the past, both on- and off-screen. And nearly anyone associated with Tommy or the show could be the killer, be it one of Lily's fierce competitors, a member of the beleaguered film crew, or even one of Tommy's fellow judges—struggling cookbook maven Claudia D'Angelo or beauty contest winner Scarlet McIntosh. Now, while she's baking up a storm for the show, Lily must also whip up an impromptu investigation . . . before the murderer rolls someone else away.

*Available in August 2022 from
Kensington Publishing Corp.*

Chapter 1

I'm a baker, not a TV personality. This wasn't my idea, and my doubts were growing steadily as the day got underway.

"Sit still," the woman growled as she dabbed muck on my face.

"Is this going to take much longer?" I asked.

"It'll take as long as it takes." She took a step backward, tilted her head to one side, furrowed her brow and narrowed her eyes as she studied me. I tried to smile. It wasn't easy. "You'll do," she begrudgingly admitted. "At least you have camera-friendly hair."

"Thanks," I said. "I think."

I eyed myself in the mirror. I'd never seen so much make-up in my life, never mind worn it. Thick black lines were drawn around my eyes, my lashes were caked with mascara, dark pink blush outlined my cheekbones, and my lips were a slash of crimson. My naturally blond "camera-friendly" hair cascaded around my shoulders in soft waves.

"You do know this isn't at all what I look like at work," I said.

The makeup artist began packing up her pots and brushes. "That's what they all say. I'll say, as I say to them all, if you want to be on TV you have to look the part."

"That's the point," I said to my reflection in the mirror. "I don't want to be on TV."

"They all say that too."

A rap sounded on the trailer door, a voice called, "Knock knock?" and the door flew open as Bernadette Murphy came in without waiting for an answer. She stopped in her tracks when she saw me. "Oh my gosh, Lily Roberts. Is that really you?"

"No," I said.

The makeup artist chuckled.

"Can you do me?" Bernie asked her.

"Not on my schedule. But I'd love nothing more than to get my hands on that hair."

Bernie tossed her head and her curly red locks bounced.

"Off you go, and"—the woman glared at me—"don't you dare rub your eyes, kiss anyone, or have anything to eat or drink."

I stood up and gave her a salute. "Yes, ma'am. An important part of my job is tasting what I'm making, but I'll do my best. Do you have a name?"

The edges of her mouth turned up, just a fraction. "Thank you for asking. I'm Melanie Ferguson." She was in her early sixties, tall and thin, with a heavily-lined face and tired eyes that said she'd seen it all.

"How long have you been doing makeup, Melanie?" Bernie asked.

"Longer than you've been alive, honey. Probably longer than your mothers have been alive. Now get out of here. Because you've been polite and not demanding, I'll give you a tip, Lily. Josh Henshaw's not a bad boss, as directors go, but he expects punctuality above all else, and I've known him to fire crew for showing up five minutes late."

"Thanks," I said. "But I don't work for Mr. Henshaw."

"Far as he's concerned, this week you do." She lowered her voice. "Josh was a big-time director, once. Now he's doing reality TV. Hard on the ego, and we all know how some men react when their ego's hurt."

"I've worked in Michelin-starred restaurants," I said. "I can hold my own against men's inflated egos. Women's too."

"Glad to hear it. Watch out for Reilly, the assistant director, too. He's on his way up the career ladder and that lot can be worse than the old guys on the way down. Here's another tip for nothing. Tomorrow, don't wear red."

"I like red."

"Too harsh under the bright lights for that pale complexion. Now, run along and have fun."

"That's not going to happen," I grumbled.

Bernie linked her arm through mine. "Always the optimist."

We left the makeup trailer and stepped into the parking lot of my restaurant, Tea by the Sea. Although, if I hadn't been aware of what was going on, I never would have recognized my place.

Trailers and equipment vans lined the long driveway, and on the lawn and the patio thick black cables crossed all over themselves. Shouting men rolled cameras and sound equipment through the gate. As I watched, one of them hit his head on a broken teacup swinging from a colorful ribbon tied to a branch of the ancient oak in the center of the tearoom patio. He rubbed his head with a muffled curse.

The patio was full, more than full, with TV people as well as guests here to enjoy afternoon tea at ten in the morning. It was a beautiful Cape Cod summer day, clear skies overhead, the blue waters of Cape Cod Bay sparkling in the background, a light breeze ruffling women's hair and causing the teacups hanging from the single tree in the center of the patio to tinkle cheerfully.

My friends and my grandmother's gardener had gone to a great deal of trouble to spruce up the space and it looked great. Moss in varying shades of green and tiny blue and white flowers peeked from between cracks in the weathered stone of the half-wall surrounding the patio and the flagstones that make up the floor. They'd refreshed the colored ribbons in the old oak from which hung a variety of teacups, repurposed when they got damaged. The flowers in the terracotta and stone flowerpots edging the patio had been deadheaded and trimmed and replanted if needed.

The people gathered here this morning either eyed the TV people with excitement, or pretended not to notice them. Each table had been set with fine china, pressed linens, and silverware, and a tiny vase of flowers selected personally from our own garden by Simon McCracken, the gardener at my grandmother's B&B, Victoria-on-Sea. Everything looked fabulous but at the same time strange, I thought, as not one person had a cup of tea or a plate of my baking in front of them.

My maternal grandmother, Rose Campbell, had taken a seat at a table for four. She saw us coming and lifted her hand in a wave. I grimaced in return. When Rose arrived at the beginning of the day to take her place, the assistant director told her to go home and change. He didn't want extras dressing up for the camera, he said.

Rose genuinely didn't know what the man was talking about. Her attire today—flowing black pants with a print of huge yellow sunflowers, purple T-shirt, red scarf, sparkly pink sneakers—was nothing more than her usual informal attire. As was also usual, she'd applied a heavy coat of blue shadow to her eyelids, dark red lipstick to her lips, and two slashes of blush to her cheeks. Her short gray hair stood straight up in a series of spikes. My grandmother is a woman who likes color. I wondered if she and I would look even more alike than usual today considering that I was now almost as made-up as she. If you didn't know better, you'd think the bride in my grandmother's wedding photo, the one sitting in pride of place on her dressing table, was me dressed in old-fashioned clothes.

"You there! Blondie. Yes, you." A man broke away from a cluster of people and waved at me. "We haven't got all day here, come on."

"Actually," Bernie muttered, "I think they do have all day. I'll go and join the peasantry. Enjoy your time in the limelight."

I growled at my best friend.

"You know you're loving it," Bernie said as she skipped off. The man sitting at Rose's table politely got to his feet as she approached. Rose had invited Matt Goodwill, our closest neighbor, to join them. I thought the TV people would be pleased about that. Not many handsome young men go to afternoon tea. Simon, our gardener, had also been invited to participate, and he'd flatly refused.

I was not enjoying my time in the limelight. Not one little bit. I hadn't expected to. But Bernie can be very persuasive when she wants to be; combined with Rose they're an unstoppable force.

I went to join Josh Henshaw, director. I hadn't met three of the four people with him, but I knew who they were. The older woman was Claudia D'Angelo, legend of the New York City baking world. The man was Tommy Greene, famously temperamental English chef and star of many a TV cooking show. The younger woman was Scarlet McIntosh, who didn't seem to do much in life other than be on TV. I'd met Josh's assistant director, Reilly Miller, several times as the plans for this event came together.

Rain was expected to move in later in the week, so the decision had been made to film outside today, and move inside the restaurant later if necessary.

"Good morning, Lily. Are you excited?" Reilly asked me as I approached the group.

"You could say that," I said.

Reilly introduced me to everyone. I gushed over Claudia D'Angelo and told her, truthfully, she was a hero to me. She smiled and thanked me. Tommy Greene gave me a wink and said, in his working-class English accent, that he was looking forward to what I had to make for him. He was in his early fifties and not a good-looking man by any means, but there was a certain presence about him. He was around my height, five foot eight-ish, thin to the point of scrawny, with a prominent nose, too large and too white teeth, thin lips, and pale blue eyes. His hair was an unnatural shade of yellow, except for the section at the front, the tips dyed a solid black, which stood straight up to frame his bony face. Scarlet smothered a yawn as she limply put her hand in mine and said, "Delighted, I'm sure." I got the feeling she expected me to be delighted, not her. She looked exactly as you'd expect a former beauty queen to look: tall and far too thin, except for the augmented breasts, with dyed blond hair tumbling halfway down her back in sleek waves, sharp cheekbones, plump lips, wide brown eyes, and red fingernails resembling talons. In contrast Claudia, who I knew to be sixty-five, was considerably shorter than me, slim and elegant. Her thick black hair was heavily streaked with gray and styled in a chic chignon, her makeup subtle, the nails on her manicured hands clipped short and painted a light pink.

Her olive skin was good, but the fine lines around her eyes and mouth were showing. She was, I thought, the sort of woman content to age naturally.

Formalities over, Josh turned to face the onlookers. "Okay everyone. First, thank you for coming today. Filming out of doors can be tricky, what with weather and all, but this garden is so lovely, we want to feature it on the show."

I glanced at the assembled guests. Edna Hartwell, who helped in the B&B with the breakfasts, was here, accompanied by her husband, Frank, editor-in-chief of the *North Augusta Times*. I recognized Susan Powers, mayor of North Augusta, sitting with her husband, Gary, a smattering of town councilors along with some of our neighbors, B&B guests, and tearoom customers who'd called to make a reservation for their afternoon tea and been told what would be happening today. We hadn't served breakfast at Victoria-on-Sea today because the breakfast chef, aka me, was otherwise occupied, so Rose had offered guests either vouchers for a restaurant in town or a chance to be on TV and enjoy a full afternoon tea, albeit at ten in the morning. To no one's surprise, every one of them had joined us.

My assistants, Cheryl and Marybeth, both of whom had been given a pared-down version of the full makeup and hair experience, fidgeted in the doorway. Cheryl wiped her hands on her apron, looking as though she wanted to flee. As for Marybeth, I hoped she'd be able to control that manic grin. They both wore their regular work clothes of white blouse with lace collar, black knee-length skirt, and a bibbed apron featuring the name of Tea by the Sea. Earlier Cheryl had asked me if her earrings were okay: silver with a stream of sparkling red stones. "One of my grandchildren gave these to me for my last birthday. She said they were good luck earrings, and she'll get a kick out of seeing them on TV." I'd told her the earrings were fine with me.

"All I need from you," Josh continued speaking to the guests, "is to act naturally. Can you do that?"

No one said anything.

"Can you do that?" Josh yelled.

The guests yelled back, "Yes!"

"Okay then. The servers will bring out your food and you'll eat it. Servings will be paced so the judges have time to visit each table to ask how you're enjoying it. Remember to be totally honest, and try to avoid grandstanding or lecturing. Say hello and answer their questions. Now, let me introduce you to our judges." He then did so. Claudia D'Angelo smiled modestly, and the older women in the crowd clapped with enthusiasm. Tommy Greene gave everyone a wave and many of the women squealed with excitement. "Now remember, ladies and gents," he said, "I know you Yanks like to be polite—"

"No we don't," Susan Powers' husband yelled. Big grin in place, he glanced around at the people at his table, checking for their reaction.

"Don't speak until you're spoken to," Reilly said.

"My bad," Gary Powers shouted. His table mates tittered in embarrassment and his wife threw him a poisonous glare.

Josh and Reilly exchanged a glance that I took to mean they'd keep their eyes on Mr. Powers.

"And, last but not least," Josh said, "our third judge is none other than the pride of Louisiana herself, Scarlet McIntosh." Scarlet took a step forward and waved her fingers. Gary Powers whistled. His wife's face tightened still further, but Scarlet gave the man a smile.

"Now remember," Tommy said, "*America Bakes!* is all

about frank and fair criticism as well as praise when it's warranted." He turned his bright eyes and toothy grin on me. "You can take it, can't you, Lily?"

I nodded.

He gave me a genuine smile before shouting, "We'll see about that." Everyone laughed once again. Everyone except Bernie, who leaned across the table and whispered something to Rose. I don't know what she said, but Rose threw me a worried glance.

"As filming progresses you may talk quietly amongst yourselves," Josh said.

"My wife's never spoken quietly in her life," Gary shouted. He laughed but no one else joined in, and Susan Powers shifted uncomfortably in her seat. I'd met Susan before but not her husband; however, I'd heard things about the Powerses' marriage. Someone had called him an anchor around her political ambitions. I could see why. It was ten o'clock in the morning. They'd been here since nine. I wondered if he'd been drinking.

"If," Josh said sharply, "I may continue. I want no shouting, and no one's to stand up without raising your hand for permission first. One crew will be out here filming, while the other's in the kitchen with Ms. Roberts. You can assume the camera's on you at all times, so don't be talking with your mouth full, no sneezing into the linen napkins, and for heaven's sake, people, no mugging for the camera. Do you get it?"

Everyone shouted, "Yes!" Rose's accent, full of the memories of Yorkshire, rose above them all. My grandmother clapped her hands. Gary opened his mouth to grace us with another charming *bon mot*, but Susan grabbed his arm and hissed at him.

"If the judges stop to talk to you," Josh continued,

"speak clearly and distinctly. Answer their questions and that's all. I don't want to hear about your new grandchild or what you're doing on your summer vacation. Get it?"

"Yes."

"Do you get it, sir?" He stared at Gary Powers, who for once only nodded.

"No eating while you're being spoken to." Josh turned to face me. "You're with me. Reilly, you have the show out here. Let's do this."

He stalked into Tea by the Sea. Marybeth and Cheryl scrambled to get out of his way.